D0876221

Cashing In

ALSO BY
Susan Colebank

BLACK TUESDAY

Cashing In

Susan
Colebank

DUTTON BOOKS
an imprint of PENGUIN GROUP (USA) INC.

DUTTON BOOKS
A member of Penguin Group (USA) Inc.

Published by the Penguin Group

Penguin Group (USA) Inc., 375 Hudson Street, New York, New York 10014, U.S.A. • Penguin Group (Canada), 90 Eglinton Avenue East, Suite 700, Toronto, Ontario M4P 2Y3, Canada (a division of Pearson Penguin Canada Inc.) • Penguin Books Ltd, 80 Strand, London WC2R 0RL, England • Penguin Ireland, 25 St Stephen's Green, Dublin 2, Ireland (a division of Penguin Books Ltd) • Penguin Group (Australia), 250 Camberwell Road, Camberwell, Victoria 3124, Australia (a division of Pearson Australia Group Pty Ltd) • Penguin Books India Pvt Ltd, 11 Community Centre, Panchsheel Park, New Delhi - 110 017, India • Penguin Group (NZ), 67 Apollo Drive, Rosedale, North Shore 0632, New Zealand (a division of Pearson New Zealand Ltd.) • Penguin Books (South Africa) (Pty) Ltd, 24 Sturdee Avenue, Rosebank, Johannesburg 2196, South Africa • Penguin Books Ltd, Registered Offices: 80 Strand, London WC2R 0RL, England

Library of Congress Cataloging-in-Publication Data

Colebank, Susan.
Cashing in / by Susan Colebank.—1st ed.
p. cm.
Summary: In the three years since her father's death, Arizona eighteen-year-old Regina has loaned her mother thousands of dollars to cover her compulsive spending and gambling, while coping with her own stress by overeating, but when her mother wins the lottery, Reg hopes their troubles are over.
ISBN 978-0-525-42151-1
[1. Compulsive behavior—Fiction. 2. Mothers and daughters—Fiction.
3. Gambling—Fiction. 4. Single-parent families—Fiction. 5. Family
life—Arizona—Fiction. 6. Arizona—Fiction.] I. Title.
PZ7.C67363Cas 2009
[Fic]—dc22   2008048976

Published in the United States by Dutton Books,
a member of Penguin Group (USA) Inc.
345 Hudson Street, New York, New York 10014
www.penguin.com/youngreaders

Designed by IRENE VANDERVOORT

Printed in USA   First Edition

10 9 8 7 6 5 4 3 2 1

This book is dedicated to the family and friends who helped me make Reggie and Gabe and Pete and Sarah who they are.

Thank you, Paige, for being born and making Mommy strive to be the best role model she can be for you.

Thank you, Susan LG, Stacey, and Shelley. My critique group is my Tim Gunn—they're always there to push me, to "make it work."

Thank you, Gig and Lia, for being my avid readers who let me know when a character sucks in a good way and when one sucks in a bad way.

Thank you, Brooke, Francine, Megan, and Tiffany, for being my focus group and letting me know when I went too Breakfast Club on you.

Thank you, Mom, for staying up all night to read the book. I know it was no Time magazine, but it meant a lot to me.

Thank you, Maureen, for being such a positive person and for wanting this book to be as good as it should be.

Also, it is said that it's never the easiest proposition being married to a writer—when a deadline looms, a case of the crazies takes over the body and dust bunnies take over the house. So thank you, Jason, for babysitting during crunch time (although next time, let's just say I wouldn't be upset if you did some housecleaning, too).

Cashing In

THREE YEARS EARLIER

This message is for Mrs. Imogene Shaw.
This is Sergeant Williams at the San Diego Police Department.
Mrs. Shaw, please give us a call as soon as you get this.
It concerns your husband.

I REMEMBER THAT THE DAY WAS HOT—no surprise there, since almost every day in Arizona is hot—and I had to put on deodorant twice. I remember how a fly buzzed over Aunt Barb's potato salad and how there was a sad brownie no one wanted to eat.

I ate it, though. I ate that, two scoops of Aunt Barb's Gourmet Marketplace potato salad, two squares of baked macaroni, and five slices of homemade bread smeared with half a stick of room-temperature butter. I ate it all in my room in the back of the house, an old converted garage that got too hot in the summer and too cold in the winter. Next week, Dad had planned to install a vent in my room so I'd get cool and hot air like everyone else in the rest of the house.

But he couldn't. He was dead and, as of two hours ago, buried six feet deep in the Waterview Cemetery.

Him being dead changed a lot. No air vent, for one. No finished bathroom, even though we just have one and the floor is now tile glue and concrete. No new lawn to replace the weeds and gravel outside.

It meant no more Sundays on our boat, *Bertha*. No more eating pancakes for dinner or birthday cake for breakfast. No more Stealthy Dad Kisses when he thought I was sleeping.

The house could get finished. Mom, Jeff, and me could work together and get it banged out in a year maybe. Even if we didn't, which knowing my mom we wouldn't, I wasn't going to miss any of that. But Stealthy Dad Kisses? I already missed those. A lot a lot a lot.

I wanted more baked macaroni and bread and potato salad. I was going to be sick later, but it was as if my brain was no longer talking to my stomach. My brain kept saying *Food, food now*. My stomach wasn't saying much of anything. It was just moaning.

"Hey, kiddo." Mom stood at the door, her eyes red, her hands shaking as she dabbed an old-looking Kleenex under her nose while also holding a half-empty wineglass between her fingertips. "Want some company?"

"Sure." I pushed the empty plate under the bed with the

heel of my black Converse. I felt guilty for eating, for being able to eat. My dad was dead. How could I eat?

I had to do something with my hands, so I grabbed Mr. Puffin. Mr. Puffin was a worn and nubby stuffed bird Dad had gotten me on one of his San Diego trips. Not on this last one, though. This last one, he'd died.

"How'd I give birth to such a pretty girl?" She bit her lip and stroked the side of my face with a thumb. I took after mom with her dark hair, light blue eyes, and fair skin. But I wasn't a size two like Mom. I had boobs and hips and a pretty fast metabolism, considering what I ate.

She sat down, the bed barely moving under her weight. "How're you holding up?" she asked.

"I'm breathing." More than I could say for Dad. I clenched my lips together and sucked them into my teeth, willing my eyes to unblur as I concentrated on the spot in the avocado carpet that my cat, Birdie, liked to sharpen her claws on. You could see past the layers of carpet fibers and foam padding and make out the gray concrete underneath.

I felt an arm drape over my shoulders, but my mom had lost so much weight this last week, her arm felt as if I was imagining it, that I was here with a ghost. It wasn't until she squeezed me that I felt as if I had someone here, someone to feel the pain with me, to remind me there used to be days when the only things I worried about were if I was going to get home in time for dinner and if my best friend, Sarah, and Pete, her significant other, were fighting again.

"Do you like?"

It took me a minute to figure out that I was supposed to be looking at the bracelet slipping and sliding between her wrist and elbow.

"It's pretty." I pulled her arm closer, trying not to wince when I felt the frailty of her bones and skin and veins. "Was this what Dad got you last Christmas?"

She laughed. "Your dad would never have bought me this. We never had that kind of money." She stroked the bracelet. "But now I'll have something to remember him by."

We owned one beat-up car, a thirdhand boat, and a fifty-year-old house Dad had christened "Our Tiny Piece of Fixer-Upper Heaven." Then Dad had died five days ago of a brain aneurysm in a San Diego Hilton.

And yet Mom had somehow found the energy to go shopping. I hadn't even found the energy to wash my hair until this morning, and even then, I lost interest halfway through.

I didn't say anything about the bracelet. Or how Jeff and me were pretty good reminders about Dad. I don't do confrontations. If I even think about the possibility of a confrontation, I want to eat an entire sheet cake.

I pressed Mr. Puffin closer to me as the fingers of my other hand played with the smooth Tahitian black-pearl pendant Dad had gotten me last Christmas. Above it was a tiny diamond, and it all dangled on a silver chain. I loved it, and hadn't taken it off since he gave it to me.

"I heard the phone ring," I said, wetting a finger to try to rub a mac-and-cheese stain out of Sarah's black dress. Sarah's an Amazon, and the at-the-knee dress fell to mid-calf on me. "Was it Jeff?"

Mom took a mouthful of wine, nodding. "He's still at McClurry's. They're giving him a hard time about the balance." McClurry's was Waterview's only funeral home. Four days ago, we'd picked out a shiny black casket with pewter hardware and a satin lining to bury Dad in. As if a nice-looking casket would get him into heaven faster. "He said he'd be here soon."

Jeff was my older brother and a senior at Waterview High. He usually wasn't much of a talker, and he'd been talking even less these last couple of days, at least not to us. He'd been on the phone with the funeral parlor, the cemetery, the life insurance people, Dad's boss at Bob Huffy Construction. Mom hadn't asked him to do any of it. But Jeff was like me—if you wanted something done right or just done in general, then don't leave it up to Mom. Unlike me, though, being proactive went against his nature.

The phone rang again. I stood up, glad for an excuse to get away from Mom and her insane purchase. "I'll get it."

"You're a good girl, Regina," she called after me, a hint of a slur in her words.

I crossed the family room, where about fifty people wearing various shades and sizes of black were eating food, drinking, crying, laughing, and whispering. I kept my head down, not wanting to make eye contact with anyone. I'd told Sarah and Pete to stay home today. I could keep myself from ugly crying if they weren't here.

Mom's room was off the hallway shared with the kitchen. I picked up the cordless right before the machine clicked on. "Hello?"

There was a pause and then a clicking. A telemarketer? Seriously? Anger burned across my skin, and I was reaching for the off button when I heard, "Hello. Hello? Is Richard or Imogene Shaw there?"

I put the receiver flush against my ear. "She's sort of busy today. May I take a message?" I found myself switch onto autopilot as I dug through Mom's nightstand. I finally found a pen and a pad of paper from a casino Mom liked to go to once in a while.

"This is Matt from Susie May Student Loans. When would be a good time to talk to Imogene?"

How long does it take to get over a husband you've been married to for twenty years? "I have no idea. Can I take a message?"

The voice on the other end started getting more assertive. "We've been leaving messages for Imogene going on three months now. We are calling her today as a courtesy, to let her know that if she doesn't make good on her payments— including penalties and interest—we will have no choice but to get a collection agency involved. Do you know what a collection agency is, young lady?"

Like I said, I hate confrontations, but I found myself having no problem going off on a nameless, faceless, clueless idiot. "Well, since we're talking about being courteous, maybe you'd like to know my dad died last week and she's sort of out of it." I heard my breath echo back to me over the earpiece, loud and harsh. "Do I need to explain what dead is?"

The guy stuttered and stumbled over what sounded like an apology. I didn't stick around to listen; I hung up and slammed my head into my dad's pillow. I smelled his aftershave, and I let myself cry as I hugged the mound of foam and pillowcase against me.

I never, ever said that sort of stuff to people. I wasn't that kind of person. Instead, I went with the flow, living my life and letting people live theirs. If Sarah had seen me just then, she would have freaked. Regina Shaw does not show people how she really feels. Ever. She just stews and thinks bad things and hopes karma burns their arm hair off.

A half hour later, my eyes had no more water in them, and my throat was scratchy and dry. But I felt better than I had all week. I stood up, brushed my fingers through my hair, and went back to face a pack of people who thought it was okay talking about my dad like he was gone.

I mean, I knew he was. But I didn't want to hear small talk about it.

"You just let us know what we need to do, Genie. If you need anything, we're here for you." It was dinnertime at Aunt Barb's house. It was Aunt Barb's idea for us to come over, something about getting away from the dirty dishes and avoiding eating one of the casseroles now stocking our freezer. I didn't point out that the dishes would still be there when we got home and we'd be pulling out the casseroles starting tomorrow. But Aunt Barb was Aunt Barb—good in a crisis, bad any other time.

I'd changed into jeans and a T-shirt but had kept on my black Converses. Mom was still in her dress and her bracelet. Jeff hadn't come back from the funeral home yet.

Uncle Mark and Aunt Barb's house was nothing like ours. Ours was an old 1960s one-story with peeling adobe and a weed-infested yard; it sat next to the highway, and we'd had to convert the garage when we moved in six months ago so that I had a place to sleep.

Aunt Barb's house had been built two years before and sat yards from the beach, with its own personal dock that held a speedboat with a bright blue sun canopy. The house itself was three stories, with a deck on each floor. My cousin, Bridget, had the third floor all to herself, with a bedroom, bathroom, sitting area, and even a bar area that worked as a kitchenette during her sleepovers.

Not that I'd ever been to one of those infamous sleepovers. We might have shared DNA, but Bridget and I were polar opposites: she was skinny, I was curvy; she was fashionable, I was whatever-was-clean; she had a million friends, I was set with Sarah and Pete. She was also a year younger than me, but the way she dressed and did her makeup, people usually thought she was older. Sometimes even older than Jeff. Mom says it's her posture. I say it's her drag-queen makeup.

Bridget and I might as well have been strangers; that's how much we knew or cared for each other. Plus, she was Aunt Barb and Uncle Mark's only child, and she had some serious issues about sharing well with others.

Some kind of morose-sounding classical music played over the ceiling speakers. The dining room table was set up with porcelain bowls, crystal platters, and Chinese takeout. But no one but Uncle Mark ate anything. We sat on the overstuffed sofas in the travertine-tiled living room watching a sitcom on mute.

"Mom." We all jumped a little, even Bridget, who'd been text-messaging and listening to her MP3 player. Jeff stood in the archway that separated the foyer from the living area, his tie undone, his short hair all over the place, a corner of a thumbnail in his mouth. "I need to talk to you. You too, Reg." He waved Uncle Mark to sit back down and told him, "I just need to fill Mom and Reggie in on some details."

We followed him outside to the enclosed courtyard, a fountain burbling softly nearby. It had been Uncle Mark's last anniversary present to Aunt Barb. Mom told us Aunt Barb had taken his credit card and bought herself a "real" gift after he'd gone to bed.

"Did you clear everything up at McClurry's?" Mom asked. She had a new wineglass in her hand and a new color of wine in it.

"Not exactly." Jeff ran his hands through his hair, which helped me figure out why his hair was so messed up. "Turns out that Dad bought out his life insurance."

The wineglass would have slipped onto the patio if I hadn't grabbed it. "Your father has no life insurance?" she asked. "But I just talked to his boss, Bob. Bob said he had life insurance."

"He used to, yeah. But then he cashed out to buy *Bertha*." He was talking about our really used, really old boat. Every Sunday, we loaded it up with food and CDs and water toys, staying out from midmorning to just after dark. Many sunburns, water-gun fights, and cans of root beer had been experienced on *Bertha*.

"Cashed out." Mom said the words with no emotion.

"Yep. So I told him to use one of the cards you gave me." He cracked his knuckles. "Nothing. All of the ones you gave me were maxed."

Mom spun her bracelet around and around and around, but it didn't look as if she knew what she was doing or how ironic it was that she was touching something that had probably maxed out one of those cards.

"So no insurance, no credit cards," Mom repeated with no emotion and some slurring. "What about the money in checking?"

Jeff nodded. "There was enough."

Mom's shoulders lost some of their tension and her eyes closed in relief. "Well, thank God for that."

"There wasn't enough for the casket, Mom, just so you know."

"How much was there enough for?" Her words were soft and barely audible.

"A pine box."

I thought back to the funeral. Me in the front row, trying to keep myself from looking at the open casket. Counting the roses in the vases around his coffin: 282 in all. Which was ironic considering they were all for a guy who had been allergic to flowers when he was alive. "That wasn't a pine box?"

"No, that had been a mahogany, satin-lined casket."

"What, like he's going to know the casket's pine now?" I didn't see what the big deal was. Pine, mahogany—wood was wood.

"It's not a casket, Regina." Jeff cracked another knucle. "It's literally a box. As in wood, nails, and six sides. There's nothing inside, just wood."

Nothing? I thought about Dad in there, no pillow, maybe even splinters. "Is the casket that much more?"

"Five thousand more."

Dad in a wood box. And Mom with that bracelet. Tears burned my eyes and made my nose run. A week of crying, and I was still a mess. An ugly, ugly mess, just like Dad in his pine box with no pillow.

"Your father deserves a damn box, leaving us with his funeral bills and no insurance money." Then, it was as if something was crumbling inside Mom. Tears came fast, her mouth and chin trembling.

"It's not like anyone's going to see his casket ever again, right?" She mustered a smile as she sobbed, as if she hadn't just cursed Dad. "The plot and the headstone, those are the important things, right?"

Jeff looked at me, avoiding Mom's eyes. "There wasn't

enough for a headstone, Mom. They said they'd put up a wood cross with his initials on it so we'd know where to find him until we can afford something else."

So we would know where to find him.

Mom's body slumped as her shoulders shook, and her sobs turned into primitive-sounding moans. I started toward her, but then the afternoon sun glinted off her new bracelet. I stopped. There was my father's headstone. Right there, on her emaciated arm.

When life got complicated, I got going, usually to the nearest cake, cookie, or candy.

In this case, I turned and walked back inside to the three kinds of cake Aunt Barb had set out.

I just stole four hundred dollars.

I can't believe I just stole four hundred dollars. I've never stolen anything, ever, except for that extra newspaper I picked up one time for Dad. It had stuck to the other newspaper I'd gotten in Gas 'n Go. I hadn't found out about it until we were home, and when I told Dad what I did, he said that sort of stuff happened. "Don't worry about it, sweetheart. They'll never miss that extra fifty cents."

But four hundred dollars wasn't fifty cents. It had been just as easy to steal, though. Too easy. I sort of saw why people did it. A misplaced receipt here, a payment in cash there, and I was able to pretend the Art Club had only made $1,500 for the year and not $1,900.

I put the twenties, fives, quarters, and even pennies in a tampon box in my bottom dresser drawer and jammed in the client receipts afterward.

It had been three weeks since Dad's funeral. Three weeks of living in a room with no air conditioner as the days got hotter and hotter. I took a shower at night, but I always slept too late to take one in the morning. Every morning, I'd put on deodorant, some perfume, and tell myself I was good to go.

But I guess I wasn't. Because one day, I went to my locker and saw *Go home and take a Shaw-er* written in black, permanent marker across the door.

I felt as if my insides were on fire. I ran to the Art room, grabbed a thick black marker, and ran back to my locker. Was this what instantaneous combustion felt like? After I had blacked out the message, I ditched my afternoon classes, and I went straight to Cashmart and shopped for an air conditioner. But they only had the most expensive ones left. And Waterview being Waterview, no one else in town sold window units.

I went home and told Mom I needed an air conditioner.

"I can't do it this month, hon." She'd been sitting at the computer, browsing eBay. "We've got mortgage and utilities left to pay." She said this as she put bids on an Adrienne Vittadini purse and a gold-and-diamond tennis bracelet.

I felt backed into a corner. I didn't want to ask the question, because I was afraid I was going to get a bad answer. But I had to ask. *Go home and take a Shaw-er* was on a ticker tape in my head. "Mom, can't we just use your credit card?" If she was bidding on eBay that meant she had at least one card that wasn't maxed out.

She'd turned around, the circles under her eyes purple and deep, her hair unbrushed and ratty. "I need these things, Regina. You've got a fan in your room. You can make do."

I didn't tell her about the locker. If I told her, it would have made what happened more real. And I didn't want it to be real. "Maybe we can use some of the money you got from Dad's boat?"

And that's when my mother changed before my eyes. The woman who used to cheer for me at soccer practice and play Name That Tune on long car rides was no longer here. In her place—well, the best way to describe her was Medusa, the one who turned people into stone with just a look. And I was getting that look right now.

"That money is gone, put down on your father's student loan. A loan, mind you, I stupidly co-signed on, and that I still owe forty thousand dollars on. A debt that's going to haunt us and keep us from fixing up this crapper of a house your dad talked me into."

That's when I realized that asking too many questions led to conversations that I never wanted to have. I didn't want to know about Dad's student loan or how Mom hated the house. No fifteen-year-old should know that stuff.

I would have borrowed the money from Jeff's stash of odd-job money, but he didn't come home that night. Years later, he told me that pretty much every night after Dad died, he went out to the desert, followed the glow of bonfires to the nearest kegger, and got drunk.

So I stole the money. And tomorrow I'm buying an air conditioner.

I had an overwhelming need to be with the pack of Little Debbie oatmeal cookies in the back of the pantry, hiding out under a ten-pack of ramen no one ever touched. But we had people over. People who'd never given us the time of day before Dad died, and who I knew would start to disappear again any day now.

The sound of Aunt Barb and Mom talking came through my bedroom door. I went out and was hit with a wave of cigarette smoke. Their clothes reeked of it, which wasn't surprising considering they'd spent the last two days in Vegas playing slots next to chronic smokers.

"Hey, Reg." Aunt Barb picked through a shopping bag and threw something black toward me. "Saw this and thought of you." It was a T-shirt with a rhinestone-covered skull and a foil rose coming out of its eye. "I got you the black one—the color will really make your eyes pop."

"Thanks, Aunt Barb." Inside, I was saying *Thanks for getting me a death T-shirt three weeks after my dad died.*

The recliner—Dad's recliner with the broken footrest—squeaked behind me. Bridget sat with one foot under her butt, the other foot rocking the chair as she text-messaged. "Are we going or what? I have to meet Nancy at the movies in like an hour and I gotta go home and take something for my cramps."

I let the moms deal with Bridget as I walked into the kitchen and grabbed a Cashmart soda. It was disgusting, but we didn't buy real stuff. We couldn't afford it. We couldn't afford name-brand soda, we couldn't afford a vent in my room, and we couldn't afford linoleum in the bathroom. But we could afford a useless bracelet and dollar slots.

I walked into the kitchen. Aunt Barb followed. "Hey, Reg, my personal trainer's cocker spaniel had puppies last week. Want one?"

I knew all about animals. My cat, Birdie, was always needing shots and flea stuff and heartworm pills. Cha-ching, cha-ching, cha-ching. "I'm not really into dogs."

She sipped her drink. "How about a kitten? My pool guy is trying to offload a few."

I shook my head. Birdie had jealousy issues. That kitten would be a midday snack.

"Hey, Reg." Mom sat in front of the TV, beyond the kitchen archway, a deadened expression on her face. Whenever she wasn't shopping or gambling, she looked like she had checked out on life. "Bridget needed to use the bathroom, so I gave her the box of tampons you keep in your bottom drawer." I barely heard her say, "She thinks she started." I was racing down the hallway to my room.

Bridget sat on my bed, the tampons dumped on top of my bed, the box on the floor.

And twenties, fives, quarters, and pennies in her lap.

CHAPTER ONE

Reg. Hey, it's Mom. You hungry? I'm starved. You feel like taking your mom out to Foster's? Their special today is pumpkin ravioli, your fave. Anyway, call me back. Love you.

THE LINE STRETCHED FROM THE ROW OF DOUBLE DOORS, down the concrete stairs, and almost to the end of the student parking lot. People wore sweatshirts, flannels, and even long pants. But everyone still wore flip-flops.

It was fall in Arizona, a Saturday. Specifically, SAT Day. Well, it was SAT Day for almost every single eighteen-year-old but me. Come next fall, I was going to be one of the few who wasn't going to be wasting money on an ugly papasan chair for her jail-cell-sized dorm room.

"But if white is to black, wouldn't it be empty is to full?" Pete Nellis flipped through the pages of a dog-eared, slushie-stained Princeton Review. He's smart, but he uses most of his brain memorizing *Star Wars* facts, *Star Wars* statistics, and *Star Wars* lingo. The only thing that will save him from living with his mom until he's forty is he's a jock, with a tan, biceps, and a crooked smile. He nailed a 360 at Waterview's water-ski championships last year, taking gold for his age group.

"Why wouldn't it be orange is to green? They're opposite each other on the color wheel, and black and white are opposites," Sarah shot back, her eyes shut as she leaned against a brick column. Sarah Bretton, my best friend since age six, had blond hair cut into a blunt bob and the ability to say whatever she wanted, when she wanted, to whom she wanted. She was also Pete's on-again, off-again girlfriend. This week, they were heading toward off-again.

"But white is the absence of color, and black is all the colors. I say the empty/full thing works."

Sarah's eyes opened and she pointedly stated, "Orange/green."

Pete frowned. "Empty/full."

This could have gone on for another five minutes, ending with Sarah saying "Go screw an Ewok" and Pete being oblivious that Sarah was mad and had stopped talking to him.

"Hey, you know what's empty?" I said, shaking my oversized to-go mug between them from where I sat against a column. "I need a refill. Think The Coffee Spot's open?"

"Orange/green." Sarah looked down at me. "You don't need any more coffee. You just drank the equivalent of four cups. One more and your heart's going to climb up your throat and run a four-minute mile."

"Four cups is no biggie."

She looked at her watch. "Four cups in an hour? Biggie."

"It's already been an hour?" I pushed up off the ground, getting dizzy for a few seconds. Okay, maybe Sarah had a point about the coffee. I dug through my canvas bag, frayed at the edges with a purple ink stain on one corner, covered with the caricatures I've been working on since sophomore year. There was Pete and Sarah and my Mom and Jeff . . . Even Birdie had made it on there. I checked the time on my cell phone. I still had twenty minutes to loiter.

Ahead of us, the doors opened. Four Waterview teachers started directing everyone inside, and the sound of kids talking and laughing slowly faded. Girls ate their hair, and the guys dug their hands deeper into their pockets. "Good luck, guys," I solemnly whispered.

"Luck has nothing to do with it," Pete said as he shoved the SAT prep book into his backpack. "Why aren't you taking the test, Reg? You're here anyway. And it's not like you have to study. You're like a savant or something when it comes to multiple choice."

"An SAT test isn't the same as a trigonometry test." I

avoided Sarah's eyes. I'd been hearing the same thing from her for the last three years. *Just take the test, Reg. It's not going to hurt anything. Is it money? It's money, isn't it. Because you know I can spot you.*

Everything I could or couldn't do in my life was always about money. But the SAT wasn't just about money. As I'd told Sarah, the SAT was for people who were going to college and didn't mind spending the next twenty to thirty years paying it off. Like my mom. She didn't seem to care about paying off Dad's student loan any time soon.

"By the way, it's black is to white." I hitched my bag up on my shoulder. I'd helped them study enough to pretty much have the stupid Princeton Review memorized.

Sarah hadn't moved with the line. She was too busy giving me her disappointment face. "C'mon, Pete," she said as she started to walk again. "So what if Reggie could ace the test? You have to preregister for the SAT, anyway. And that means planning for the future. Putting something in motion now in order for something to happen later on, like taking the SAT."

I didn't follow them. Why would I? So I could hear Sarah go on about how I should live my life? The distance widened between us, but that didn't keep Sarah from throwing over her shoulder, "And as we both know, Reg doesn't like planning for the future."

I only listened with half an ear as Pete argued with Sarah that you could register the day of, as long as there were enough empty seats.

Walking on the dirt shoulder of the road in front of Waterview High, I headed toward the highway. Instead of four hours of filling in bubbles and calling it a day, I'd be putting in a sixteen-hour shift.

Waterview has two gas stations, one grocery store, a combo movie/arcade/mini-golf course, three elementary schools, and one high school. It also has one chain discount store. Cashmart is one of about five hundred in the United States and Canada, according to the brochure in the photo department that I've been reading over and over and over again for the last two years.

Cashmart was pretty much a warehouse with rows upon rows of neatly piled merchandise. The walls were white, the ceiling was made up of exposed steel beams, and the only bit of color anywhere was on the red-and-white signs that told customers windshield wipers were in aisle three and a twenty-four-pack of baked beans was in aisle twenty-two.

I worked in the Say Cheese! photo department. I'd been there two years, starting the day after my sixteenth birthday. My time was spent developing pictures, taking family portraits, and using the photo-editing program to draw mustaches on customers who had forgotten to take their antipsychotic meds. I liked the job well enough. I would like it even better once I was made photo manager. Starting pay? Twenty-five thousand dollars. A semester making that kind of money would get me out of Waterview, no problem. And a year or two making that kind of money? Even better.

A well-fed guy fighting a losing battle with hair loss came up the aisle toward me. "Miss Shaw, it's nice to see an employee who values company time." Dwayne Fellers was general manager of Cashmart. He could tell you what time the bathrooms were cleaned and how much mint-flavored Crest was this week. "Only ten minutes early today?"

Fellers and I had a running joke about me coming in half an hour early, and anything less was "late." "Sorry about that. I had to pull a bus off an old woman. Oh, and then there was that thing with the baby carriage and an oncoming train." I liked Fellers. Over the last couple of months, he'd been hinting about promoting me to photo manager.

"Sounds like the perfect day to bring in help, then."

"Help?" Currently, me and Clarissa Healy held down the fort in Photo, sometimes Pete when he wasn't needed in Electronics. Sure, Clarissa couldn't count out a drawer to save her life, and Pete spent way too much time trying to talk people into the R2-D2 backdrop, but we did well enough.

"His name's Gabe Donaldson. Starts later tonight during graveyard so he can learn the lay of the land without too many customer interruptions. Since you're taking over Healy's shift, I'd appreciate it if you showed him around." He lowered his voice. "I'm taking the wife to Laughlin for our twenty-year. All-you-can-eat buffet, keno, an Engelbert Humperdinck show." He winked at me. "It'll make her forget all about me, uh, overlooking her birthday."

I could think of better places to take your wife than Laughlin, Nevada. Like taking her to Waterview's one swanky restaurant, Foster's. Even the Waterview Sewage Plant had to be a better date.

"Sure thing, boss. I'll show him where everything is. You want me to give him a PhotoBrush tutorial?" I pulled out the two-inch-thick PhotoBrush user manual. I had spent the last two years improving it, inserting Post-its and legible block print that told users things like the real way to arrange contrast settings to hide the blotchy skin of a three-year-old in the middle of a tantrum.

Fellers shook his head. "He's already familiar with PhotoBrush. He's coming to us from that big Cashmart down in Phoenix. He could probably even teach us a thing or two."

The big Cashmart? The last person who'd come out of the big Cashmart was now manager of Electronics. My brain started to feel a little numb, like I was a first-grader trying to work out a trigonometry question. "So he's a transfer?"

"Yep." Fellers stepped out of the way to make room for a mom coming toward us, her arms holding a wiggling toddler as she navigated the Personal Care aisle that led up to the photo department.

"He was an associate there?" I asked.

"Yep."

My heart was jackhammering. Maybe Sarah had a point about OD'ing on coffee. Not like I'd take her advice; my entire life was one big cautionary tale about overconsumption.

"He has four years of experience and plans to stay in Waterview for a while." He backed away, making room for the mom who was still busy putting back everything the boy had pulled off. Fellers seemed to be overly interested in the Charmin display in front of us. "He's our new photo manager, Reg."

"Photo manager?" I repeated. I pressed my fingers over my chest. Into my chest, really. Willing my heart to stay in my chest cavity. That was my job. *My* job. The job that was going to help me pay my way out of Waterview.

MY JOB.

The mom was now in front of me, scanning the photo packages on the lit board above me, the little boy screaming in her arms.

Fellers cleared his throat, looking as if he wanted to say something. But the decibel level wasn't going to cooperate. Instead, he knocked on the glass countertop, raising his voice as he said, "I'll check in with you later, Reggie."

Later. He'd check in with me later. I watched him go, and I didn't say anything. It had nothing to do with me not liking confrontations, though.

It had everything to do with me not going ballistic. Fellers had literally robbed me of twenty-five-thousand dollars. Money that could've gotten me out of Waterview faster than I was going now.

The boy's screams filled the air, bouncing off the walls, the rafters, the linoleum floor.

I knew exactly how he felt.

"Wow. You look awful."

"Gee, Mom, thanks." We sat in our booth at Mr. Wong's, which was in the same side-of-the-highway strip mall as Cashmart. Mandolin music played overhead, and the lights were dim and shaded with dusty red lampshades. I'd read somewhere that the color red and low lighting increased your appetite. Not today, though. I think I'd managed half a piece of sweet-and-sour chicken before my throat remembered to close up again.

"Well, you do." She pushed her designer eyeglasses up

her nose and took another bite of Peking duck. "You've got the face going. What made you get the face?"

"DNA. Age. Forgetting to put on sunscreen that one spring break." I sipped my green tea and focused on the Lucky Cat statue by the cash register. I knew I had a face going, but I didn't know how to stop it. Ever since this morning, when Fellers told me someone was taking the promotion that should have been mine, I'd been trying to keep that prickling sensation in my nose from turning into some major bawling. I couldn't cry, though. I still had eleven hours left on my double shift.

"Regina." She tilted her head and raised her eyebrows, giving me the look I used to get right before a time-out. "You only have so much time to spend with your mom. Can we somehow have a nice conversation over a nice meal?"

I wouldn't call Mr. Wong's All-You-Can-Eat $3.99 Buffet a nice meal. It was a cheap meal. And when you left, you smelled like fried food until you were able to take a shower and wash your hair. But it was what I thought we could afford when I chose the place; Mom had wanted to go to Foster's, even though I knew she'd seen the water bill we got yesterday, a bright red SECOND NOTICE box stamped on the front.

I had a feeling that I'd be writing a check for it. But I never did it until Mom asked. I never wanted her to forget for one minute that she had to ask her eighteen-year-old daughter to help out with the bills. Not that it had ever stopped her.

"What do you want to talk about, Mom?"

I heard her bracelets clink together. One bracelet was Dad's Funeral Bracelet, the other one an eBay "steal." "I won it for just under two hundred," Mom had told me, still on a high after getting into an online bidding war against Love2Shop. I didn't quite understand how you "won" something if you still had to pay two hundred bucks for it. And I had a feeling she had really paid four hundred, but two hundred had sounded better.

I popped out of my thoughts when I saw her finger pointing at me. "I want to talk about you. And the face."

I shrugged.

"Are you still thinking about the necklace?" she asked. "You've got to stop getting yourself sick about it. It'll turn up, I promise."

For just a few minutes, I had forgotten about the black-pearl pendant Dad had given me.

My hand went up to the space between my collarbones, and I shook my head. "It's not that." I didn't want to talk about that. Ever. "I didn't get the photo manager position."

Mom didn't say anything. She just shrugged and went

back to her duck. No surprise there. She had no idea how important this job was to me, or how much I hated living under her roof, with her bills, with her constantly asking me for money. She just thought working overtime at Cashmart was my hobby, like basketball or Key Club.

Mr. Wong's bell chimed as an old man held the door open for his equally old wife. I shifted in my seat, my butt asleep. Mom still hadn't said anything about my news. The chicken I had managed to swallow had stopped moving and begun to expand into something constant and uncomfortable.

Not wanting her to take my own silence as an opening to ask another question about the necklace, I changed the subject. "How's the Berger sale going?"

She crunched ice and played with her red plastic glass, sliding it back and forth between her hands. "I finally got an offer, a real, bank-backed offer. And what'd Andy Berger do? Turn it down because it was ten thousand dollars less than the asking price! I told him he was lucky anyone even wanted to buy that dump, especially in this market." She went on about closing costs and inspections and pissing contests. This was the part of the conversation I always tuned out. It'd been six months since Mom had sold anything. Which meant money wasn't coming in, but then again, not that much had been coming in before. Mom hadn't been a top earner at Southwest Real Estate for a long time, having decided there were better things to do on a weekend than host an open house, like playing video poker or selling bargain-bin items from Cashmart on eBay.

She'd worked there too long to get fired, especially since the owner was this grandma type who didn't believe in giving up on people. But the grandma wasn't an idiot, either. Mom was now stuck selling Waterview's fixer-uppers and trailers, and she sucked at that, too.

"So I'll need you to give Barb her order tonight," she was saying, a piece of ice garbling her words. "She hasn't been returning my calls. Again. As if I'm some telemarketer she's trying to avoid."

I had definitely missed something, tuning in just as Mom went into her Aunt-Barb-never-returns-my-calls spiel. "Give Barb her order," I repeated. "You know I have the late shift at Cashmart, right?"

"You know, if I tuned out on you like that, you'd have a fit." Mom pressed her lips together and focused her attention on the condensation dripping down her glass. "Barb ordered some stuff from Pretty Lady." Mom was a sales rep for Pretty Lady, which was sort of like Avon but sold stuff made out of placenta and fish eggs for five times as much. She didn't use that money for bills, though. She used it for eBay and lottery tickets. "I'm hitting the road after this, so I told her to stop by Cashmart during your shift." She arched an eyebrow. "Notice that I listen when *you* talk."

A tiny Asian girl slipped a plastic tray with the bill on the table. Sitting on top were two fortune cookies.

"Ooh, my favorite part." Mom was already taking the wrapper off her cookie, breaking it open before grimacing. "What a dud. 'The trees whisper to those who hear.' I'm definitely not playing the numbers on that one." On the bottom of Mr. Wong's fortunes, there was a list of five numbers. Perfect for the Arizona Five, which Mom played every week. She pushed the other one toward me. "Open yours."

I read mine. Then I read it again and tried not to snort. I finally said out loud, " 'The future is yours to make.' " Sarah would have so loved to rub that piece of garbage in my face. She'd probably make me stick it up on my mirror and repeat it to myself a hundred times a day.

"Ooh, I like that one," Mom said, grabbing the slip of paper. She stuck it in her wallet, and then spent a few seconds going through the wallet's compartments. "Hon, I don't think I have any cash on me."

I couldn't help the short, audible breath that pushed out. I love my mother. She bakes me Grandma's upside-down apple cake when I'm sick and lets me stay home when I need a mental health day. But I could see the tip of a bill peeking over the edge of her Louis Vuitton wallet. (Another eBay "steal.") "You have no money. Absolutely none?"

"Just my Vegas money." She pulled out the bills, still crisp from the ATM, and fanned them out in front of her, staring at them as if they might multiply in front of her from pure strength of will. It looked like around two hundred dollars. "I feel tonight's the night, babe. The right machine, the right hand, and the max bet could have us on easy street for the next decade."

I kept my eyes down and away from my mom's flushed cheeks and bright, overly optimistic eyes. I couldn't look ahead ten years. I couldn't even look ahead a month. The best I could do was two weeks. Every two weeks, my paycheck was direct-deposited into my checking account; as of last week, I'd passed the five-thousand-dollar mark. I was finally—FINALLY!—getting somewhere, even as Imogene Shaw's personal ATM. As long as my mom didn't bum major money from me, I'd soon get to the six-thousand-dollar mark, and then seven thousand dollars. I might even be at five figures by graduation. More, if I had gotten the photo manager position.

I faced the check toward me. It was under twelve bucks, thirteen with tip. It wasn't going to break me, but I'd learned a long time ago that a lunch here, a book there, a Starbucks everywhere started to add up. Plus, I wasn't going to put a dent in my five thousand dollars. "I can't cover it."

Mom paused in putting on her blazer. It was black silk, an Oscar de la Renta from guess where. "Don't you keep an emergency twenty on you somewhere?"

I did. I do. But it was *my* emergency twenty, not *her* emergency twenty. And the whole reason I'd started carrying an emergency twenty around was due to our getting stranded on I-95 with no gas, no gas money, and no charged cell phone. Getting into a car with a creepy-looking guy who constantly touched my mom's thigh. I'd been carrying around a cell phone and stuffing a twenty in my sock or my bra ever since.

I concentrated on the small mound of spring rolls in the center of the table my mom had taken from the buffet but were now going to be wasted. Typical. Mom always wanted more than she could possibly eat. Or wear. Or use. "I have some money, but I still can't cover it." I wasn't exactly lying. I hadn't said that I didn't have *enough* to cover it, just that I *couldn't* cover it. "Just use a card."

She made a raspberry sound with her lips as she finished shrugging into her jacket. "Uh, okay. Which one would that be? The one I'm two months behind on or the one that's four months behind?"

I peeled my eyes off the spring rolls and turned my

attention to a grain of rice I didn't even know I'd been rolling between my finger and the table. We'd been having this exact same conversation for the last three years, and it hadn't been getting any better. And it wouldn't get any better as long as eBay was still out there and shiny objects caught Mom's eye. I pushed my finger into the rice, keeping my eyes down and words light as I smashed the sucker into the lacquered table, my stomach all twisty-turny. "Are you sure you should be going to Vegas? Don't we still have to pay off the water bill?"

I officially wanted to throw up. This was why I avoided confrontations. To avoid this horrible, gut-wrenching, can-I-just-disappear-now feeling.

"Bob's covering gas, the hotel, and food." Each word got louder and louder. Mom jerked on her lipstick as she ignored my question. Bob was Bob Huffy of Bob Huffy Construction. He'd started dating Mom about six months after Dad died. They hadn't started dating right away; they weren't that gross. But when Bob Huffy would stop by to check on Mom once a week, bringing her candy or frozen turkeys he'd found on sale, he'd started wearing Mom down until they were going out to movies and having overnighters at his house.

I hated the guy. I hated him for being Dad's old boss. Bob Huffy had no idea how much money Mom blew through. He definitely didn't know how she didn't pay the bills. Him not knowing the real Mom made me feel a little better, though. But I didn't understand why Mom kept her money issues a secret, as if she were embarrassed or something, and yet she wasn't embarrassed enough to stop going to Laughlin or to Vegas or on eBay. Or to stop lying about how much she really spent on things.

She was throwing her lipstick back into her purse when she said, "Oh yeah. I have something for you."

Mom pulled out a brown bag, one of those thin, flat kinds that cards come in. The kind of bag airport and casino gift shops use. TREASURE ISLAND was printed on the outside, and it was crumpled around something round and small. I took the bag and forced myself to smile. Inside was a snow globe, two inches tall, a ceramic pirate ship its base. White snow and gold coins swirled with each tilt.

"I didn't think you had Treasure Island yet. Do you?"

"No." And then, because it seemed to come out harsh and bitter and confrontational, I added, "Thank you."

"Is this number twenty-nine?"

"No. Thirty. You came home with a Harrah's one last weekend." When I was five, I loved snow globes. I loved shaking them, analyzing the way the snow drifted inside, listening to the tinny music that most of them played. But over the years, especially over the last three, the snow globes had gone from Tinker Bell and the Grand Canyon to the Luxor, the Bellagio, the Excalibur, even the Bellamy Roadside Café and Casino that was on a Native American reservation twenty miles away.

"Those are some good memories." She nodded at the snow globe in front of me. She twisted Dad's Funeral Bracelet. "I told your dad I was pregnant with Jeff there, while we were waiting in the buffet line."

I didn't get warm fuzzies over that image. And I didn't want snow globes. I wanted paid bills, a paid mortgage. I wanted five digits in the bank. The security to leave Waterview. To leave her.

I scraped what was left of the rice off my finger and onto the edge of the table, and focused on the spring rolls that were still piled up on the table. My mother sat outlined behind them as she pulled out her cell phone, a gift from Bob Huffy of Bob Huffy Construction with a monthly service charge of eighty dollars. A service charge I'd given her money for. Five times.

I couldn't seem to stop the tension mounting inside me. And unlike the girls at the SAT this morning, I wasn't a hair eater. Instead, I did what I could do: I shoved a cold, wet spring roll into my mouth. It triggered my gag reflex, but I made myself ignore the feeling. I ate first one roll, and then another. I had barely eaten anything, and so Mom didn't know that this was weird behavior, eating gross food that I didn't even want, fast and mindless.

I started in on a third one as my mom pressed her cell phone to her ear, punched in her account number when prompted, and figured out which one of her cards wasn't past due.

In the end, I gave her my twenty. I'm an idiot.

CHAPTER TWO

Reg? Are you there? Pick up. Pick up!

IT WAS ALMOST MIDNIGHT, and the spring rolls were making a valiant effort to come back up. The eight cups of coffee I'd had in the last twenty-four hours weren't helping, either.

And tired or not, I couldn't keep the words from blurring together as I reread the department e-mail for the tenth time:

Gabe Donaldson is joining us from Phoenix this week, and will be our new manager in the Say Cheese! photo department. Please make sure to give him a warm Cashmart welcome when you get the chance.

I was no longer angry about Gabe Donaldson, photo manager. I wasn't that kind of person. Sarah would have said

I was in denial. The same Sarah who'd been texting me all night, too hyper to sleep and second-guessing her answers to the SAT verbal. I had been ignoring most of them as she paraphrased the questions and gave me her answers, mainly because I didn't text at work. But also because I didn't want to tell her that based on my hours of helping her and Pete study, most of her answers were definitely wrong.

"Hey." A girl with a messy ponytail and a chain that went from the dog collar around her neck to her belt stood half hidden on the other side of the computer monitor. "Are you still taking pictures?"

I knew this girl. Liberty, Liberty Woodson. She'd moved to Waterview sophomore year, and we'd taken three or four classes together. "Yeah, I am." I looked at her outfit. "You thinking about the Hello Kitty backdrop?"

She snort-laughed. "I don't do pictures." She looked over one shoulder and then the other. I noticed that she actually was really pretty. Minus the heavy, uneven black eyeliner and neck tattoo. "It's for him."

I thought for a second that "him" was code for an imaginary friend. I suddenly didn't feel so tired as I leaned toward her and, in a conspiratorial whisper, asked, "Him who?"

Liberty put her camouflage backpack on the counter and lifted the flap. "Joe at Joe's Family Pictures told me to get out when he saw him this afternoon."

"Well, you're in luck. At Cashmart, we'll take your money for any kind of picture, barring nudity and blood."

She pushed her bag toward me and I looked inside.

It had officially become The Best Night Ever.

"Do you think you can get Simon to stand on his tiptoes?" I adjusted the focus on the camera.

"He's done it before, but I don't know. He's looking pretty tired." Liberty cradled Simon against her stomach. "I've seen him do it for peanut butter."

We both studied the rat, who studied us right back, his legs poking out between Liberty's fingers, kicking like he was running in place. To give him credit, Simon didn't look like a creepy, red-eyed Rat of NIMH. He looked more like one of those rats that had helped those birds sew Cinderella's dress together. Wait, those had been mice. Same diff.

"Will a Reese's Peanut Butter Cup do it?" a voice behind me asked.

I was still thinking about Simon as I turned around and looked up. And up. The guy was tall. He was way over six feet and had the wide shoulders and chest of a surfer but the skinny hips of a skater. A tattoo poked out from beneath the sleeve of his thermal henley.

Bob had a tattoo in that same area, but his was of Popeye, a memento from his days in the Navy. Mom was always after him to get it lasered off, but Bob wasn't into pain, which was ironic considering he worked construction and was constantly dropping heavy things that made his toenails turn black and fall off.

"I don't know if chocolate is safe for rats." I kept my attention on Simon. Many cute customers had come and gone in the history of Say Cheese!. A couple had even asked me out. But I had no time for cute when I barely had enough time to sleep and shower.

Of course, none had been this cute. Dark, shiny hair fell to his chin, with the front tucked behind his ears, and I think his eyes were brown-green, with long, thick lashes. But he wasn't one of those pretty boys. He wore a red-and-black plaid flannel shirt tied around the waist of his faded jeans and a pair of scuffed black boots on his feet.

"If garbage doesn't kill them, a little chocolate isn't going to hurt." He leaned against the counter, and a grin crossed his face. That's when I noticed the dimple.

"Exactly what I was thinking." Liberty's voice reminded me we had an audience. "Got any?"

Flannel Guy nodded and pulled out a Reese's Peanut Butter Cup from his jean pocket.

"That's convenient," I said.

"My philosophy is never leave home without one."

"Funny," I said, watching Simon's whiskers dance as he

gnawed the chocolate, "because my philosophy is never put candy in my pocket where it can turn into soup."

I saw him reading my name tag. "I'm sure the Photo Goddess understands the need for an emergency stash of chocolate," he said.

I didn't have my name on the badge, just the words PHOTO GODDESS. One night a few months back, a customer had told me that I was a goddess after I got a great shot of his three kids smiling, sitting still, and not killing one another. After five minutes alone with a label maker, I'd officially become the Photo Goddess.

If I didn't know better, I'd say I was being flirted with. But I was too fat for a guy like this. A guy like Flannel Guy needed a girl who didn't have body fat or a penchant for sweatpants.

"Rachel?" Liberty was kissing the top of Simon's head, telling him, "Good boy. Pretty boy."

I'd already told her twice my name was Reggie, but it hadn't stuck. She wasn't being mean, she just didn't care enough to remember, like some grandma who wanted to only talk about her soaps. She hadn't even cared enough to notice I'd been in three classes with her. But if the rumors about her were true, she might have had more than a few brain cells chemically fried over the years.

"Since we only have a couple of shots left," she went on, "I was wondering if we could do a costume change?"

I nodded and stepped back from the camera. "Go for it."

Liberty tugged off the pink tulle tutu Simon had been wearing and pulled out a tiny red triangular hat with a cotton ball attached to one of the corners. "C'mon, Simon, Mama needs some Christmas pics."

Simon hadn't minded the tutu on his waist, or the bow tie on his neck before that. But the little Santa hat on his head made him frantic and crazy-eyed.

I stepped behind the camera and fiddled with the zoom until Liberty's hands pinning his arms to his sides were no longer in the picture. I adjusted the dials until his eyes and nose were in sharp focus. "Hey, Simon. Si-mon." I sang his name. I even put it to the tune of "Twinkle, Twinkle, Little Star." By the end of the second line, he stopped fussing and, without pausing, I snapped the last two pictures.

"And Photo Goddess earns her title." Flannel Guy was still smiling, and the dimple in his cheek had deepened. He only had one, but two would have been overkill on this guy. I got ahold of myself, though. This guy liked Liberty. Plain and simple. I was just getting part of the smile that he was flashing Liberty's way, I told myself.

Liberty put Simon back into a Caboodles-like mini-carrier that she slipped into her bag. "You said they'd be ready Monday?"

"After some minimal cropping and retouching, yeah,

we can get them to you then." Turnaround for portraits was usually seventy-two hours. But I was fast and a perfectionist and worked almost every day.

All qualities that any good photo manager should have, I couldn't help but think. Bitterly.

"You rock, Rhonda." And she was off, her ponytail a little messier than before and one sugar-hyped rat scratching at his carrier from inside her backpack.

"So, Photo Goddess." Flannel Guy stood by the counter. "Or is it Rachel? Or Rhonda?"

We no longer had an audience, and I turned back to the computer. The coffee was definitely out of my system, and I had to focus on getting my hands and brain to work together as I reduced red-eye and cropped out hands. If this guy was here to amuse himself at my expense, I was ready to freeze him out. He was cute. Okay, he was out-and-out gorgeous. But I didn't have time for gorgeous. Plus, he was probably waiting around to get me to tell him Liberty's phone number. No way was I going to tell him, though. It was against Cashmart policy. It had nothing to do with me feeling the teensy tiniest bit jealous he was attracted to a space cadet like her.

"That rat thing. Does that happen a lot?"

"I wish." I moved on to the next Simon picture. "That was a once-in-a-lifetime experience."

"Well, that's good to hear." He leaned on the counter and flipped through the PhotoBrush book I'd personalized. "Wow. There are notes on every page." He squinted at something I'd written. "This must've taken you a while."

I shrugged. "Yep." I wasn't going to get into a conversation about PhotoBrush with some bored customer looking to liven up their night with the Photo Goddess. If he wanted time with me, he could pay for a portrait.

"Impressive," he said, closing the book. There was just silence, and I finally looked up. He studied me with his hazel eyes for way longer than was humanly appropriate. Before I could think too much about it, I ducked down and pretended to be looking for something. Partly because of the stare. Partly because him looking at me like that was giving me very, very nice tummy wiggles.

"But I still have to write you up."

I straightened up. The dimples were gone. So were my tummy wiggles.

For a few seconds, all I could absorb was the Celine Dion song playing in Electronics and Simon's nose being too blurry in the picture in front of me.

"Gabe Donaldson. The new photo manager." I didn't even form it into a question. I knew. The sinking feeling in my stomach told me.

"Gabe Donaldson," he confirmed. "The new photo manager."

"Why are you writing me up?"

He gave me a half smile. But I ignored him and his fake smile. "Cashmart doesn't allow pet pictures. Something about health inspectors and Cashmart having a food court and a Grocery section."

I know what Cashmart does and doesn't do, I wanted to scream. But it was 1 A.M. and the food court was closed, and Grocery was like two football fields away, on the other side of the store. But I didn't do confrontations. And so I had to remove myself from Gabe Donaldson, new photo manager. I wasn't mad because he was now my boss. I couldn't change that. I was mad because he had been an accessory. He'd given that dumb rat chocolate. Pulled it out of his pocket and everything.

And he was going to write *me* up? He could take his pen and—

I pushed away from the counter and made my way down the Personal Care aisle. He didn't try to stop me, and I didn't turn around to tell him I was going on a break.

I passed Electronics and the fifty TVs all set to some benefit concert. I passed the food court and its stale-popcorn smell. Instead, I thought about the cupcakes up in the break room. They had Cookie Monster–blue icing, which was cracking off chunk by chunk after two days of being ignored on a grease-bottomed paper plate.

The blue icing tasted like a mix between a plastic Barbie head and a Pixy Stix, and the cake was dry. I still inhaled them in under two minutes, scraping the cupcake paper with my teeth and then using the inside of my sweatshirt to wipe my mouth clean.

I felt sick. But that didn't stop me from wanting more.

Dawn was still an hour away when my shift ended. My wordless, tension-filled shift, with Flannel Guy trying to ask questions and me ignoring them as I put together Simon's portfolio. It took me three hours to do a job that normally took an hour.

I got home and went immediately into the shower to start scrubbing Mr. Wong's fried sweet-and-sour chicken out of my hair. While I was at it, I was hoping some of the anger I still had for Flannel Guy would circle down the drain, too.

I scrubbed harder. What kind of guy wears flannel? Fellers should have docked points for that. *Docked points? Geez, Reg, get a hold of yourself.*

"Reg? Reggie?"

I grabbed the shower curtain, soap stinging my eyes. "Mom?" The shampoo blinding me, I had to depend on my hearing. It sounded like Mom. But Mom was in Vegas mode, and nothing ever snapped her out of Vegas mode. Never.

"Yeah, it's me." Her voice was near, like she was in the bathroom with me. I pulled the curtain more tightly around me. Mom hadn't seen me naked since I was around five, a hundred pounds and one mushy stomach ago.

"I thought you were in Vegas with Bob."

"Nope. We decided to come home early." Semi-hysterical laughter punctuated her words.

I turned off the shower and smoothed my hands down my wet hair. I heard the shampoo crackle from where it still clung to my hair. "What's wrong?"

She'd never come back early from a casino. Ever.

"Nothing. Nothing's wrong." She lifted her head from where she was bent over the chipped bathroom sink and turned toward me, and her smile was so wide I could see her molars. "Everything is great. Better than great. Everything's"—she took a breath, her eyes trying to search for an answer in the toothpaste residue in the sink—"everything's perfect."

"Perfect." I felt the word fill my mouth, and it came out like a foreign language. Nothing had been perfect for a long time, if ever.

She straightened up, her hands rubbing her stomach. "Well, for one, Bob popped the question."

Suddenly I felt cold. I didn't understand my reaction, since I had known this day was going to come eventually. *Get a grip, Reg.* It wasn't as if Dad had been gone for three months. It'd been three years. Three long, un-perfect years.

"Yay, Mom." I mustered a smile. She deserved a smile. I was going to be gone in eight months and she'd be alone. No matter how I felt, I knew that she didn't deserve to be alone. Even if she was with Bob Huffy, Dad's old boss of Bob Huffy Construction. Bob Huffy, the guy who gave me Bob Huffy Construction calendars and store gift cards for Christmas.

She put her left hand out, and I squinted. The ring was old, the gold dull and the stone red and cloudy.

"It was his grandma's. The stone's a ruby, but I'm going to change it out next week. Bob said I could."

It didn't surprise me that she was going to change the stone. This was the same woman who'd thrown away all her perfectly fine fifty-dollar discount designer sunglasses and now wears a pair of three-hundred-dollar Diors.

"Bob's going to spring for a new diamond? I didn't know the construction business was that lucrative."

"Oh, he's not buying it. I am."

The bathroom fan started to hum louder. Or at least it seemed like it. "A diamond?"

"Flawless and at least three carats," she confirmed.

I took a couple of steps backward, letting the curtain fall between us. I grabbed the towel I'd put over the curtain rod and wrapped it around my shoulders. I realized I was shaking.

"Reg, I have something else to tell you."

What more did she have to tell me? That we were going to sell the house and squat somewhere under a cactus, sleeping at night with the lizards and scorpions and rattlesnakes? That we'd use her diamond ring to blind the jackrabbits we'd be killing for food?

"I made good tonight, Reg."

My mind tried to decipher that. "What's 'good,' Mom?"

I didn't hear anything from the other side of the curtain. I wrapped the towel under my arms and pulled back the curtain. Mom was bent over the sink again. "How 'good' did you do in Vegas, Mom?" I couldn't keep the sarcastic tone from surfacing briefly.

Her voice was muffled, and I had to work to hear her. "It wasn't in Vegas. I mean, I found out there, but I didn't make good there."

"What did you find out, Mom?" The last time Mom had been this spacey was when she found out Dad had died. She'd been doubled over then, too. I flipped through a mental Rolodex. Both sets of grandparents were dead, and our only relatives were Aunt Barb and her family.

"Barb's okay, right?"

"I found out last night, when I watched the news. I wanted to call you, but I knew you were working and you don't answer your phone when you're working. And you don't sleep enough, so I didn't want to call you when you got home." She wasn't making a lot of sense, and I tried to piece together anything that sounded sane. She'd been watching the news and she didn't want to tell me whatever it was over the phone.

"Oh my God." Aunt Barb was supposed to have come last night and gotten her Pretty Lady products. I had forgotten that she was supposed to come until I was getting ready to go home and saw the pink bag in my work locker. "It's Aunt Barb, isn't it?" I stepped over the lip of the tub.

"Barb's fine."

"Then what did you hear on the news that made you freak?"

"I'm not freaked. I'm … I'm … I guess I am freaked, huh?" She let out another shaky laugh. "Reg? It happened. It finally happened." She whispered, "We did it, babe. We finally won the lottery."

CHAPTER THREE

This message is for Mrs. Shaw. This is Paris at Expressions.
We were able to get you in with Fabian for a cut and color and
a deep-tissue massage with Alicia. Blaze said she could get you
in for a facial, too. Give us a call to confirm. Also, we need a
three-hundred-dollar deposit to hold the reservation.
Okeydoke. Bye!

WHAT DO YOU THINK ABOUT butterscotch chocolate crumble with a cinnamon graham cracker crust?" It was Monday morning, and Sarah stood over me, her backpack with a Yoda zipper pull dangling by her hip, the computer lab crowd typing around us.

"Any cream in it?" My body had no problem with milk or cheese, but anything that used pure cream—like ice cream or whipped cream—made me throw up like someone who's ridden the Tilt-A-Whirl twenty times too many.

"None."

"Then it sounds like a winner." My words came out peppy. I was never peppy, especially with no caffeine in my system. It must have been the

ONE POINT SIX MILLION DOLLARS.

That's how much Mom won. That *we* won.

And I hadn't stopped thinking about it since. That's why I hadn't slept yet and why I'd been in the computer lab since it had opened at 6:30 A.M.

I had ten more minutes and one conclusion paragraph to go before the bell for homeroom rang. Adrenaline was getting me through this paper. Pure, lottery-fueled adrenaline.

Sarah looked at the computer screen, unscrewing the lid from her water bottle. "Wow. You're working on a paper that's due today? That's a first. Did you finally decide that getting zeros sucked?"

I'd decided to finish the paper after I realized I couldn't go to sleep last night. And I couldn't procrastinate by calling Sarah; her mom was a Nazi when it came to anyone calling or texting during Mrs. Bretton's 8:00 P.M. to 7:00 A.M. do-not-disturb hours, and I couldn't call Pete because Sarah would have killed me if I'd told him before I'd told her.

She stood there, drinking her water, waiting for an answer. But I didn't have one to give her. After all, how do you tell someone you've won the lottery? That you've won one point six wonderful, beautiful million dollars? So instead I started typing the conclusion and tried to lower the decibel on the big, booming voice that kept shouting

ONE POINT SIX MILLION DOLLARS

in my head.

"Yo, Regina. You okay?"

I clicked the save button and turned to her. I opened my mouth, the words there, teetering on the precipice that separated dream from reality. Once I said it out loud, it would be real.

Before I could get a consonant out, some kid from my sophomore year chemistry class walked by. "Nice stain."

I looked down, and sure enough, a coffee stain the size of a golf ball was on the stomach of my dad's Diamondbacks jersey. I hadn't seen it because of my boobs. They weren't big boobs, but they weren't skinny girl boobs either. I felt my face burn, and I put my palms on my cheeks, trying to cool them down.

Go home and take a Shaw-er flashed like a neon sign in my head. I grabbed Sarah's bottle and put the mouth against the stain, soaking it. I used my nail and scrubbed. When that didn't work, I took my sweat jacket off the back of my chair and tied it high around my waist. I was wet and cold, but at least I didn't look dirty anymore.

"Her stain beats your fashion sense any day of the week, Melman," Sarah called after him. I didn't do comebacks, since that fell under the heading of *confrontations*. But that was part of the reason we'd been best friends for so long—Sarah said stuff Pete and I didn't.

"As always, you're my superhero, S." My eyes caught the second hand of the clock. "But unless you've got the power to stop time, I've got two minutes left to run spell-check and print this out. Talk later we will?"

"Talk later we will," she Yoda'd back to me.

As she walked out, I looked at the clock. Where was a wormhole when you needed one?

"So, I heard."

Bridget leaned against the locker next to mine, school over for the day. She smelled like the three-hundred-dollar-a-bottle perfume Aunt Barb wore. She was wearing a junior varsity cheerleading sweater and skirt, and even though it was late October, her legs were tan. Circling her neck was my black-pearl pendant necklace.

"And what did you hear, Bridget?" I pulled out a book, trying to keep my eyes off the necklace, and saw Sarah walking down the hallway. She slowed her pace when she made out who I was talking to. She grimaced and sat down on a bench, hugging her backpack while she waited Bridget out. Sarah couldn't stomach my cousin; join the club.

"That you're, like, rich now." She smiled, but it looked

tight and unnatural on a face that was used to pouting and judging. "It was something like two million, right?"

I pulled out my phone and punched in "Like, gag me." I sent it to Sarah. A second later, I heard her snort from her bench. "Something like that."

I knew immediately this was the wrong answer. I should have known by now to stick to yes or no answers with Bridget. The less she knew, the less she had to work with.

"Wow." The bored look that was usually in her eyes when she had to talk to me had disappeared. "Any plans for the money yet?" Her eyes wandered from my stretched-out jersey to my three-year-old sneakers. "Like, a new wardrobe should be first on your list. Just say the word and we'll go to Vegas and close down the shops at Caesars Palace. I'll give you the benefit of my eye for style, and you can buy me a purse and some shoes and we'll call it even."

Caesars Palace had the best shopping in Vegas: Versace, Louis Vuitton, Christian Dior. I just nodded as Bridget kept talking. About money and how to spend the money and where to spend the money. Mom had already done the same monologue yesterday when I was still dripping on the bathroom floor.

"So, you know how I play the Arizona Five?" she'd said, still propping herself up over the sink. "I played it yesterday, using the numbers off your fortune cookie from Wong's."

We won the lottery. We won the lottery? Finally, I said, "Oh my God. You won the stupid Arizona Five?"

She straightened up from the sink and turned on the faucet. She picked up the bar of soap and started scrubbing her hands. "Sorry it isn't the Powerball."

I moved so I was standing on the side of the sink, and I couldn't really comprehend that we had won money and yet I was standing barefoot on cold, cracked concrete, bits and pieces of the old linoleum still stuck in the corners of the room. Another Dad project that hadn't been finished. "I don't care about Powerball, Mom. The Arizona Five is huge! Think about all the things we could pay off."

She shrugged and scrubbed harder. "It's not like we won three hundred million dollars or something."

And finally, her words started sinking in. And I started a conversation I never thought I'd have in a million years. "Mom, us winning anything right now is good news. We don't need three hundred million dollars." Three hundred million was overkill. We didn't need that much money. But . . . "A million. A million would be awesome. It would get us out of debt. We could finally get a good house!"

"There's nothing wrong with this house." She stopped scrubbing her red hands. "This was your father's dream house."

I tried to keep my eyes off the concrete floor, the pink

tile in the tub, and the chipped pink sink. Proof that I wasn't being crazy asking for a good house. This might have been my dad's dream house if he had stayed alive long enough to finish it, but it was so not mine.

I 'tried to backtrack. "Mom, I'd be happy no matter what. A million, a hundred million, same difference. We can pay off our bills and stuff, right?"

She ignored my question. "Well, we won, all right." She turned off the faucet and pulled a white slip of paper out of her jean pocket. She finally was smiling again, but it didn't seem to spread to her eyes. "The big prize was one point six million bucks, give or take a few dollars for taxes."

One point six million. Enough for our bills and Dad's student loan and Mom's past-due notices. Enough so maybe Mom didn't have to hawk Pretty Lady on the weekends.

Pretty Lady . . . I opened the door to my locker wider and looked inside, Bridget still talking purses behind me. I wiggled the mangled bag out from underneath my six-hundred-page trigonometry book. "I forgot. Aunt Barb's order came in."

Bridget ignored it and asked, "So, are you up for it?" I had never really met anyone—outside of Pete—who had such a one-track mind. Being an only child with access to too much money had made Bridget's me-me-me tendencies get worse and worse over the years. Pete, on the other hand, at least tried to think of someone else on those occasions when we called him on it.

"Am I up for what?" I was tired, glad that tonight was my night off at Crapmart. I wasn't ready to quit. I might have been one point six million dollars richer, but until I saw the money, felt the money, and rolled in the money, I wasn't giving up that paycheck.

Bridget's smile started to look less sincere. "Vegas. You know, the city that never sleeps, the 'what happens here stays here' place? Or does leaving Waterview freak you out? Maybe you'd be perfectly content staying here in Waterview, marrying your Waterview husband and raising your little Waterview kids in a trailer behind your mom's house until the day you die."

My hand that was holding out the Pretty Lady bag lowered. Is that how people saw me? As someone who never, ever wanted to leave Waterview? Who was just one bad debt away from trailer trash? I wanted to leave Waterview more than anyone in my senior class or Bridget's junior class. People who didn't know the first thing about me.

I didn't even realize my arm had moved until Bridget yanked the bag out of my numb, immobile fingers. "Call me if you're ready to cut the umbilical cord with Waterview."

She left, and I watched her and her designer purse and the neck wearing my necklace grow smaller and smaller.

Bridget knew how to spend money and how to flutter her eyes at Daddy to get more money. She'd learned from Aunt Barb. And Aunt Barb had learned from Grandma, who had had five husbands, rich tastes, and the belief that she deserved nice things, no matter what.

"So what did the Golden Child want today?" Sarah stood in front of me, but her eyes were following Bridget as she clip-clopped down the hallway. She knew that Bridget had nice things and a bedroom that could rival the presidential suite of any hotel, but she didn't know that our relationship had nothing to do with family and everything to do with blackmail. "I'll kick her ass if you need me to. Just blink your right eye and my foot will connect with that stick in her hole."

I shook my head and made myself smile. "Just the usual Golden Child stuff." I physically forced myself to stop thinking about Bridget's parting words. I leaned my ear against my shoulder and did the same thing on the other side, popping the tense muscles in my neck.

"Where's Pete?" I asked. I had to tell her about the lottery before Bridget opened her fat mouth around her. Not that I was too worried. They didn't exactly run in the same circles.

"The career lab. He's going over his essay for North-western with Ms. Parker." Sarah looped her arm through mine. "Feel like going and filling out some applications? C'mon, fill one out and I'll treat you to dinner."

"Actually, that's what I wanted to talk to you about."

"What are you going to spend the money on first?" Sarah asked the question as soon as we were seated at one of the best white-linen-covered tables at Foster's. Our view was the marina and the sun setting over the Chemehuevi Mountains. The only other people around us were a couple in their fifties with a champagne bucket next to their table.

It took a second to hit me: I was treating my friends to dinner at the fanciest restaurant in town. I still hadn't seen the lottery money, but knowing it was there was good enough. Anyway, taking my friends out to dinner wasn't anything like blowing money on clothes in Vegas.

And I had to hand it to Pete and Sarah, they had taken the news pretty well. Sarah had said "Shut up" about twenty times, and Pete had looked up long enough from his video game to give me a high five.

"Well, the first thing I'm spending the money on is this dinner." I tore into the herbed focaccia in the center of the table.

"Besides that," she said. "I mean, what big-ticket item do you have your eye on?"

"Um, the mortgage payment this month?" I said around

a mouthful of bread. They knew about Mom's spending habits, so I didn't have to really explain this one.

"Boring." Pete crunched the ice from his water goblet. "How about some vintage *Star Wars* memorabilia? I know a dealer out in Sherman Oaks who says investing in top-of-the-line collectibles is better than buying a Picasso."

"She's not wasting the money on Yoda crap," Sarah snapped back. The couple next to us looked over. Even I was startled. Sarah had been on edge tonight, especially with all things Pete. To me she said, "But you should start thinking what you want to use the money on."

"For instance?" I asked.

"For instance, college tuition." The way she said it, Pete wasn't the only one she was on edge with.

Copying Pete's inflection and nasal tone, I said, "Boring."

"How about a car? You're always complaining about having no wheels," Pete said.

Out of all the ideas they had—tuition, *Star Wars* Camp, a diamond-encrusted class ring—that was the best one.

We were still on the salad course when I saw Bob Huffy of Bob Huffy Construction come in. Or I guess he was Bob Huffy, Mom's New Fiancé. His daughter and seven-year-old grandson sped by me, each giving me a quick wave.

"Nature calls," Bob chuckled, stopping at our table and

gesturing at his speed-walking companions. "I didn't expect to see you here, Regina."

I hated how he called me Regina. Like I had done something wrong.

"Hey, Bob. You know Sarah and Pete, right?"

He nodded, giving them a polite smile. Of course he knew them. You don't come around for three years and not know your girlfriend's daughter's friends. You might not know your girlfriend's daughter too much, but oh well.

"You celebrating your mom's lottery win?" he asked.

Bob did have a way with stating the obvious. I nodded.

"Well, make sure you don't get in too late. Your mom said that you worked real late at Cashmart last night. If you miss out on too much sleep for too long, you'll get yourself sick."

Uh, whatever. As if he even cared. He'd been feeling uncomfortable around me and Jeff ever since he started dating Mom. Of course, Mom said it was because he thought we might feel weird about him being Dad's old boss. Ya think?

He left, and dinner ended up lasting two hours, with the bill coming to $320. We'd had lobster, scallops, filet mignon, and anything else that was on the higher end of the menu. Both Pete and Sarah started complaining of being stuffed halfway through our third course, but I told them they could take what they wanted home. It was my treat, after all. Inside, I hyperventilated a little. I thought of all the bills I could have paid with that money.

"I think that's a little excessive, Reg." Sarah pushed her plate away, scrutinizing me. "A little too Imogene, don't you think?"

I rolled my eyes at her, but she had a point. I gave the waitress my debit card so she could electronically take some of my in-case-Mom-makes-us-homeless money. As soon as the Arizona Lottery Commission released the money to my mom next week, I'd put the money back into my account. Mom owed me a ton of money, and I was finally going to get it back.

"What do you think, Reg? The forty-two-inch, or should I just say screw it and buy the sixty-five?" Mom stood next to me, both of us in the only TV store in town: dear ol' Crapmart.

It was late, almost eleven, and I was overwhelmed by LCDs versus plasmas, Sonys versus Panasonics, HD versus non-HD. But I didn't let my eyes wander from the wall of TVs. Electronics was directly in front of Say Cheese! and Flannel Guy.

"Do we even have cable?" I asked, trying to distract myself. Cable had been cut off a couple of months ago; we wouldn't be able to get it reinstated until we paid off our bill and put down a five-hundred-dollar security deposit.

Mom studied a product card mounted in front of one of the TVs. "I'll take care of that later. Anyway, there's always DVDs." Mom started jabbing the buttons on a remote pasted to a stand in front of a plasma. "Feel like a movie tonight on our new big-screen TV?"

"Our new big-screen? I thought we were just window shopping." I realized I had crossed my arms in front of me, and I forced myself to uncross them. To keep my body language passive and not defensive. "Did the lottery people already put the money into your account?"

She faced me, the TVs forgotten behind her, and pulled my hands into hers. "I know I've been bad in the past about paying you back." She squeezed my fingers. "But, honey, we've won lots and lots of money. We don't have to worry anymore. *You* don't have to worry anymore. Those times are behind us. Gone. See you later alligator."

I tried to slip my fingers out of hers, but she held on to them. I knew we had money, but I also knew my mother. I looked into her eyes, a bright light blue like mine, the blue of a tidal wave before it hit a city and demolished it. But I couldn't say no and risk her throwing a tantrum here. In front of Say Cheese!. And *him*.

"You *promise* me," I said, emphasizing the *promise*,

"you'll pay me back when the money comes in?" We'd won the lottery. Mom had to pay me back.

Right?

The first time Mom borrowed money from me, I was two months old. Grandpa Shaw had given my mother a hundred-dollar bill to start a savings account for me. At least, that's what he'd told me when I was six and spent a week at his farm outside of Phoenix.

When I came home, Mom had asked me how my visit with Grandpa Shaw had gone.

"Grandpa said I have a hundred dollars."

"Yeah?" Mom continued to read the *TV Guide*.

"He said he gave me a hundred dollars when I was a baby."

Mom had finally looked at me. "That's right, he did. But I used it to buy you diapers and a stroller." She patted my hand. "Your dad and I didn't have much money back then."

Dad had been sitting at the kitchen table, working on a puzzle. We were living in an apartment on the other side of Waterview, and Jeff and I shared a room with each other and the washer and dryer. "That money helped us raise you, kiddo."

"But I need it now," I'd said, pouting.

"Oh? What do you need it for, baby girl?" Mom had

pulled me onto her lap and blew raspberries against my neck.

"A pink bike. With blue and purple streamers in the handlebars."

"That's very specific," Dad had said, hiding a smile.

"Sarah got one last week, and I want one, too."

"Oh. That explains everything." He didn't even try to hide the smile this time.

Dad had made his way over to sit next to Mom, where he started blowing raspberries against the other side of my neck. "I heard a rumor that Santa is bringing that for you."

"Christmas isn't until next year!" I'd said with a six-year-old's sense of time.

"It's in four months, Reggie. You can wait four months, right?"

The raspberries had begun doing their magic. I dissolved into laughter and forgot all about Grandpa Shaw's money.

The second time I could remember my mom borrowing money from me, I was eight. This time at a gas station on our way back from Disneyland.

I'd still had ten dollars of birthday money left; I had started the trip with fifty, but one Minnie Mouse T-shirt, a set of Mickey ears, and too many bags of candy later, I was down to ten. While Mom paid for the gas, Dad cleaned the windshield and Jeff went to the bathroom. I was at a turnstile that sold key chains. I stopped at the *S*'s, and pulled down one that said *Sarah*.

I'd gone to the counter where Mom stood, eyeing something under the glass counter.

"You ready to go, Reg?" she'd asked, not looking up.

"I have to buy this for Sarah first."

That's when Mom had looked up. "How much is it?"

I looked at the sticker. "Four ninety-nine."

Mom took the key chain from me and examined it. "Does Sarah really need a key chain?" She softened the words with a smile. I shrugged. "I dunno."

"Why don't you give her the Minnie Mouse shirt you bought?"

I looked at her as if she'd grown a second head. "That's my shirt."

"But we got you Goofy and Donald Duck already. You don't need another one."

I looked at the key chain, at the rainbow on the front, at the *Sarah* on the back. It wasn't a very good present. Sarah didn't even have a key.

I took it back to the key chain stand, placed it with the other Sarahs, and started toward the front door.

"Hey, Reg, you have cash left over from Disneyland, right?"

I nodded.

"Care to give your mom a loan?"

"A loan?"

Mom nodded toward the glass counter. "Those lottery tickets are calling our names, don't you think?"

I'd stood there, head cocked, and listened. "No," I finally said.

"It's a figure of speech, babe," Mom laughed. From the back of the gift shop, Jeff came out of the restroom and paused at a machine churning red and blue ice.

"Mom, can I get a slushie?"

"It depends on your sister, Jeff." Mom gave a tiny smile. "What do you say, Reg, you in? I'll give you half of anything I win."

It wasn't till I was older and overheard my parents talking that I found out that Dad monitored Mom's credit card usage, and so she couldn't just slip ten dollars' worth of lottery tickets onto a gas bill. Instead, she used her eight-year-old daughter as an ATM.

Reluctantly, I had given the crinkled, sweaty ten-dollar bill to her. She bought seven lottery tickets, a small blue raspberry slushie for Jeff, a roll of LifeSavers for her and Dad, and a king-size Kit Kat for me.

That day, my brother's tongue stayed blue for seven

hours, Mom won two dollars, and I felt sick from too much sugar. I hadn't even been hungry.

Mom had given me half of her winnings, as promised: one dollar. But she never paid back the original ten-dollar loan.

"More to the right. Yeah. Yeah, you've got it." Mom stood by the cart, directing everything with the earpiece of her Dior glasses.

Flannel Guy shifted the TV box to the right.

Trust me, I wished I could have found somebody else, even one of the retired guys who bagged groceries with their slow, arthritic hands. But it was late and the pickings were slim. And out of everyone working, Flannel Guy was the only one who hadn't been with a customer, didn't have a broken arm or wasn't five foot two with no upper body strength.

It was cold, and I zipped up my sweat jacket and tucked my chin inside. Flannel Guy's hair fell in his face as he battled the box into the trunk. I forced myself to look up into the moonless night and tried to keep my eyes away from the hair. And the body.

It was hard staying pissed, knowing that Flannel Guy was turning out to be pretty decent. He'd pushed the cart for us, even when Mom made him take a detour through Grocery to load up on cases of Dr Pepper. The real stuff, not the generic Crapmart brand. He'd even reorganized the trunk to make room for the box. He hadn't said one word as he moved the giant Cashmart bags holding four-for-five-dollar photo albums and almost-expired lipstick tubes tagged with yellow clearance labels, stuff Mom had all these grand plans about selling on eBay. Me, I was mortified. I gnawed on a thumbnail until I tasted blood, and even then I didn't stop. I wanted food, and this nail just wasn't doing it for me. But at least the pain took some of the bone-throbbing embarrassment away.

"I think you're all set, Mrs. Shaw." He finished tying down the trunk to the bumper with a few plastic bags he'd knotted together. He wiped his hands on his apron and stepped back, still looking at the makeshift lock. He hadn't looked at me since he had told me he'd help. "Anything else?"

"I think we're good." Mom put out her hand. But it wasn't to shake Flannel Guy's. It was to hand him something. Mom wasn't one to give tips, which meant she wasn't very suave when she handed the folded bill to Flannel Guy. Which meant that I saw the twenty as it dropped on the ground. He picked it up and pocketed it without looking at it, thanking Mom for it.

I knew we had just won the lottery. But twenty bucks for

ten minutes of work? And my emergency twenty, too? After just loaning my mother somewhere just south of three grand, even though I had promised myself I would never, ever loan my mother a penny? I dug what was left of my fingernails into the sides of my legs and repeated in my head,

ONE POINT SIX MILLION.

ONE POINT SIX MILLION.

"I can tape a bag onto the box so people know it's over-size and won't ram into you," Flannel Guy said, a frown on his face as he looked over the dimensions again. On the side, you could see 65-INCH LCD TV. I wondered what the good people of Waterview would think about seeing a TV like that sticking out of the trunk of a car with red tape on both its taillights and a V-shaped dent in the bumper from the time Mom backed into the mailbox.

Mom groaned. "Reg, I forgot the DVDs. I'll be right back." Mom started speed-walking toward the store. Over her shoulder, she said, "Don't worry about putting anything on it. We live less than a mile from here. We'll be fine."

After she left, Flannel Guy stayed. "You've been quiet."

The words were soft, but I could hear them perfectly. There was zero wind, and the crickets that were usually rubbing their legs together had finally shut up.

I nodded and made my way to the passenger door. Gabe Donaldson was dead to me. Dead. D-e-a-d.

"Pretty nice TV."

I leaned against the car, facing away from him but still seeing him out of the corner of my eye.

"My roommates have a thirteen-inch TV," he added. "It doesn't have color, though, and we have to use a clothes hanger if we want to watch, you know, *Mister Rogers* or *Barney*."

I felt my mouth being pulled into a reluctant smile. A tiny smile. Very, very tiny.

"I have to admit, though, I'm more of an Elmo guy."

I stole a look behind me but didn't see Mom. If I was being totally honest, I was glad Flannel Guy was trying to get on my good side, if only so I wouldn't be standing here all alone in a cold, dark parking lot next to a major highway. I'd heard serial killers loved highways.

I breathed onto the slick surface of the hood, and used my finger to make a design in the condensation left behind. I was glad he was here, but I still wasn't going to talk to him.

But Flannel Guy wasn't giving up as he kept up his end of this one-sided conversation. "We live over at the Waterview Apartments. You should come over sometime."

I stopped making designs on the car. I forgot for a moment that he was d-e-a-d to me. "You want me to come over to your apartment?"

"So you can see that I'm not some ogre who likes writing up people."

"Too late." I continued with my design. Actually, I was now making words. Bad words, too, with Flannel Guy's name attached to them.

"You should come over. Meet my roommates, Paul and Deadhead."

"Deadhead?" This made me look up, and I made eye contact with Gabe for the first time that night. The parking lot lights and the night around us were doing great things for his face, creating angles and shadows that played up his eyes and lips.

Oh, get a grip, Reg. Next thing you know, you're going to be writing sonnets about his nose hair.

"He likes the Dead. And waterskiing. With Waterview being sort of a water sport mecca, we decided to put down roots here."

"You're a skier?"

"I'm passable." He laughed over the word. "If you squint and I'm far, far away."

Someone's car alarm started going off. It was beeped into submission about ten seconds later.

"I hear you're friends with Pete," Flannel Guy said. "He's a great skier."

I nodded, tensing up as I prepared to defend him. Sarah and I could make fun of him, but no one else could.

"Interesting guy." Gravel rubbed against asphalt as he shifted his feet. "I saw him lip-synch the entire *Star Wars* movie when it was playing in Electronics yesterday."

"Yep. That's Pete." And because I was remembering his Dr. Jekyll and Mr. Hyde routine with me, I added, "You're not going to write him up, are you?"

"I wasn't putting him down. I think it's kind of cool. The level of dedication he has is …" He paused, and for a minute, I didn't think he was going to finish his thought. "It's pretty enviable."

I leaned my cheek against the car, and the cold metal reminded me that I was tired, my feet were starting to hurt, and I had goose bumps pretty much everywhere. Talking seemed like a good way to forget all that. "You know that bar in *Star Wars*?"

"The cantina?"

"Yeah. You know the songs that play in the background? Pete plays them on this electric keyboard. He can't play anything else—he doesn't even know chords or scales or anything—but he knows how to play that cantina music."

"See what I mean? That's dedication." Flannel Guy

smiled, and the dimple made an appearance. I turned away. I was not going to get swayed by The Dimple.

"So Reggie, listen."

I saw Mom hurrying toward me. "Looks like Mom's back." I pulled open the passenger door without giving him another look. But I had to throw Flannel Guy a bone for making an effort. "'Night, Donaldson."

CHAPTER FOUR

*Reg, it's S. What's up with not telling me about
the hotness that's Gabe Donaldson? You didn't even
mention him. What's up with that?
Unless you're not interested. [Pause.]
If I didn't have Pete, I'd be all over him.
Be thankful you don't have a Pete dragging you to stupid comic
book stores and video game stores and arcades and Star Wars
sing-alongs . . . [BEEP!]*

THE NEXT MORNING, I had a hard time trying to keep my eyes open as Ms. Moore droned on about Virginia Woolf. I hadn't made it home until after midnight, and then it had taken another hour to set up the TV and then another two-plus hours to watch the high-def version of *Pulp Fiction*. And now I was dragging, daydreaming about The Coffee Spot. It was just a small cart set up in one corner of the lunchroom with a pretty limited drink menu, but it had a dollar cup of coffee that acted like that shot of adrenaline John Travolta punched into Uma Thurman's heart.

I doodled a Chihuahua in the margins of my notebook, trying to look as if I was taking notes. I liked Ms. Moore. She'd been my art teacher freshman year, before budget cuts made her take an English position. I liked art a lot because of her. And I even liked English because of her.

But I could never get comfortable around her. I'd stolen four hundred dollars when she was the Art Club adviser, and I could barely look her in the eye ever since.

"Regina, do you have a sec?" Ms. Moore stood over my desk, and only a few kids were still in their seats, gathering their things. I guess I'd zoned out the bell. Not for the first time, either. But it was usually because I'd worked a double shift, not because I was up watching John Travolta's hairline in high def.

She slid into the desk across from mine, her dull blond bun tilting to the left. By the end of the day, it was going to be half-up and half-down her back, making her look like some half-crazed cat lady.

"If you're willing to write a note for my next class," I said.

"Great." She picked at a red pen mark on her thumb. "I wanted to talk to you about your last paper."

I didn't say anything. I was waiting to get reamed for improper margins or an incomplete thesis statement. At least I had turned it in this time.

"I noticed how well-argued it was, and the amount of research you incorporated in support of your argument was remarkable."

"Cool." Inside, I did a mental cartwheel. Maybe twelve years of grammar and sentence structure had made their way into the dormant crevices of my brain after all. I closed my notebook and slid it into my bag. I still kept my eyes away from Ms. Moore's as I drew on my bag. Today it was a caricature of Pete in Spock ears.

"I've been seeing tiny bits of this writing in your other papers, but this was the first time I saw an entire assignment—out of the few that have been turned in, of course—that was worthy of an A."

"I got an A?" I dragged my backpack on top of my desk and put my chin on it. That was a first. I don't usually do so hot on written stuff. I usually didn't have the time to read a book, do research, and then spend time typing two thousand words. But then you win the lottery and can't sleep and somehow you find the time to apply yourself.

"Yes, you got an A." The room was silent, and I realized we were the only ones in here, even though the second-period bell was about to ring. It must have been Ms. Moore's free period. "But my question is, why haven't I seen this quality of work from you before?"

Because I've been working almost thirty hours a week? Because whether I get A's or C's, I'll still be done with school in June? Because my GPA was so screwed, what did it matter?

I shrugged and played with the zipper on my bag. I avoided her eyes and told her what I thought she wanted to hear and would keep me away from a confrontation: "I'm sorry, Ms. Moore."

"Don't be sorry, Reggie. My feelings don't get hurt when you turn in a bad paper." She took in a breath and slowly exhaled it. "Anyway, I wanted to talk to you because you're failing this class."

"Failing?" The word made my heart stutter. A C was one thing. An F? Not in the plan. "I thought I had a solid C."

"You didn't turn in two papers."

I opened my mouth to argue but then stopped myself. She was right. I had decided that working double shifts was worth more to me than that paper on *Robinson Crusoe* or the essay about post-colonial something or other.

"You need to turn in at least B-quality papers for the remainder of the semester in order to pass. And they can't be late."

"No problemo." It's not as if I'd have to work sixteen-hour shifts like I had these last few months. I didn't even have to work, period, if I didn't want to. The thought left me momentarily breathless. I didn't *have* to work. For the first time in three years, I could quit if I wanted to.

Once the lottery money came in, of course.

"Keep in mind that these papers have to be pretty much perfect. With a good argument. Good research. Typewritten, not handwritten. Now that I've seen you do it, I know it can be done. The question is, do you have it in yourself for repeat performances?"

Before the one point six million, it would have been a problem. By next week, I'd have the best laptop lottery money could buy and more time on my hands than I'd know what to do with. When June came, I needed to be out of Waterview, not stuck in summer school. "I promise, I can write more good papers. You'll see."

When you've never had a lot of money, you learn to do things that require no money. One such thing is hanging out. This can mean cruising, where you drive around town with music thumping on the subwoofers installed in the trunk of some crap car. This can also mean loitering in the school parking lot.

As it turned out, Pete, Sarah, and I liked loitering, especially since it fit in rather nicely with any spare time we had between school ending and work beginning and, in Sarah's case, pie experimenting. If we weren't at school, work, or home, we were in the Waterview High School parking lot. Talking, arguing, eating crap. It was pretty much the highlight of my week, actually.

"So, Reg, I saw you getting all cozy with Gabe Donaldson last night." Pete turned on the car's CD player, cranked up the sound, and settled next to Sarah on the hood of his meticulously maintained but majorly old Honda CRX. I sat across from them on a retaining wall, my sweatshirt under my butt, thinking about how the clouds looked like little Mini Coopers as I tore open a two-pound bag of Twizzlers.

How much was a car nowadays? Because I wanted one. A lot. And I could get one with our

ONE POINT SIX MILLION.

Suddenly, the air smelled crisper, the bare, desert mountains looked bluer, and my mood improved drastically.

"Reg?"

"Huh?" I focused and tried to remember what Pete had asked. "Oh. He was helping us with that ginormous TV Mom bought." I filled my mouth with licorice and mumbled, "And I wasn't getting cozy with him."

Pete ripped off a piece of candy with his teeth. "Good."

"When do you care about my personal life, Peter?" I asked. Pete barely paid attention to his own personal life.

"It's just that I don't think he's all that great," he said.

"Actually," Sarah said slowly, taking off her cardigan and situating it over her eyes to block the sun, "I think your exact words were that he looked like a wannabe serial killer."

"He has that drifter, charmer quality about him. Like Ted Bundy," Pete explained.

"You look more like Ted Bundy than Gabe does," Sarah argued. She readjusted herself, and the hood made a crumpling noise beneath her. Pete jerked his head up at the sound. "Plus, you got that loner geek side of you that screams slice-and-dicer."

A car honked as it went by, and I saw Ms. Moore waving from the driver's seat. I nodded to her and chewed off another hunk of licorice, pretending like my throat hadn't just closed up.

"Pete, did you stay up all night and have another *Star Wars* marathon?" Sarah shifted her weight again, the hood popping under her. "Is that why it seems like you're on something? Lack of sleep and too much Han Solo?"

"That's not the point." Pete's head was still up and looking at Sarah. "Can you pick a spot and stop moving? I don't need a Sarah butt print in my hood."

"Your big head is going to do a whole lot more damage than my butt ever would." Sarah lifted her head and pulled the sweater from her eyes to look at me. "Don't tell me you didn't notice how cute Gabe is."

Pete scowled. "Will you stop with the 'he's so cute' thing? He's a guy who's got a major flannel fetish and, who knows, may have some cut-up man-meat in his freezer."

I didn't get between them. They were seriously close to breaking up again, and I learned a long time ago I couldn't take sides. I'd done that once during freshman year, and both of them ganged up on me when they were on-again.

"Trust me, I noticed the dimple," I said. "But then he played the control-freak card, and any and all attraction disappeared." I snapped my fingers. "Poof."

"It's because he wrote you up, isn't it?" Sarah said knowingly.

"Of course it's because he wrote me up." I took another mouthful of licorice, a chokable amount, actually. It kept my mind off Gabe at least, the whole trying to breathe and survive thing.

"Is that what you're mad about?" Pete said after a minute. "You shouldn't be."

"And why is that?"

"You deserved it." He said it so matter-of-factly, I had a momentary vision of me taking the Wookie bobblehead glued to Pete's dashboard and smashing it on his hood. Sarah's butt print would be the least of his worries.

"And why are you okay with this? What happened to him being a serial-killing plague to all womankind?"

"He still is. But he was within his rights to write you up. I heard the district manager was there and saw you with that rat. He *told* Gabe to write you up."

So Gabe was just the messenger. Well, messengers had a way of getting shot. "Fine. So I revise what I said. Gabe's just a big Cashmart suck-up."

Pete didn't try to correct me. Instead, he glanced over at Sarah, who'd put the sweater back over her eyes. "I heard he's rooming with meth freaks, too."

I didn't like Gabe, but I also didn't like rumors. Years in Bridget's sphere of influence had taught me that. "Gabe said they were skiers."

Pete leaned back on the car, his forearm shielding his eyes from the sun. "Yeah, sure. That's why I never see them on the water. Cuz they're such serious skiers. They must work out in the other lake. Wait a minute, there *is* no other lake." He put down his arm and squinted into the sun. "You could say they were dingoes teaching aliens how to do origami, and I'd believe that more."

The conversation trailed off at that point. I wasn't in the mood to talk about Gabe Donaldson, and Sarah and Pete were in the middle of some sort of cold war.

"Hey, did we figure out what we were doing for Halloween yet?" Pete asked. He never liked silence for too long.

"Darcy's," Sarah and I said in unison. We always went

to Darcy Huber's Halloween party. No matter what, Sarah made me take the night off for, as she called it, "teenage frivolity." Darcy's party usually started with a scavenger hunt that was more Truth or Dare than any sort of hunt. It was kind of insane and really fun.

Around us, the last of the high school students peeled out of the parking lot, on their way to football practice, friends' houses, volunteer activities that would pad their college applications. A quick glance at my watch told me that our loitering for the day was coming to an end.

"C'mon, slackers," I said. "I need a ride."

Three months ago, Birdie got into a fight with Mr. Brendon's Shih Tzu. She came home with a torn ear, a bloody side, and a pretty scratched-up eye. I was almost hysterical. Mom was in Laughlin with the Clunker, our only mode of transportation, Pete was out of town at a *Star Wars* thing, and I couldn't reach Sarah. I guess I could have called Bob, but I didn't have that kind of relationship with him. He seemed busy with his daughter and grandson, and a lot of the time, I think he saw me and Jeff as temporary fixtures in my mom's life.

I'd walked Birdie to the clinic, blood on my T-shirt, on my arms and face, on the towel I'd cradled Birdie in. I guess I'd been a sight, because Doc had taken Birdie out of my arms, a silver cane hanging from a cuff on her forearm, and limped into surgery without even talking to me about payment first.

Doc was Dr. Maggie Hutton, the owner of Paws and Claws Veterinary Clinic which, like almost everything else in this town, was in the same shopping plaza as Cashmart.

When Doc got out of surgery, she'd told me Birdie would be as good as new, minus one eye. I'd almost crushed the doc as I hugged her when she told me Birdie was going to be okay.

I'd pulled the debit card out of my wallet, not even thinking twice about using the money I'd been painstakingly saving for the last year. "How much do I owe you, Doc?"

She hadn't looked at me, instead focusing on picking at a loose thread sticking out from a shirt button. "Between surgery and aftercare costs, the bill comes to around six thousand dollars."

At the time, I'd only had four thousand in checking. "Six—six *thousand* dollars?" I felt something dark and sickly pulling at me. I should never have gotten Birdie. If I couldn't afford her medical care, then I didn't deserve to have a cat. She didn't deserve to have *me*, a girl who had a wet noodle of a backbone when her mom asked for Venti lattes at Starbucks or an advance for her cell phone bill.

Doc had put her hand out, pushing the debit card I was

holding back toward my wallet, a crappy Velcro thing I'd decorated with a Sharpie and caricatures of Sarah and Pete. "You work over at Cashmart, don't you? I think I've seen you in Say Cheese! when I'm shopping there."

I'd nodded, still pretty deaf, dumb, and mute after the six-thousand-dollar quote.

"I see you there a lot. Are you working there full-time?"

I was still feeling numb, so I rattled off numbers. I was good at numbers. "I'm only allowed to work twenty hours since I'm still in school. But I usually work thirty if I can pick up other people's shifts."

She'd nodded and gestured toward the stark-white walls in her waiting room. "How are you with a paintbrush and paint?"

"Why?"

"I'm thinking maybe you can work off the bill."

I looked around. The walls looked as if they could use a coat or two of a boring beige or slightly less boring sage.

"How are you with painting animals?" she asked.

I said the first thing that came into my mouth: "Depends. Are you holding them down and I'm roller-brushing them?"

She'd laughed until she started to hiccup. "I mean painting animals on the walls. Can you draw?"

"A little." I hadn't picked up a stick of charcoal, a watercolor, or even a colored pencil since ninth grade. Not since Dad and the air conditioner and the Art Club money. All I did nowadays was doodle, constantly.

"You must have some sort of artistic gene to be working over at Say Cheese!. And I saw your wallet. You did some pretty amazing work there." She bumped my elbow with hers and said, "C'mon, give it a try. You can at least try, right? There's no time limit. Come in when you can, cuddle a few cats, paint. What do you say, huh?"

And now here I was, three months later, a tabby, a black Lab, an African gray parrot, and a partially done Chihua-hua under my belt. I figured it would take me until the end of senior year to get it all done. But Doc didn't seem to be in a rush. That wasn't her style. I think it was because she'd been forced to be patient after her leg got crushed. She's been through nine operations since the car accident, with another operation planned in a month. In the meantime, she used a silver cane that cuffed to her lower arm and spent two hours every morning with a physical therapist in a pool and on weight machines.

I didn't understand all the time and money she was putting into getting a perfect leg. It wasn't as if the leg or the cane got in the way of how she removed tumors, set bones, or stitched up messed-up cats.

I concentrated on the mural in front of me. "That Chihuahua is looking like a cat, isn't it?"

"A little." Doc limped toward the wall and put on her reading glasses. "But you've nailed the Lab. Those eyes are almost human."

I headed into the restroom off the waiting room and fished under the sink for my supplies. "I can fix that."

"Don't you dare!" I heard her scold behind me. "Labs, out of almost any other dog out there, are very humanlike."

"So you're okay with the eyes?" I asked doubtfully. "I can change them. My feelings won't be hurt."

"I'm more than okay with the eyes." Dr. Maggie took off her glasses and put her hand in the middle of the mural, her fingers spread out like she was protecting the dogs, cats, and birds that had been created with a little bit of acrylic and a lot of elbow grease. "I love the eyes. You've got a gift, Reggie, a real gift."

I looked down at my palette, suddenly very interested in getting the brown and white and yellow to the exact tan I needed for the Chihuahua. I guess it was cool to have a gift. It would have been nice to have a gift in chemistry or math so I could make a buttload of money being a heart surgeon or a stockbroker. But art? Art wasn't going to give me any sort of real job. A stable job. With a 401(k) and benefits and pet insurance, like the kind that came with the photo manager position. That *had* come with the photo manager position.

"How's ol' Birdie doing, by the way?" Doc asked.

"Good." I filled a plastic cup of water. "All healed and adjusting to her new sense of depth perception." Every once in a while, she'd run into a wall, but she always played it off as if she'd meant to do it.

"Still staying indoors?"

"Yes, Doc, she's one hundred percent indoors." That had been part of the deal. Paint the mural and make Birdie an indoor cat and that six-thousand-dollar bill was settled.

Doc smiled and pulled back her white coat sleeve, glancing at her watch. "Say, I have a checkup in a couple of minutes, and Bev's still getting coffee over at Cashmart. Wanna help?"

I tightened the lids on the baby jars holding the acrylic paint I'd been using. "I don't know how good I'll be."

"You ever held a pissed-off cat before?"

Every single day. Birdie wasn't exactly Miss Congeniality. "Yeah, definitely."

We headed toward one of the examination rooms, and Doc, a playful gleam in her eyes, turned around to add, "Mrs. Haskell's cat can be a real butthead. Just stay clear of the back paws and you should be fine."

I thought about Birdie and Pete and Sarah. But most of all, I thought about Gabe Donaldson. "Lucky for you, Doc, I speak fluent butthead."

CHAPTER FIVE

Reg, it's me. Sarah. Sarah Henrietta Bretton.
Don't even think about canceling tonight.
I know you want to. But just remember,
I know your social security number.
If you don't want to end up joining the Navy, the Army,
and Future Farmers of America,
you will go out with me tonight.

I HATE A LOT OF THINGS. I hate my house with the worn carpet and the eBay boxes everywhere. I hate that my Dad died.
I hate that my mother is a fool when it comes to money.

And I hate Halloween.

My family was never big into traditions, but Halloween
was different. There are some people who go all out for
Christmas; with my family, it's Halloween. We might have
been living in an apartment, but Dad still outlined the
windows in black lights and the railing out in front with

orange pumpkin lights. Mom would dress like Morticia Addams, Dad would be Gomez, and Jeff and I would be Wednesday and Pugsley. Some years I was Wednesday, some years I was Pugsley. We probably bought three hundred pounds of candy, most of it family-sized Hershey bars. We were *the* apartment to go to on Halloween.

We haven't had that kind of Halloween for three years. Jeff tried that first year, but we fought over who was going to untangle the lights, who was going to buy the candy, even who was going to be Gomez. As it turned out, that first Halloween after Dad died, Mom was in Laughlin, Jeff was at his girlfriend's, and I ate the bowl of candy I'd bought but was too depressed to hand out.

A lot of things died with Dad, and Halloween was just one of them. It started with us no longer going out on the boat, and then us eating dinner separately. At Christmas, everyone still sort of tried. At least we used to until we forgot to buy a tree two years ago. Then last year, Jeff didn't even try to make it home; he called us the day before Christmas, saying gas was too much, the drive was too long, blah blah shut up already.

Sarah knew I wallowed on Halloween. That's why she'd made it her mission to drag me out for Darcy's Darkest Hour Scavenger Hunt.

"House key?" Sarah stood in front of my yard, a brown

wig from what looked like the 1800s on her head, a dark green dress fanning from her hips to the ground.

I patted my cleavage. "Check."

"Mother?"

"Vegas."

"Of course. Party face?"

I gave her a wide, cheesy grin.

"We'll work on it," she said, pulling a list out of her dress pocket. "We've gotta go to The Coffee Spot first, and one of us has to either tell our bra size or chug down ten espressos in under a minute." She punched my arm. "We've totally got that one in the bag."

I was pretty sure she meant the espresso, although I wasn't shy about my bra size. I had boobs. I wasn't going to pretend I didn't. "Is the school even open?" I asked.

"I don't think so. But Darcy's dad is the main janitor or something, so he probably pulled a few strings." She studied the list while I rubbed my hands up and down my arms. I thought about backtracking inside and grabbing a sweatshirt, but Sarah seemed to be studying me now. "What exactly are you?"

"Uma. Thurman, you know? From *Pulp Fiction?*" I had on a white shirt, Spanx in order to fit into the shirt, a black wig, and red nails. I also had the most ridiculous five-inch stilettos on. But Mom had insisted that the look wasn't complete without them. I sort of agreed. I definitely felt more like Uma Thurman with them on. It was better than being a storm trooper again.

"Where's Pete?" I asked.

"Frankly, my dear, I don't give a damn."

I scanned Sarah from her head to her toes. "You're Scarlett O'Hara? I totally thought you were some Jane Austen chick."

Sarah ignored me as she continued to look over the list. "Uh-oh."

"What?"

She looked up at me. "You know what? The scavenger hunt is dumb. We'll go to the party and just say we did it."

I rolled my eyes at her. "Whatever. You live for this stupid hunt."

"You say that now. But when you see number five, you're going to want to have me gutted and dismembered."

I made a face. "Nice visual. Anyway, I don't care what number five is. We're doing it."

I hated number five. I hated it and Darcy and the universe and its stupid, stupid, *stupid* sense of humor.

"Only one of us needs to go up there. I'll do it." Sarah had been saying the same thing over and over again, ever since I pretend-fainted when I read number five. I seriously considered her offer, but something in my gut wouldn't let me take her up on it. Pride? Anger? Curiosity? I shook my head. "No. I'm going to do it. I've worked here for two years. The Photo Goddess does not just scurry off into the night, her tail between her legs, licking her wounds."

Sarah gave me a look. "Yeah? Then what exactly would you call all the name-calling and stewing you've been doing these last couple of days?"

"Shut up." I drew in a deep breath and blew it out. She was right. I had been a wuss. But now I was a rich wuss. I was no longer You-Stole-My-Job Reggie. I was Yay-You-Stole-My-Job Reggie. "Let's just say it's time to take the upper hand back. I'll see you in a minute."

We stood just inside the front entrance of Cashmart, the automatic doors opening and closing. In front of us, a man with a white jumpsuit with gold sparkles walked in, muttonchops down to his chin, a pair of brown-tinged aviator glasses on. "Good evenin', ladies."

"Hey, Elvis," Sarah said.

Elvis wasn't just dressed for Halloween. Elvis dressed this way every single day, and was sort of a year-round fixture in Waterview. No one knew his real name or what he did for a living or where he lived, but everyone knew him, waved at him, and talked about him.

"Are you sure you don't want me to at least come with you?" Sarah asked.

"I'm afraid you'd take Truth. And I don't trust you with truth, Big Mouth Bretton."

She made a face. "Whatever. I wouldn't tell him how you have to sleep with Mr. Puffin every night. Or that you eat like a termite when you're stressed."

Sarah really did know too much about me. I stuck out my tongue at her and made my way across the linoleum toward the back of the store. I only slipped about three times in those stupid stilettos.

I'd managed to learn how to walk by the time I reached Photo. Gabe was by himself, studying the computer screen.

"Hey."

"Hey." He looked up, and the smile that had started seemed to stall. "Wow."

My confidence experienced a surge with that one word, like the kind that powers up a city block after a blackout. But I ignored the feeling. Gabe was still d-e-a-d to me. Well, maybe he was more living dead to me. It was Halloween, after all.

"How'd you get on Darcy's scavenger hunt?" I asked.

"My roommate dates her sister, and she asked me to be a part of tonight's festivities."

"Deadhead's girlfriend?"

"No, Paul's." He smiled. "Deadhead sort of has a thing for pretty girls who don't really have anything else going for them."

"He sounds like a winner."

Gabe leaned on the counter. "Compared to Gabe the Write-Up Jerk, he is."

Again, I couldn't quite contain a tiny smile.

"So, which is it?" he said. "Truth or Dare?"

"Dare."

He leaned forward, pulling and pushing a pen cap on and off. "Are you sure? The truth might be easier."

Darcy had written out the Truths and Dares on her Scavenger Hunt, so I was well aware of which truth I'd have to tell Gabe.

"I'm not telling you my weight."

"What's the big deal?"

"The big deal is you'd have to immediately die after I told you."

The Dimple made the ever so slightest appearance. "Fine." He wiped an imaginary speck off the counter and pitched his voice into a low bass. "Regina Shaw, Photo Goddess Extraordinaire, your Dare is to give me the one thing in the world I won't be able to say no to."

Sarah and I had already talked this through. When it came to boys, there were a lot of things they couldn't say no to. As it turns out, the list is sort of long. And scary. So I had picked the least-scary option.

I reached into my bra, my hand closing on what I needed. Without looking away, I came back with what he couldn't say no to.

A pack of Reese's Peanut Butter Cups.

He laughed. It was loud and abrupt and real. "I guess this qualifies." Gabe took the package, and he raised his eyebrows. "And where exactly is the candy that used to be in here?"

"Oops." I pulled away from the counter, and once again I was aware of the bad pop music in Electronics and the harsh fluorescent lighting. I grinned and rubbed my tummy. "Yum-yum."

"You're such a brat."

"And you're a jerk."

Was this flirting? I had no idea. I hadn't gotten a lot of practice in the last eighteen years. Could I count out a drawer to the last penny? Check. Could I scrub scuff marks off the linoleum? Check. But flirting? That box was empty.

All I knew was that this thing between us felt comfortable. Cozy almost. And I was feeling a little drunk from it, which was the only explanation for what I said next: "You suck for writing me up."

"I know." He leaned on the counter, and a mixture of musk and spices hovered between us.

"And just so you know, you suck for getting the photo manager position over me."

"I know," Gabe said. I must have looked confused, because he added, "Pete filled me in with the backstory. How Fellers promised it to you and how you thought it was in the bag."

I should have been mad at Pete, but I wasn't. I was glad that the messy details had been passed along by a third party. "Okay, then. So, we've come to an understanding?"

He nodded, an earnest look on his face but something else sparkling in his eyes. "Yes. I suck, you look awesome, and we are on the schedule together tomorrow. Fresh start?" He held out his hand. I took it, and instead of a shake, it was more like a squeeze. A warm, electrifying squeeze.

"So, how'd it go?" Sarah asked when I got back.

"Good." A grin split across my face. The skin over my cheeks actually hurt, they stretched so much. "Great, actually."

"Excellent." We headed back to her car to get to our next spot, the Waterview Public Library. "So now would be a good time to tell you that I helped Darcy pick the spots for the scavenger hunt?"

I grabbed her skirt, and she jerked to a stop. "What if things had gone horribly, horribly wrong, you wench?"

"I had faith in you." She started walking again. "He's too cute for you to mess things up too much."

I wanted to die. And if anyone was listening Up There, I wanted to share a room with Princess Diana and James Dean and Betty Crocker.

I think the dip at the party had cream in it, and cream was my kryptonite. Pete could tell you exactly which color kryptonite, but all I knew was the color of the vomit coming out when I staggered to the toilet at 3:00 A.M. And 5:00 A.M. And 7:30 A.M. It was now after 9:00, and I gingerly pulled the quilt up to my chin, not wanting to upset the delicate balance between my stomach and my mouth. The quilt was a relic that had more stuffing on the outside than the inside, and it was one of the few things we got from Nana Shaw when she died. In hindsight, I should have wrapped it in tissue paper and put it somewhere safe. But the garage got pretty cold during the winter, even if it was the desert, and preserving the quilt and Nana Shaw's painstaking work would have just been dumb. Colossal dumb.

Mom-with-money dumb.

I managed to fall asleep again and woke up sometime after 1:00 P.M. to the sound of talking. I moved my head, waiting for something to happen. Nothing. Then I pushed myself to a reclining position on my elbows. Still good. I pulled on my slippers, slipped into a sweatshirt, and headed to the living room, carefully putting one foot in front of the other like a drunk with a massive hangover.

"What number do you have over there?" Mom knelt on the ground, holding the end of a tape measure. She had jumbo pink rollers in her hair and Dad's old blue robe on. A little kohl was still edging her eyes from dressing up like Cleopatra for the Luxor's Halloween party, where keno was two for the price of one.

"Eighty-two and a half inches." Aunt Barb read off the numbers, her khakis slim-fitting and wrinkle-free, a pink-and-white button-down shirt flared open at the cuffs, a pink cardigan tied over her shoulders. She pressed a button and the tape whirred back into its silver box. She wrote something on a pad of paper before sipping what looked like orange juice from a champagne flute. Knowing Aunt Barb, there was more champagne than OJ in that glass. "You can do a sectional or a couch and a love seat. A glass coffee table in the middle, maybe a glass end table on one side." She looked up. "Hey, Reg."

"Hey, Aunt Barb."

"Wasn't today picture day? I could've sworn it was

today. I let Bridget borrow my Pucci scarf and my diamonds because she told me it was picture day."

Yeah, it was picture day; it came to me around seven, when the only thing that made me feel even a little better was being curled in the fetal position and hugging my knees to my chest. Anyway, the thought of missing pictures didn't stress me out. I never bought the yearbook anyway. What a waste of forty dollars. I'd have forty bucks to spare this year, but I wasn't buying something I wasn't in anyway. Don't get involved in school; don't get your picture taken.

"Reg, you're missing pictures?" Mom rubbed the spot between her eyes. "You should've told me, babe. You're a senior. And it's not as if we don't have the money."

"If you want my picture that badly, there's always retake day. I'll just slip in there."

That seemed to appease her. Mom slipped an arm over my shoulders, careful to keep her Velcro rollers away from my bedhead. "You feel like tea, kiddo? Maybe some toast?"

Aunt Barb headed toward my room. "I'll take measurements while you're up."

I rubbed my stomach, the contents inside still curdled. "I'm barely handling saliva, so no to the tea and toast." Barb's words suddenly sunk in. "Why do you need my room measurements?"

"We're redoing the house." Mom threw her arms out and turned around, excitement lighting up her face, looking like Julie Andrews during the opening credits of *The Sound of Music*. "Every nook, every cranny. And you know what that means?"

I didn't. But knew she'd tell me.

"It means we're putting a vent in your room!"

A vent. Three years ago, before Dad's aneurysm, he'd talked about putting a vent that connected my room with the rest of the house's heating and cooling system. But then he died and I stole four hundred dollars, for an air conditioner that leaked and rattled and reminded me every day about stealing four hundred dollars.

"And that's not the only thing we're changing in there, Reg. We're going to paint, put in hardwood floors, maybe even get one of those fancy chandeliers to put in there."

"A chandelier?" The only light I had in there was the desk light by my bed. And now I was getting a chandelier. It had taken three years to get real air-conditioning, but only a few days after winning the lottery to get a chandelier? I struggled to keep that thought to myself, to keep from disturbing the happy mood that this house hadn't seen for a while. "What's with the sudden urge to decorate?"

I heard Aunt Barb's voice from the kitchen. "Probably

due to the sudden appearance of all that money in your mom's account this morning."

"Seriously?" I think the word came out more as a squeal than a question.

Mom pulled the robe tighter and nodded, her face a study in mock seriousness. "Seriously."

Mom had money in her account. One point six million. Well, more like a million after taxes and fees for taking it as one lump sum. But still. WE HAD MONEY!

"In that case, can I get a new bed instead? Maybe a king, one of those pillowtops maybe?" A bed, at least, I could take with me and actually use eight months from now. One that didn't tilt to the side.

"Reggie, your mother's won the lottery. I think she can afford to give your room a total makeover." Aunt Barb came out of the kitchen and jerked her thumb toward the back of the house. "And the kitchen. Imogene, please tell me we're ripping everything out and starting from scratch. I'm seeing a bay window over the sink, maybe copper tiles on the ceiling."

They both disappeared into the kitchen, and I flopped down on the sagging sofa. On top of the coffee table were what looked like hundreds of loose magazine pages. I picked up a handful, riffling through them. They were pictures of wedding gowns, engagement rings, and wedding cakes with notes like *pretty bodice* and *gold or platinum?* and *three-tier or four-tier?* The nausea I had thought had disappeared made a brief reappearance.

Instead, I picked up the remote and turned on the sixty-five-inch TV. Mom hadn't hung it yet, and wires snaked out of it into tangled, confusing piles across the avocado carpet. Under the coffee table, our new DVDs were still in their Cashmart bags, still shrink-wrapped. The nauseated feeling was replaced with a cold wave of anger.

Mom had money, but she still wasn't taking care of the things it bought. I'd read once that the relationship you have with money and the things it can buy and the people that are in your life are all interconnected. So if you treat money like crap, you also treat your things and your people like crap.

I turned on the Food Network, settled on a show about the history of cupcakes, and started opening DVDs, one by one.

And I tried really, really hard not to feel like crap.

"You're not contagious, right?" Sarah put a hand between me and the bowl of cherries, sugar, and cinnamon she was stirring.

It was a few hours later and I was leaning against Mrs. Bretton's granite countertop. "No, Sarah. My intolerance to cream is not catching. Unless, of course, the Food and Drug Administration is keeping something from us."

She put down her hand. "I just can't afford to get sick. The Bake-Off is in two months, and Mom is putting the pressure on." She poured the filling into a piecrust. Sarah and her mom made awesome piecrusts, with just the right amount of flakiness and sweetness. It was no surprise that it was awesome: Mrs. Bretton had been entering the Southwest Bake-Off for twenty years, and had finaled almost every single year. She'd never won, though. This year, she was on a mission.

"How crazy has she gotten?"

"We aren't Stage Five yet. I'd say a Two, maybe a Three." Mrs. Bretton was a control freak, and could be a little intense. This was the worst she'd ever been, though, micromanaging everything in the kitchen, even the portions people ate. She was also on Sarah's case to clear up her acne because, well, no judge wants to taste-test a pie with a zit looking him in the face. "So far, she's only had to drive to Phoenix twice. Once to get some organic peaches from a tiny farm that she swore by. The second time to get a pie stand she saw online and didn't trust them to ship."

"A pie stand?" Peaches I could understand. Something that didn't even go into the pie? Not so much. Affecting her mom's soft, prim church lady voice, I said, " 'Presentation is everything, Sarah.' " I used my finger to swipe a taste of cherry filling.

She scowled at the finger in my mouth. "She only gets like this right before the Bake-Off. I can put up with it if I know there's an end in sight." She slapped my hand as I tried to take a second swipe. "Anyway, my mom's not the only crazy one around here. At least she's not trying to buy a marble toilet."

"I told you already, Mom was kidding about that."

Sarah wiped her hands on a towel and leveled a long look at me. "Are you sure she was just kidding?"

Sometimes I forget that Sarah's been around a long time, and that she's seen a lot. Like the time Mom bought an eight-hundred-dollar dress to perk herself up after the electricity got turned off, and it didn't even fit. She has yet to wear it.

"You know, that money's yours, too." Sarah leaned on the counter, using her finger to draw a design in the flour she'd rolled the piecrust out on. "She doesn't have the right to do whatever she wants with it. Especially considering how she hasn't paid you back yet."

"She will." Even I heard the defensiveness in my voice.

"Yeah, right, because she has such a great track record for paying you back," Sarah mocked. Behind her, the refrigerator crackled as it made ice.

I rubbed my neck, working at a knot that hadn't been there a second ago.

Sarah stood up and brushed her hands together. "Change of subject?"

"Change of subject," I agreed.

"So, you're really not going in today to work for, like, the first time ever?"

I looked over my shoulder at the clock. It was almost five, the start of my shift. In the past, if I'd been sick I would have missed school but still showed up for my shift—through the flu, through a migraine, even through a bad case of hives.

"I wasn't a slacker. I called in sick," I said defensively.

"Why don't you just quit? You're on easy street now."

I shrugged. I couldn't exactly say why I wouldn't quit. Maybe it was because Cashmart had become a habit. I didn't know what it was like *not* to work. Work was my identity. If I didn't have it, what did I have? Basketball practice? Prom committee? United Nations ambassador?

Exactly.

"So," I said, drawing out the word and trying to shut my thoughts up, "is Pete coming over tonight to sample the goods?" Pete was the master taster around here. He had taste buds that could pick up the subtle difference between clove and allspice and ginger and nutmeg.

"Nope." Sarah started filling the sink up with water. Dishes clattered as suds formed.

"But it's Fruit Pie Day. He's always here on Fruit Pie Day."

"Things change." Sarah turned the water on a higher setting, and I had to focus on hearing her above the din. So. It looked as if their relationship was officially off-again. I flipped through Mrs. Bretton's recipe cards and started to organize them alphabetically. "What'd he do this time?"

"It wasn't one thing. It's never really one thing. It's a combo of things until one thing finally sets me off." Her back was still to me, her head down as she scrubbed.

"What was it, Sarah?" I didn't give up.

The steel pad she was using on a pie pan seemed to grow louder. I didn't hear what she said at first.

"Can you repeat that? I couldn't hear it past you torturing that pan."

"I said," she enunciated, "that he didn't call me to watch a *Star Wars* act-along down in Phoenix. He went with one of his online game people instead."

"I'm sorry, but I thought I heard you say you got your feelings hurt about not being asked to be bored out of your mind at a geekfest to end all geekfests."

She stopped scrubbing, and her whole body seemed to sag against the sink. "I did." She looked over her shoulder at me. "He's turned me into a geek, Reggie, and I think I liked it." Her eyes widened when she saw what was in my hands. "You didn't mess with those cards, did you? Please tell me you didn't alphabetize them."

"I was just trying to help," I said lamely.

"Please, don't help." She took the cards and manically started redoing them. "If you want me to survive the Bake-Off, just don't help."

I left Sarah's after eight. Mom had let me borrow her car, and the gas needle was almost on "E." Usually, I'd just return the car with no gas, especially when I figured out that she'd only let me borrow the car when it was running on vapors and I was forced to pay for gas. But Mom had shoved a hundred-dollar bill in my hand when I left for Sarah's. "A little something for being my daughter," she'd said.

I would rather have gotten three thousand somethings. I still hadn't gotten paid for the monstrosity currently collecting dust in our living room. But I didn't want to disturb the new peace between us, this happy place, so I'd taken the bill and put it next to my emergency twenty in my bra. And now I was at the Gas 'n Go, sucking on a raspberry slushie, trying to listen to the car's preset classic-radio station rather than the bad country on the gas station's overhead speakers.

The counter was at ten gallons when I heard, "Hey."

I shifted to the side, to see around the gas pump, and there was Gabe. His hands were in his pockets, a gray and green flannel over his hips. He leaned against a big truck as he waited for the gas nozzle to switch off.

"Hey yourself."

He pushed himself off the light blue old-fashioned truck with rounded tire wells and a big round hood. Rust clung to the edges, and all in all, the whole look fit Gabe. I don't know why exactly, but I just knew that he wouldn't have gone with a Corvette or a Hummer or a Honda Accord.

"You ditched Photo tonight," he said.

"I did not ditch. I called in sick." I heard my gas pump click behind me, the tank full. "Bad stomach."

He took in the slushie. "I can see that."

"Hey, I haven't been able to get anything down until now." Which wasn't exactly a lie. I hadn't until around three hours ago, when I sampled Sarah's pies. "I've been sick all day."

"You know why, don't you?"

I started telling him yes, I knew exactly why. And then I saw how relaxed he was and how that dimple grazed his cheek. I realized that he might be flirting with me. And I realized that I didn't know what to say, or where I wanted all of this to go. I finally settled on, "Why?"

I couldn't believe he was actually flirting with me, me in my sweatpants with the Mickey Mouse patch on the butt.

"It's the gods frowning down upon you for eating my Reese's Peanut Butter Cups."

Before I could think of something that was equal parts cute and witty, a car pulled up behind mine. That's when I realized every spot was full, and in some cases, the wait was two cars deep.

"I'd better get going." I took the pump out of the gas tank and screwed the cap back on.

"Hey, Reggie?"

"Yeah?"

"I like your pants."

"I need a favor." Bridget stood on my front porch, her jean jacket buttoned to her neck but her legs bare in a skirt.

Talk about buzzkill. The last time Bridget had needed me was when she was going to Paris and wanted me to take her photo for her expedited passport. I opened the door wider, mainly because it was cold and I was in just a T-shirt.

Bridget stepped into the house. And for once, I didn't care about the eBay boxes lining the wall, the plastic storage crates filled with Cashmart markdowns piled three to a stack, and the air smelling like my quick dinner of boiled hot dogs.

Her mom's Pucci scarf was in her hair, her mom's diamonds dangling from her ears. And when she took off her jean jacket, I saw my black-pearl necklace encircling her throat.

"That guy you work with. Greg?"

Okay. Hadn't been expecting that. "Gabe," I corrected.

"Yeah, Gabe. Set me up."

Suddenly feeling a little unsteady, I went over and sat down on the couch. "Do you even know Gabe?"

"I know he's cute."

"Yeah, well, I don't have much pull with him." Plus, I didn't hate him that much. Come to think of it, I didn't even dislike him that much. Or at all, even.

"Huh." She digested the info. "Then set me up with your geek friend."

"Pete?" Bridget wasn't the most logical person I'd ever met, so I struggled keeping up with her.

"Yeah, the *Star Trek* dude." I didn't correct her. *Star Trek, Star Wars.* It all fell under the same geek subcategory to most people.

"You want to date Pete. Pete Nellis. The guy who put on Yoda ears for his senior picture today?" Sarah had told me about his fashion statement. She'd even teared up when she told me, like she was already missing Pete and his socially awkward tendencies.

Bridget crossed her arms and shrugged. "I like funny guys."

She thought he was funny? I took in her ramrod-straight back, her ironed jean jacket, her Coach bag that still smelled like a new car. Bridget had a sense of humor?

"He doesn't seem like your type."

She shrugged. "What can I say? I'm a Trekker."

I didn't bother to correct her. "What's going on, Bridget? Gabe and Pete are polar opposites, and you're okay being set up with either one of them?"

She studied a nail. Long with healthy cuticles. The complete opposite of mine. "You know that dude Dead-head?"

Deadhead. The guy who liked girls who only had pretty going for them? "Gabe's roommate?"

"Yeah. I wanna meet him."

I tried visualizing Bridget with Deadhead. I didn't know what he looked like, but a name is worth a thousand stereotypes. "And you think that either his roommate or another skier like Pete is going to help you get in with him?"

"That's the plan."

"Why not just, I don't know, ask him out?"

She rolled her eyes. "Because he has a girlfriend. And if I'm either Patrick's—"

"Pete."

"Whatever. If I'm Pete's or Gabe's girlfriend, then I can hang out, get to know him better, make him break up with that skank he's been with after he is educated about our shared interests."

"And what exactly are your shared interests?"

"Him being hot, me being hot," she said.

I walked to the door, my hand on the knob. Hint hint. "I don't have time for crazy, Bridget."

She didn't move. "Regina, Regina, Regina." She shook her head. "Do I really need to remind you that I own you body and soul?"

For three years, I'd washed Bridget's car, I'd lied for her when Aunt Barb thought she was sleeping over at my house, I'd lied to Mom when Bridget borrowed some designer thing of hers and I played it off like Mom had probably misplaced it somewhere. And it was all starting to feel as if I had a size-two monkey on my back.

"I think you've gotten your money's worth out of me." My eyes fell on the pearl necklace around her neck. My black-pearl necklace. The one that she demanded I give her before freshman homecoming because it matched her dress.

I had never out-and-out asked for the necklace back, though. I'd hinted at it. I'd even stared at it pointedly. But either Bridget hadn't noticed or hadn't cared.

Scratch that. Bridget noticed everything.

Which meant she just didn't give a crap.

Which meant even more reason to hate her. But would

I ever tell her that? Not to her face. Just the thought of doing that made me light-headed and feverish. Instead, I bit my lip so hard, I tasted blood.

"I don't think I've gotten my money's worth at all, Regina." She put herself in front of me, our noses so close I could smell the Tic Tac in her mouth. She waved her cell phone from side to side. "I have half the school programmed in here. One text message, and no one would think you were trash. They'd know you were trash."

CHAPTER SIX

Yo, Reg. Regina. Genie. [Pause.]
Hey, your nickname's like your mom's. [Pause.]
Oh, I forgot. You don't like that nickname. [Pause.]
Anyway, it's Pete. Bring some Hot Tamales when you come,
okay?
Sarah likes them with her popcorn. Awesome. Bye.

TWO LARGE FRIES AND TWO APPLE PIES TO GO, please." I pulled out my emergency twenty as the Clunker idled next to the intercom, spitting out a cloud of smoke each time the car shuddered.

I was on a mission, and it included salt, sugar, and fat. I pulled up to the drive-through window, and a forty-something woman with a mountain range of red bumps on her chin passed the drinks and food to me. "That's six-fifty."

I swore she was looking in the car, for the other person who was getting an apple pie and large fries. I passed the twenty-dollar bill to her. "Keep the change. I've gotta get Mom's fries to her before they go cold."

I pulled into a furniture store parking lot a block away, parked by a Dumpster that shielded me from the street, and unwrapped the first pie.

Ten minutes later, I was licking the salt and pie crumbs off my fingers, but I was still hungry. Not in a stomach-gurgling sort of way. More like a nervous-stomach sort of way. Like if I didn't fill up my stomach, I was going to drive to Bridget's house and punch the veneers out of her mouth.

But I never did that sort of stuff. No, I did stuff like order two large fries and two apple pies and then inhale them in ten minutes.

My cell rang and the caller ID lit up. A two-minute conversation later, I pulled out of the parking lot and checked my teeth for trace evidence.

I walked past the glass case of apple fritters, Boston creams, and DD's famous Reese's Cup in a Hole—part candy, part glazed chocolate donut. I didn't even look at it, but not because my stomach was two thousand calories fuller. My big brother was back.

"Jeff?"

"Hey, squirt." He stood by the hostess stand, still tall, lanky, and bad with combing his hair.

I threw my arms around Jeff, breathing him in: soap and deodorant. It smelled like Sundays on the lake with *Bertha* and eating buttercream roses at 7:00 A.M. on the day after someone's birthday.

"What're you doing here?" Jeff walked over to a booth where Mom was sitting. I slid in next to her, and Jeff sat down on the other side. In the back of my head, I made the connection that we were sitting in our old booth. It had been three years since we had been to DD's Donuts, but it felt as if only a week had passed since Dad had bought a dozen donuts and pretended to get mad when we stuck our fingers into the jellied ones to figure out which ones were lemon and strawberry and not the gross boysenberry.

"I have no idea why I'm here." Jeff opened his eyes wide and shrugged. I knew him well enough to know that he was being sarcastic. "Just passing through town, I guess. I smelled the donuts and had to stop."

"Jeff," Mom said, her hand squeezing Jeff's, "is here because I asked him to be here. To discuss the money." Then her tone got all serious. "But before we talk about money, I want to talk about protecting ourselves."

"Protecting ourselves?" A brief smile came and went on

Jeff's mouth. "Is the Arizona mob planning to whack us or something?"

"C'mon, I'm serious here, guys." She sat up a little straighter, her voice lower. "I want us to keep the lottery under wraps."

The scent of too much rose-scented perfume blew by. DD Harris, the owner of DD's, was taking a pot of coffee around, filling up mugs. "Why do we want to keep it a secret?" I asked.

"Not so much a secret as just, well, private," Mom said.

"Sounds like a fancy way of saying a secret," Jeff said.

"Well, that's not what I intended," she said. "But I've read about how some second cousin raising pigs in Florida can show up at your house one day looking for a handout."

"And you're afraid someone in Waterview, living three thousand miles from Florida, is going to know this pig farmer?" I asked.

"You don't know who knows who," she said defensively.

I thought about her request. "Can I tell Pete and Sarah?"

"Are they good with keeping secrets?"

I thought about how they'd never told anyone how my Mom sucked with money. Not even their parents. Sarah was a great secret keeper. Pete—well, he wasn't so much a secret keeper as he was a secret forgetter. "Yes," I said.

She nodded and looked at Jeff. "Are you in, bud?"

He shrugged. "Whatever."

"Great." She sipped her coffee and leaned back in the booth. "Then let's talk dreams. What do you want? Name it."

I played with a napkin. I knew what I wanted. I knew exactly what I wanted. I just didn't want to be the first one to blurt it out.

"You sound like a genie granting us three wishes," Jeff said. Then he laughed, and it was a pure Jeff sound—like a pig snorting. "Hey. Genie. And your name's Genie. Cool."

I kept tearing the napkin, waiting for Jeff to say what he wanted instead of wasting time on the old, tired joke we've been using since we saw *Alladin*.

"I guess it'd be nice if my car was paid off," he said.

"Done." My mom banged the side of her fist against the table, causing her coffee to spill down the mug. "What else?"

"I like those new Nike trainers?" He said it as if it were a question.

"Done!" Mom looked like a little kid at Christmas. Except we were the ones who were opening the presents. "What else?"

Jeff shook his head. "Dunno."

"Anything in the world, and you don't know?"

"Mom, we're not billionaires." Jeff grabbed the pile of

napkin shreds from me and started creating a pattern with them. "It's not as if I can ask for a Learjet or something."

Mom didn't say anything for a minute, and I thought maybe she was mad. But when I looked at her, she was concentrating on the ceiling. "But you could rent a Learjet if you wanted to."

Jeff pig-snorted. "So I can fly from here to my apartment in Phoenix three hours away? That's a little overkill. Not to mention bad for that ozone thing up there."

"Ozone thing?" She plicked his hand. "Maybe you should take some of the money and finish your degree. What do you think? We can afford it."

Jeff shook his head. "Nah. The job in tech support is working out. I don't really need to go to school to help people debug their computers."

I felt her tense up. "That's not a good lesson to pass on to your sister, Jeffrey."

Both Jeff and I exchanged a look. This from the woman who made us lie to the collection agencies on a day-to-day basis, such as she couldn't come to the phone because she was in the middle of chemo?

"Reg is a smart girl," Jeff said. "She'll do what she needs to do."

Mom groaned. "Fine. Be a hardhead. What about you, Reg. What are your big dreams? Anything. Just name it."

I knew exactly what I wanted. I took a deep breath and, for once, said exactly what I was thinking.

"A car would be nice." *And my three thousand dollars.* First, though, I wanted to ask for something that would make her happy.

"Done!" She banged her hand against the table, more coffee spilling everywhere. "We'll go car shopping ASAP. What're you thinking about? A Mercedes? A Lexus?"

"Something that doesn't spit exhaust would be a good start."

"What, the Clunker isn't your dream car, Reg?" Jeff asked, the shreds of napkin in front of him in the shape of what looked like a donut. "Shocker."

Mom took a new napkin out of the holder and a pen out of her purse. "So, just to recap. Jeff needs his car paid off and new Nikes. Reg wants a new car. Mom wants a new car." She tapped the pen on the table. "What else, guys?"

Everyone was in a good mood. It was time. Time to let my sash for Non-Confrontation Queen slip a bit.

"What about paying off the bills?" *And my three thousand dollars?* I was slowly working my way up to it.

Mom rolled her eyes. "There's no such thing as paying off bills, Reg. Water's always going to get used, same with electricity."

"But we can pay off the overdue ones," I said quietly.

"Already done."

I felt my head snap up, and I was dizzy with shock for a second. "You paid them off?"

She nodded, her attention on a baby at the next table. She waved at him and he giggled. Mom was a charmer when she wanted to be. "I took care of most of them as soon as I got the money."

"Even Dad's student loan?"

The smile that had been on her face disappeared. "Reg, that's one of those bills that's just always going to be there."

I pressed my hands together under the table, my fingers biting into each other. The "right time" was officially drawing to a close.

"Don't you want to get rid of the loan, Mom?" Jeff asked, his eyes on the spilled coffee Mom hadn't cleaned up, a muddy river widening between her and us. "It's been, what, twenty years?"

Mom shook her head, and I noticed she was wearing the black pearl earrings Dad had gotten her for their anniversary. He'd gotten them at the same place as my necklace. The necklace I wanted more than a car or even my three thousand dollars.

"Forget the loan." She sounded mad, which I think

she realized, because her next words came out almost like baby talk. "That's no fun. C'mon, Reg, there has to be something else you want. You too, Jeff. What else do you want?"

Want is an interesting word. It's not a need, like food or one pair of working shoes or a plunger. I guess you could say I *wanted* electricity. I *wanted* cable. I mean, you can live without electricity or cable.

What did I *want*? I looked up and saw the old TV DD's had had since I could remember, a fuzzy, too-yellow news show on, the sound turned up too high.

I knew exactly what I wanted. I wanted the money Mom borrowed from me. I wanted my necklace from Bridget.

Mom leaned forward. "C'mon, guys. Something frivolous. Something fun. Don't we deserve that?"

Speaking of fun things, Elvis walked in. No-name, no-home, no-clue-who-he-was Elvis. Today he was wearing a black jumpsuit with silver sparkles, the front unbuttoned to his waist. He ordered half a dozen powdered donuts. For a second, my mind wandered and I wondered if he was able to eat them without getting any on his very black outfit.

The smell of a new batch of donuts coming out of the fryer hit me. Fun and frivolous. Mom wanted fun and frivolous.

I wanted my three thousand dollars. But after seeing her

reaction about the bills and student loan, I wasn't about to bring it up now.

Pete's living room looks a lot like that house on *The Brady Bunch*. There's lots of wood, ugly couches, and high ceilings. He also has a lot of siblings—four brothers and two sisters— that were all married or in college. His parents are kind of old, more grandparent-looking than parent-looking. That meant he pretty much did whatever he wanted, when he wanted, like two-day *Star Wars* marathons. Pete was a geek even when he was being rebellious.

"So you're set. You got your sodas?" he said, like a dad reading off a list before a road trip.

"Check." I held up my Dr Pepper. Sarah ignored him on her corner of the couch and tore into a bag of licorice. They might have been in their off-again stage, but they still hung out.

"You got your assorted chocolates?"

"Check." I held up the one-pound bag of peanut butter M&M's. It was more for Sarah and Pete than me since I really didn't eat a lot in public. Which was a good thing, considering I'd weigh two hundred pounds if I ate whatever I wanted all day long, every day.

Sarah didn't say anything as she sat on the corner of the

couch, her feet under her, twisting the top of her 7-Up open and closed, hiss and click.

"You both have gone to the potty?" Pete asked.

"C'mon." I threw an M&M at him. "Get the show on the road already."

"Just checking, females." He held up a plastic case in his hand. Cradled it, almost. "Once this DVD starts, there is no stopping, pausing, or rewinding."

"It's not as if we haven't seen it five times already," I muttered. But Pete still heard me.

"Must I go into again how imperative *The Wrath of Khan* is to the *Star Trek* history? It was voted the best of any *Star Trek* movie. This is, after all, where Spock perished, people. Have some respect."

"Aren't you being a traitor to your *Star Wars* peeps if you watch a *Star Trek* movie?" I asked.

A sigh ran down Pete's body. Literally. You could see it slump his shoulders, knock in his stomach, and weaken his knees, like Gumby taking a punch. "I am not a traitor. I am a fan of the science fiction genre, which *Star Trek* falls under."

"Didn't Spock show up again in *The Search for Spock*?" Sarah asked, a scowl on her face as she stared at the ingredients list on her soda bottle, her fingers picking at the label, purposely not looking at him.

"Don't make me ask you to leave, Sarah Bear." He bent and put the DVD in. It was obvious Pete didn't know Sarah had started break-up proceedings.

I leaned back, ready to enjoy the show. And I'm not talking about *Star Trek and the Wrath of Whatever*. Sarah and Pete was the oddest coupling I'd ever seen, and their uncouplings were just as odd. Sarah would ignore him but still come and hang out while Pete had no idea they weren't talking. Or broken up.

"Anyway, why aren't we watching this on the movie screen at your house, Reg?" Pete asked, pushing buttons on three different remotes.

"It's not a movie screen."

"Might as well be."

The licorice package crinkled. "So after your mom blows money on stupid stuff," Sarah said, holding a licorice vine out to me, "is she going to put aside anything for college? Or paying you back?" The way she tore into the licorice, I knew she was taking out her Pete frustrations on me.

I took the licorice and then spent a lot of time fluffing the pillow behind my back. If she wanted a fight, I wasn't going to play the role of Surrogate Pete.

"Has she?" Sarah pressed.

"I have no idea."

"You need to find out. Then you can get going on late admissions."

I finally got the pillow just so. Pete was still fiddling with the remotes, and I got interested in a year-old copy of *Scientific American*. I flipped through the pages, more to keep my hands busy than anything else. Beside me, Sarah chewed on her licorice like a cow chewed its cud, loud and obnoxious.

"Have you seen my grades?" I finally said. "Colleges sort of don't like GPAs to be under 2.5."

On the screen, loud previews started to play. "Hey, deaf guy! Turn it down." Then Sarah focused her attention back on me. "Bad grades don't mean no college. You can start at WCC, bring your GPA up, and apply at universities later on."

Waterview Community College was a two-year school that a lot of Waterview High students went to. A lot of people would never make it out of Waterview. You'd have to chloroform me and duct tape me to a desk before I ever stepped foot in there. To me, WCC was just Waterview High, the sequel.

I threw the magazine back on the table. "I'm not going to WCC so I can hang out with the losers."

"Oh?" Sarah crossed her arms and leaned away from me. "I'm going there. Does that mean *I'm* a loser?"

Sarah was a brain, and had entered and pretty much won every spelling bee and science fair since I'd known her. She didn't do well on standardized tests, though, because she second-guessed herself too much. Which meant that she would probably be going to WCC until she could get a score that would get her accepted into Berkeley, her dream school.

"You know what I mean." I sighed. Sarah was beyond touchy about this subject.

"No, exactly what *do* you mean?"

"Females, please." Pete got up. "The night's young. *The Wrath of Khan* is all set to go, Reggie's paid for all of tonight's assorted tooth-decaying foods, and I get to go play mini-golf this Friday for the first time in forever. Can life be any better?" He rubbed his hands together, a goofy grin on his face as he headed to the kitchen. "I'll go get our popcorn."

Sarah sat up a little. "Mini-golf?"

Pete's grin was still in place as he said, "Yeah. I'm going with Reg and Bridget."

"You have a date with Bridget?" Unlike most girls I knew, Sarah's voice got lower and softer when she was angry.

"It's not a date." Some of his smile disappeared. "She's just going to be my partner. Plus you hate mini-golf." He sniffed the air. "I think I smell burning. I'll be right back, Sarah Bear."

Sarah slowly pushed herself off the couch. "A double date?" She turned to look at me. I found I couldn't meet her eyes. "Isn't that interesting." She grabbed her jacket. "I gotta go."

"C'mon, Sarah. You're blowing this out of proportion." But she wasn't. I hadn't told her about mini-golf because I hadn't wanted to deal with the fallout. So much for that.

She shook her head as she walked to the door. "What exactly am I blowing out of proportion? You calling me a loser? Or you pimping out Pete?" She seemed to do a double take. "And why are you even setting him up? And with Bridget? That girl is horrible, Reggie, and you know it!"

I tried to deflate the situation by not even attempting to explain the Bridget thing right now. "I'm not even going to college, so I don't see what your problem is."

Sarah's eyes looked as if they belonged to a puppy who'd just been smacked on the nose, and I wondered how the night had gotten so off track. I'd come to eat candy and watch William Shatner overact; I hadn't expected to get into a discussion about Waterview Community College and my stupid cousin.

"My problem," she said, her voice so low I had to strain to hear it above the TV volume, "is that you're the only loser here, Regina. You've known it, this town's known it, but I've been too blind to see it." She walked to the door and slammed it behind her.

"Where'd Sarah go?" Pete stood in the living room, a bowl in his hands. "I made her her stupid popcorn-Hot Tamale bowl."

Loser.

I sank into an ugly Naugahyde chair, curled into a ball, and shoved a pillow in front of my face.

"Reg?"

I shook my head. If I pulled my face away from the pillow, I was going to lose it.

"I can make you a popcorn-Hot Tamale bowl, too."

CHAPTER SEVEN

You're taking me to play mini-golf? Are you serious, Regina?
I wanted to talk to your nerd friend, not deal with sun
cancer and hanging out with the kind of losers who mini-golf.
Whatever. You're paying. For everything.
Including my gas there.

REG, you are a genius."

I paused, my paintbrush over the tips of the Chihua-hua's ears, trying to make them less catlike. I didn't turn to face Doc. My eyes were red, the spaces under them gray from lack of sleep. "Yeah?"

I could feel her studying my face. "You're sure here early."

"Yeah." I mixed more gray with white, swirling it together for longer than I needed to. "The cleaning crew let me in. I hope that was okay."

"Of course it was." I heard Doc move closer, but I still didn't turn. *Loser.* That's all I kept hearing in my head. *You are a loser. You've known it, this town's known it.*

Loser, loser, loser.

I was so, so tired. And the new king-size pillowtop mattress that came yesterday had felt nice—very, very nice. But when I still hadn't fallen asleep by 5:00 A.M., which was when the construction crew came to tear out the kitchen, I got up, pulled on jeans, my dad's old University of Arizona sweatshirt, and my three-year-old Converses.

Being here, in this tiny waiting room with the morning light coming in, was nice. Simple. Calming.

So, on the plus side, at least I was calm while the word *loser* echoed in my brain.

"What do you think of it?" I finally asked. I said it sort of quietly, a small part of me hoping she wouldn't hear me, that she wouldn't tell me what I was thinking: *It sucks. You suck. Sarah was right, loser.*

"I think," Doc said, slowly, deliberately, "that you have a real talent."

"Yeah?" I stepped back. The Chihuahua had lost its cat appearance, and I'd started on a guinea pig between one of the dog's ears. My freehand attempt at PAWS AND CLAWS VETERINARY CLINIC had turned out crisp, in a burnt sienna that complemented the sage wall really well. "I don't know if it's good enough."

"I do." I felt Doc move to stand next to me, where she

seemed to still be studying my face. "So, do you think you're rediscovering your love of painting again?"

I hadn't thought about that. Did I love painting? It had been a long time since Art Club, but the ability to figure out colors and perspective was still there. Plus, painting had a way of really calming me down on days like today.

"I guess I am. Especially knowing I'm working off my debt to you." I paused, trying to figure out how to put into words what I was feeling right now. After my fight with Sarah, I wanted to make sure I said exactly what I meant. "I just want it to be good, you know? I haven't really done the whole art thing for a while."

Doc didn't say anything. Then she tapped my leg with her cane. "You think you may want to study it?"

My mind was coming up blank. "Study what?"

"I see you're wearing a University of Arizona shirt. I've heard they have a good art program down there."

"Oh." I dabbed a tiny bit of white onto my brush and concentrated on brushing highlights into the animals' eyes. "College really isn't in the cards for me, Doc."

"Really? Hmm."

I turned and saw that Doc was looking at my mural, a frown on her face.

"Don't feel bad for me. I never thought college was in

the cards. I don't have the grades." I didn't get into winning the lottery. I hadn't told anyone outside of Pete and Sarah. And Bridget, but I hadn't exactly told her as much as just confirmed it.

"What are your plans, then, when you graduate?"

My plans used to be to work at Cashmart until I could make the first month's rent, last month's rent, and security deposit for a Phoenix apartment. Until I could afford a car and gas for that car and insurance for that car, too.

But then one point six million dollars showed up.

I told her the one thing that hadn't changed. "I plan to get out of Waterview."

"And?" Doc prodded.

"And that's it. Get out of Waterview."

"I understand that. But get out and do what?"

I had never really thought that through. I had only been focused on making money and saving money and leaving. I had figured the rest would fall into place.

"Maybe I'll work at the Phoenix Cashmart," I half-joked. It wasn't like one point six million was going to last forever. Anyway, working had become a habit. And it was hard to quit a habit. Like binging on junk food and avoiding confrontations.

Doc stopped studying the mural to look at me. "So ten years from now, you plan on still being at Cashmart?"

I shrugged. I hadn't really thought about it. I'd been too busy just trying to get through the day at times.

"I'm just not seeing you looking up the price on a pair of underwear missing a price tag, Reg."

I thought about some of the older people who worked at Cashmart. Single moms and retired navy guys. "There's nothing wrong with that kind of life."

"No, there's nothing wrong with that kind of life at all," she agreed. "But I just don't see a girl like you being happy with that kind of life."

Working at Cashmart had changed. Knowing that I didn't have to work had made the days go faster. I also started feeling lighter, no longer afraid I was going to lose my job or worried about not becoming photo manager.

I also started thinking Gabe was getting cuter. And nicer. I think I was even starting to flirt with him.

Me, Regina Shaw, the girl who had always been too busy to notice the opposite sex.

"Okay, Nicole, I'll say one, two, three, and then you'll smile and say 'flannel,' okay?"

"Okay!" The seven-year-old clutched her one-eyed bear closer and grinned, showing every single one of her baby teeth.

"Okay, then. One, two, three—"

"Flannel!" she yelled. I took five pictures, and checked them for any crossed eyes, lazy eyes, or closed eyes.

I had never been so glad to be at work. School had sucked; there was no Sarah to sit next to at lunch, no Sarah to hang out with after school. There was Pete, but Pete isn't Pete without Sarah, if that made any sense at all.

"Did that girl just scream 'flannel'?"

"Yes, she did." I didn't look up and instead focused my camera. Gabe had been in the stockroom, and I had had the feeling Nicole Brady yelling "flannel" would get his attention. "I told her to yell out the most disgusting fabric she knew."

I could feel him standing next to me, and I swear the air got warmer. "Do you think flannel's disgusting?" he said. I couldn't help thinking his voice sounded like a warm brownie with ice cream melting on top.

Get a grip, Reggie. You're sounding like one of Sarah's stupid romance novels. And you're no romance heroine.

I shrugged. "Depends who's wearing it."

Nicole's mom tugged down her dress and put a pair of felt deer antlers on her head. "Let's say it's Fellers," Gabe breathed.

"Disgusting."

"How about Pete?"

"Platonic."

Gabe was now standing beside me, his arm brushing against mine and causing thousands upon thousands of tiny fireworks to launch themselves up the skin of my arm.

"And if it's me?"

I made sure Nicole's antlers—all three feet of them—were in the picture before I snapped it. "Let's just say I'd find that interesting."

"Not disgusting?"

I shook my head.

"Or platonic?"

I found myself fascinated with getting Nicole's red eye erased as I answered him, more Mumble than English.

"I'm sorry. I didn't hear that." Gabe bent down to my level, his hand hesitating next to my face before swiping a lock of hair behind her ear. As he did so, a wave of musk and rain and soap went up my nostrils and into that part of my brain that makes my knees weak.

"I said 'definitely not platonic,'" I enunciated.

"Good to know."

A mom with two rambunctious twins came to the counter, and Gabe went to help them.

Good to know.

It was good to know that he thought it was good to know.

◊ ◊ ◊

Two hours later, I was in the break room changing out of my apron.

The door opened behind me. I knew who it was even before I looked up. Ever since it had started to thaw between us, the air seemed to crackle when we were within twenty feet of each other.

"Hey." The word came out as a squeak, and I ended up saying it more to my open locker than to Gabe.

There was no response, and I kept my head in my locker, pretending to keep busy, but also trying to hide my flushed face until I felt it turn back to a normal color again.

"So, I was thinking." Gabe sounded as if he was standing on the other side of my locker door.

"Yeah?"

"You bought that big-screen TV, and I know you're a movie fanatic, and I know I'm a movie fanatic, and I was thinking you'd want to show me what a sixty-five-inch TV can do." He pulled the locker door toward him, exposing my face. "You pick the movie, and I'll bring the popcorn."

I took a minute fishing the keys for the Clunker out of my purse, hoping my hair was hiding what was left of my blush. "The house is sort of a mess right now. And plus my brother's visiting, so his crap is all over the place." Mom had turned Jeff's room into storage for all her eBay tchotchkes, and he was relegated to sleeping on the lumpy couch.

"I've got a TV," Gabe said.

"Your thirteen-inch with bunny ears?"

He grinned, and the effect that had on my stomach was like flipping a gas fireplace on. "I did say that, didn't I? I was hoping you'd forget that." He rubbed his jaw, and I caught a scent of musk and something else. Something rain-ish. How did he always smell like rain in the middle of the desert? Whatever it was, the combination made me want to put my nose where his neck met his collarbone and stay there for an hour or two. "How about going to a real movie, in a real theater?"

"Sounds sort of nice." I grabbed my purse and pulled it across my body.

"Great." He moved toward the break-room door and held it open for me, a grin flashing across his face. "And don't even think about paying."

"Oh, you're paying. That's the guy's job." The happy feeling I had suddenly didn't feel so happy. I stopped by the door. "Why. Do you want me to pay?"

"Why would I want you to pay? I'm the one asking you out."

Something was off here. "You know, don't you?"

"Know what?"

"Um, I don't know, that the sun is round and hot?" I scowled. "You know about the lottery."

He shifted his weight, propping the door open with his body. He shrugged. "Sure, I know."

"How?"

"Pete told me."

"Pete," I repeated. So much for Pete being a secret forgetter.

Gabe no longer had a smile. He actually seemed to be the one scowling now. "I don't see what that has to do with movie night."

Of course he didn't know. But what I knew was that he was good-looking and I was a girl who liked sweatpants and her dad's old Suns T-shirts. I was already picking up the tab for Bridget; I didn't feel like doing it for yet another person who felt they were gracing Regina Shaw with their presence. "I gotta get going."

"What's going on, Reg?" He just stood there, holding the door open. I had to hand it to him—he looked confused. Or at least he *acted* confused.

I walked out and mumbled something like, "I've gotta wash my cat." I can't remember. I was feeling kind of sick inside at the time. I think he even called my name, but I didn't turn around to check.

If I remembered right, there was a Little Debbie display up front. I was in the mood for a Little Debbie. Or two. Boxes, that is.

"Regina." I turned and saw Fellers in his office, his door open, a box of Little Debbies open beside him. The irony wasn't lost on me. "Come in a sec. I want to talk to you." He gestured to a chair. "Sit down."

"No thanks." I didn't think my knees could bend at that moment. I felt like every part of me was strung tight as Sarah's voice played over and over in my head. *Loser, loser, loser.*

"I wanted to talk to you about the photo manager position."

I impatiently waved my hand at him to get him to stop talking. "I understand. Gabe has more experience, he's from a bigger store, he doesn't have school. He's a better guy to promote." I had come to terms over the promotion. One point six million dollars had helped me come to terms. Plus, I wasn't in the mood to discuss the jerk.

"Oh." He shuffled some papers on his desk, looking sort of lost about what to say next. "I'm glad you understand." He looked up. "Want a Little Debbie? They're on sale today."

As I stood there, Fellers tore open a cellophane wrapper and popped a Little Debbie in his mouth. He was almost dainty about it, barely getting anything on his lips as his teeth cut it in half.

"I'm good, Mr. Fellers. Thanks." I shoved my hands into the pockets of my jeans. I liked my Little Debbies in a room or a car by myself, so I didn't have anyone looking at me like I was looking at him—with disgust and horror.

"Anyway, I wanted to tell you that if you keep your record clean, in a year you can seriously look into a manager position here at Cashmart."

I stopped focusing on the Little Debbies. I had to wait a year until I could be a manager. That part sank in, no problem. I wasn't planning on being in Waterview in a year. If I'd been given the job, sure, I would have been tempted to stay, if only to save as much as possible. But the part that stuck, that scraped its nails down my back, was "if you keep your record clean."

I had been coming to work early and going home late for years. I had cut classes for Cashmart, gotten C's for Cashmart. I had turned around pictures to customers way faster than Cashmart asked for.

And I was being told that none of that mattered by a guy with pie cream in the corner of his mouth?

I pressed my fingers against the headache building behind my right temple. First the thing with Gabe, now this. The twenty hours I was scheduled to work this week felt like a prison sentence.

"Mr. Fellers?" At first, I couldn't get the rest of my words out, and I closed my eyes. I'd spent more waking hours at Cashmart than at home or at school, even. The clock behind Fellers's desk ticked, and the smell of popcorn from the food court floated in.

Behind my lids
ONE POINT SIX MILLION
flashed.

"I quit."

Pete stood in front of a massive clown head, his black golf ball having gone through Bozo's eye, around his left nostril, and out his tongue to land five inches from the cup. Bridget's pink ball was five inches away on the other side.

Bridget scowled at Pete, looking over his shoulder at the scorecard. "I did Hole 10 in four strokes, not six. Get your math right."

We were at Golf, Movies, and More, a combo movie theater/arcade/mini-golf course, which had twenty holes with windmills, water hazards, the works. It also had an arcade with about fifty video games, and an ice-cream parlor with six flavors of soft serve. It was pretty much the most popular date spot in Waterview. The only date spot, too, that didn't involve the middle of the desert, a bonfire, and three kegs.

I lined up my shot and tried to keep from looking at Bridget looking at Pete as if he was a waste of a good pair of muscles. Not that he noticed. He was too busy checking the wind with a saliva-moistened fingertip.

My date, on the other hand, was at Buzz's Ice Cream. I use the word *date* loosely. And he wasn't one of Pete's cute water-ski buddies, either. He was one of Pete's other friends—the kind with a serious video game addiction. He was an online buddy, which meant they were on a make-believe team that worked together to kill make-believe things. I've seen Pete when he's playing: he wears a headset and talks to guys who could be anywhere or anyone, like some eight-year-old in Japan taking a break from drawing manga and studying for Harvard.

The guy was Brad Watts. He'd dropped cherry bombs into C Hall's toilets freshman year and got suspended for two weeks. Everyone knew Brad Watts. Of course, he hadn't known me. Since he had gotten here, he hadn't paid attention to me or to the game. He'd been too busy straining his neck to see if his favorite game, Death Dude, was free yet.

I hit my ball and it went through the clown's eye and back out again. I slammed it harder, and it came out the tongue and within two inches of the hole. I should really envision the ball as Bridget's big, manipulative head more often.

"Reg, you saw me hit that ball in four, didn't you?" I looked up and saw Bridget glaring at me.

"Sure." I hadn't been paying attention. Instead, I kept thinking about Gabe. The more I replayed the break-room scene in my head, the more I thought about how I might have overreacted. I also kept thinking about quitting Cashmart. I had *no* regrets there, though. At least, not a lot.

"Hey, guys, you want to just do twelve holes?" Brad was back, holding four drinks in a cardboard carrier, a new cola-colored stain on his shirt, which asked: GOT GIGABYTE? "That way, we can catch a movie or something. I heard the new *Doom Day* movie is good." *Doom Day* is one of those video-games-turned-movie. I noticed the line for Death Dude had doubled, which explained the sudden ADHD interest in *Doom Day*.

I'd have to remember to thank Pete for this oh-so-stellar date.

"As soon as I beat Pete here first." Bridget folded her hands on top of her golf club. "But instead of that dumb movie, how about we go do some paintball? Reggie's treat."

Bridget sounded like my cousin and looked like my

cousin, so why did she want to extend this horribly uncomfortable day? Then I remembered. She was grounded, and could only go out with family members. Which meant it was us and paintball or her alone in her TV-less, computer-less, phone-less room.

She'd been using me a lot more lately. The mini-golf fees today, a nonfat, sugar-free vanilla café au lait here and there, me buying fifty chocolate bars the cheerleaders were selling for new pom-poms next year. That one I hadn't minded, though.

The problem was, Bridget knew about the credit card. My ten-thousand-dollar credit card. Jeff had one, too. One of the upsides of being lottery winners was that credit card companies were willing to expedite cards to you.

The card didn't have a cash advance on it, though. I'd already checked. Otherwise, I could have stopped waiting for Mom to pay me back and would have paid myself already.

Pete hit the ball. "I could go for paintball. But Reggie doesn't have to pay for me. Brad guessed it would only take eighteen torpedoes to blow up the Boss in *Outskirts of Hell*, and it was forty-two, like I said."

"So?" Bridget looked bored. Deadhead was supposed to come out with us today, but instead, we got Brad. Mainly because I hadn't told Pete to bring him. I hated confrontations, but my passive-aggressive skills were top-notch.

"So, Brad has to pay every time we go out for the next month." He pointed the end of his golf club at Brad. "Sucker."

"He can pay for you some other time. I say Regina needs to pay." She looked straight at me, as if she was daring me to disagree.

"Did you lose a bet, too?" Brad asked as he slid a mouthful of ice into his mouth.

Before I could even open my mouth, Bridget did the work for me. We were on the longest hole—thirty feet—with me still at the tee and Bridget over at the hole. Her voice carried to me, and everyone else, as she said, "Regina's mom won the lottery."

Did everyone just stop talking, or had it always been this quiet? And had my cheeks always felt like they were about to burn off my face?

"You won the lottery?" Brad looked at me, this time in the eye. The first time he'd done so since we'd met in front of Golf, Movies, and More.

"You're up, Reg." Pete, as usual, was oblivious to what was happening around him.

I pushed the cup into Brad's chest until he figured out I wanted him to hold it. As I bent to set up my shot, I envisioned the ball as Bridget's face with her Bridget headband and Bridget diamond earrings and Bridget necklace.

No. *My* necklace. The one I hadn't confronted her about yet. But I would. I was almost there. I could feel it, sort of the way I could feel when I had nailed the Chihuahua's ears at Paws and Claws.

"How much did you win?" Brad asked, his voice carrying past me, past Bridget, past Pete at the far end of the hole. A couple with a baby and a five-year-old looked my way. Behind them, two girls who I think I'd seen outside freshman gym stopped talking and started to pretend they weren't listening.

"They won, like, two million dollars." Her words reached a couple of girls reading a text message and a Golf, Movies, and More worker who was switching out trash bags by the ninth hole.

I concentrated on the ball. I figured if I ignored everyone, they'd shut up.

"Two mil? That's insane! Way cool." I hadn't taken Brad for the excitable type. At least not around anything that didn't involve blowing the head off some alien-slash-god-slash-hellbeast. "If you feel like giving to a charitable cause, I'm your guy. I mean, how sad is it that I still just have the PlayStation 2?"

"Shut up, Brad," Pete yelled out. "Let Reggie take her shot."

"If I'd won the lottery," Bridget said, balancing the foot of her club on the toe of her platforms, "I'd go to Paris for the summer. Maybe the year."

I tried to block her out. But I made the mistake of looking at her as I made my final visual with the hole.

"Regina, I think you should take me to Paris."

And that's when I swung, and the club hitting the ball sounded like a crack of lightning. That's what it looked like, too, as it spun through the mouse-sized hole that bypassed the windmill, swooped up the Astroturf, sideswiped a fake rock . . .

. . . and glided into the hole.

"Way to go, Millions!" Brad slammed his hand against my back. Just a few minutes ago, he'd been finding any excuse to get away from me. Money, I was coming to find out, was a great equalizer.

He bent his head, and I could see his scalp through his short, spiky hair. "Rub my head for luck, will ya, Millions? We have an online tournament tomorrow and I need all the luck I can get."

I didn't touch his head as we headed back to the cash register and handed over our clubs and balls. I didn't hold his hand when his brushed against mine while standing in line at Buzz's. And I definitely didn't give him my number when he asked for it in the back of Pete's car.

"Hey, can you come in for a second?" Bridget had a wide smile on her face. I wasn't fooled, though. Bridget was never, ever happy.

Pete had dropped off Brad and we were now idling in front of Bridget's three-story Spanish-meets-Tuscan house. I was tired and just wanted to take a hot shower and forget about the "Rub my head for luck, will ya?" dude.

"Can it wait?"

"Aunt Genie wanted to get some phone numbers from Mom. Florists and bakers and stuff." She held up her phone. "Mom texted me a minute ago about it."

The day was getting colder; the sun was all but gone on the horizon, and there was a slight breeze rustling the mesquite trees dotting the edge of the driveway. "Fine." I got out and told Pete, "Wait, you will."

He gave me a salute. "Wait, I will."

Inside, it smelled like the usual mix of potpourri, floor cleaner, and pumpkin candles. Bridget picked up what looked like a magazine, folded open to the middle. "Here."

I looked at it. It was a purse catalog. "Mom wants a Coach for the wedding?"

"No." She drew out the word, condescension reeking from it. "It's for me."

She held out the catalog, but I didn't take it. I looked at the page again and the expectant look on her face. And that's when it hit me. "You want me to buy you," I said, stopping just long enough to look at the list price, "a six-hundred-dollar bag?"

"Yep."

"Don't you already have one?"

She stood next to me, stroking the image with her finger. "Not this one. It's pretty."

She sounded as if she had lost her mind and about fifty IQ points. Coffees and mini-golf fees were one thing, but six hundred dollars? "Why don't you just whip out your own credit card?" I knew that Aunt Barb had given her one in ninth grade for "emergencies." I didn't know that acrylic nails once a week, highlights once every four weeks, and a shopping spree about once every other day constituted emergencies.

"Mom took my card," she said, a scowl settling on her face. "Something about me needing to pull up my AP Calc grade." Did I mention Bridget was smart? It was a shocker for me, too.

She turned and started walking up the spiral staircase, the wall curving up to the second floor painted to look like an old Italian village. Mom once said it had cost almost as much as our house.

"So why don't you just wait until you get the card back?" Washing her car and spotting her here and there was one thing; spending six hundred dollars on leather, a zipper, and a brand was insane.

"Because I don't wanna wait." She stopped at the top and leaned over, a cold smile on her lips. Her cell phone was in her hand, her past threat hovering between us. "And Regina? I want the red one."

CHAPTER EIGHT

Hey, Reg, it's Pete.
Is Sarah mad at us or something?

I WAS IN HEAVEN. And I needed heaven after a run-in with a girl who called hell home.

"Six blueberry-cake donuts, three buttermilk bars, two lemon-filled, and—" I studied DD's case. So many choices, so little time to take everything home and eat it before anyone saw the evidence. "And one Reese's Cup in the Hole."

DD herself was at the counter today. She still smelled like too much perfume, but I had learned to take shorter, shallower breaths when she was around. Her donuts were too good to get scared off by bad perfume practices. She was putting in the last donut when I heard, "Great minds think alike."

Gabe. The very, absolute last person on Earth I wanted to see. *Liar.*

"Hey." I slipped my new credit card out of my wallet, avoiding eye contact. He'd asked me to the movies and he'd gotten *Psycho*. The real-life version.

"I heard you quit."

I shrugged. My talk with Fellers seemed like a lifetime ago. Me embarrassing myself in front of Gabe, though, felt like just five minutes ago.

"Did you quit because I wrote you up?" he asked. I had to lean in to catch what he said.

"I would have a pretty slow reaction time if that was the reason."

He nodded. But then something passed across his features. Anger? "Fellers didn't do anything to you, did he?"

"Fellers? The two things he loves most in this world are his wife and Cashmart." I shook my head. "He wouldn't do anything to mess either of those things up."

I saw the tenseness leave Gabe's shoulders. "Okay. Good."

More silence. And then: "You treating your mom and brother to breakfast?"

I nodded, staying focused on the napkin dispenser and pulling out what I needed and not just a huge wad. If he hadn't been there, I would have done a wad. But he made me feel nervous. Plus, I didn't want to look like a pig around him.

Says the girl with a box of a dozen assorted donuts in front of her.

"You ready to order?" I heard Gabe say.

I looked up and realized he hadn't been talking to me but to a girl with long dark hair, small bones, and large hazel eyes.

That was all I needed to get my butt into gear. I shoved the napkins in my purse, grabbed the box, and started for the door. I hoped Gabe was very happy with the emaciated ten-year-old.

I knew I'd be happy with my donuts.

"Hey." My elbow got grabbed from behind, jerking my body one way while my donuts went another. The box fell out of my hands and onto the ground, donuts scattering everywhere.

"Nice going." This came from the gorgeous girl with the birdlike bones, who moved past me to the end of the line.

Thinking she was talking to me, I started scooping up donut parts and kept my head down, willing my hair to cover my red cheeks and watery eyes.

"Shut up, Sylvie." Gabe squatted next to me, his hands faster than mine as he tossed cake and jelly into the box. "What a waste." He held up the Reese's Peanut Butter Cup that had fallen out of one donut. "If I didn't believe in the two-second rule, the Reese's would be mine."

Through the red cheeks and the burning in my eyes, I managed, "Ten-second. In my family, ten seconds and you're free and clear to eat whatever hits the ground."

"Yeah?"

I looked through my hair, trying to keep my face hidden while trying to gauge if he was holding a grudge about the movie thing. "Definitely."

He knocked his elbow against mine. For a second, I thought it was accidental, but then I saw the Dimple. I forgot what I was doing as I took in his smile, the flannel stretched across his broad shoulders and the sudden heat in the air.

"Dare me?" He had the Reese's Cup out of the box and between his fingers, his mouth open.

Then I heard myself say, "Can I pick Truth instead?"

He lowered his hand, and the moment between us seemed to stretch into something infinite as voices, the TV, and clattering dishes faded away, and I could swear I heard only the two of us breathing.

"I don't care about the lottery, Reggie—"

"I know. I was dumb." I paused for effect. "*Really* dumb."

His eyes, greener than I had ever seen them, seemed to darken as he smiled. "Ask away."

The words rushed out as I busied myself with closing the box and standing up again. "Who's the girl?"

It's always loud in DD's, and Sunday mornings are always the loudest. But the last table could have probably heard Gabe's laugh. Maybe even the store next door, which was separated by a brick wall.

"Sylvie." He called her name as he took the box out of my hands, and whether he knew it or not, kept me from bolting out the door in utter mortification.

The girl with the ten-year-old's body came over to us, a bag in her hand. The crowd was growing, and she had to fight to make it to our circle of two, and a sliver of me hoped her tiny bird bones would get smushed. She snapped her wallet closed, her eyes on me as she put her wallet back into her bag. "Are you okay? I'll beat him up if you want. He's always been a bully, so he has it coming."

She looked at me with wide, serious eyes. Hazel eyes.

"Reggie, this is my sister."

I didn't realize how tense I was until relief flooded through my body like some hard-core muscle relaxer.

"I'd shake your hand, but it's sort of—" I held it up. Lemon jelly, powdered sugar, and dried blueberries warred for space.

"Looks as if you owe the girl some donuts," she said to Gabe.

"Just what I was thinking." Gabe gestured toward the counter, where a line now thirty people deep waited.

I held my hands out, trying not to get anything on me. I didn't feel like waiting. More important—much more important—I wasn't hungry anymore.

"I think I'm good." When it looked like Gabe wanted to talk me into it, I interrupted with "Really. Let's not dishonor the dead and departed with quick and easy replacements."

Sylvie grinned. "I like the way this girl thinks. It looks as if your taste in girls is moving up in the world, Gabriel."

His taste in girls? I was one of his girls? I felt myself blush hard and fast.

She held up the bag in her hand. "I got six donuts in here. Want to go to Gabe's and have breakfast with us?"

Gabe put his hands together, fingers pointed up, and mouthed "Please." I nodded and couldn't stop smiling. I raised my hands. "Soon as I wash up."

"Gangbusters." Sylvie grinned.

Gabe leaned toward me, a lock of his hair an inch from brushing my face. I looked down, away from the intensity in his eyes. I felt his hair touch my temple, and I tried hard to keep breathing. "*Gangbusters* is Sylvie's new word, which means 'great idea.' It's a stupid word. But I definitely agree that you coming over is a great idea. But I don't want you to feel as if you have to come."

"Trust me," I swallowed and made myself look at him.

I almost forgot that I was supposed to say something. "I think that going over to your house is gangbusters."

Gabe might have lived in a run-of-the-mill apartment from the outside, but on the inside, it was a different place. A different world. A different social class.

"Where did you get this stuff?" I ran a hand down the back of his black leather couch. It felt just as nice as the leather of one of Aunt Barb's winter jackets. I took in the pool table where a dining table would have been and a TV that might have been bigger than ours hanging over a fancy-looking aquarium.

"My old bedroom."

This stuff came out of his bedroom? I thought about the Goodwill bed frame I used to have, the saggy mattress, the rip in my carpet. "So. You're rich."

Sylvie came out of the kitchen with two plates: one holding assorted donuts and a smaller plate carrying a single pink-frosting-and-sprinkles donut. "Dad's the one who's rich. We just benefit when it comes to material things."

I took in the audio system, the quality pool table with its carved legs and rich green felt, the hot tub plumbed into the back deck. "You have all this, and you work at Cashmart?"

"Being rich doesn't mean you're lazy," he said, the words blurring together as he said them in a rush. "And Cashmart's an honest living."

It was. But why work when you didn't have to?

"Okay, you two, I'm going to go sit on the back deck with my donut and my iPod." Sylvie stood by the sliding glass door, her hands balancing her plate and a bottle of water, looking pointedly at the handle. I experienced a flash of Bridget-ness, but it disappeared as Gabe opened the door for her, and for a minute, it seemed as if she gave him a quick, pointed look. "Feel free to pretend I've disappeared."

Gabe closed the door behind her and gestured to the sofa. "Make yourself comfortable." He picked up the bigger plate Sylvie had left on the pool table. "Drink?"

As he went to get my water, I sat down and studied the contents on the coffee table. A fancy laptop, a universal remote, a toy that looked an awful lot like the one I had for Birdie. "You have a cat?"

Gabe came out of the kitchen, handed me a water bottle, and put the plate of donuts between us on the middle sofa cushion. "I do. Don't tell me you're allergic."

"If I am, I'm pretty screwed." I opened the bottle and took a swig. "I have a cat, too."

We spent the next ten minutes talking cats (his: Oscar), hairballs (Birdie's), and raising them as indoor cats (both of us). Also about cats who could dial 911 (neither of ours, but we were both trying).

The conversation dwindled into silence as Gabe ate his third donut and I drank water. I honestly wasn't hungry. I mean, I was never binge-hungry in front of anybody, but I wasn't even hungry-hungry. My stomach was sort of busy with other things, like butterflies and roller coasters and warm fuzzies.

Gabe wiped his mouth and moved the plate to the coffee table. "Can I ask you something?"

"Sure."

"You were pretty mad the other night, and now you're sitting here, drinking my water, enjoying my couch." He grinned, and then his face softened into something that was half curious, half... I don't know. Whatever it was, it made him explore my face as if it was the most interesting thing he'd seen in a while. "What made you change your mind?"

He was leaning forward, his arm along the back of the middle cushion, his fingers an inch and a half or so from my shoulder. *Should I lean back?*

I shrugged, struggling to stay where I was and just enjoy the moment. There was nothing wrong with just enjoying the moment. I didn't have much practice with living in the here and now, but I was willing to try. "There was no *one* thing. It was just a feeling, that maybe you were a good guy and you really did want to go to a movie because, well, you wanted to go to a movie."

"When did this feeling happen?" he asked. The next instant, I felt pressure against my shoulder, and saw that his fingers had reached across the inch-and-a-half gap between us. I bit my cheek and leaned into them, nervous, waiting for him to push me away. He didn't.

"Playing miniature golf." I laughed at the memory of Brad asking me to rub his head and buy him a PlayStation. I guess I should have thanked the guy for showing me what a true creep looked like.

"Yeah?" Gabe seemed to be pushing on my shoulder, moving me in his direction. I scooted a few inches toward him, and I swallowed back a nervous laugh.

"Yeah."

"It's not because you found out I had a sixty-inch TV?" he whispered.

I pulled away, but I didn't go far. His hand pulled me toward him, and this time I found myself in the curve of his arm, his lips just inches away. How had that happened?

"I'm joking, Regina."

"Reggie. Or Reg." I swallowed again. "People who aren't my friends call me Regina."

He brushed a piece of hair off my cheek and tucked it behind my ear.

I cleared my throat. "So where's that thirteen-inch with rabbit ears you were telling me about?"

He chuckled. It was low and deep and made me want to hear more. He followed it up with brushing another piece of hair behind my ears. "That was my feeble attempt at trying to appear cute and spend time with you."

"You wanted to spend time with me?" My lips were dry, but I didn't lick them. I think that would have been a weird thing to do in the middle of the conversation we were having, as close as we were having it.

"Yep." He pulled me closer, and I smelled that dizzying combination of musk and shampoo and rain. "I had to spend more time with the Photo Goddess who could get a rat to play to the camera."

The millimeters between us disappeared, and I forgot all about dry lips. Gabe had a great technique for making me forget.

CHAPTER NINE

Hello, Imogene. This is Mattie from across the street.
I believe you know that I work for Waterview Today.
Well, they'd like to feature you and your family
in an upcoming edition. Isn't that wonderful?
Please call and let me know what would work best for you.

TWENTY-FOUR HOURS LATER, my lips were still numb—in a very, very good way. Ms. Moore was up front, droning on about Jane Austen and some Brontë sister. I pretended to take notes, but I was really reliving the Kiss

It had started slow, Gabe's lips soft and firm, mine pliable. I didn't know what to do, so I followed Gabe's lead. When he opened his mouth, I opened mine, and when the tip of his tongue caressed mine, I returned the favor. He tasted like mint and chocolate, a very, very good combination. I hadn't known where to put my hands, so I kept them in my lap. Or at least I tried. By the time we came up for air, my hands were tangled in the silky strands of his hair.

As first kisses went, it had been pretty darn near perfect.

"Psst."

Something tapped my elbow and I turned. Martha Hingby, a girl who always wore her red hair in a braid to her butt and played some sort of flute/clarinet thing for band, had her eyes on Ms. Moore as she whispered, "Did you really win the lottery, Regina?"

The Kiss was forgotten. For now. "Who told you that?"

She pushed a copy of *The News* across her desk, a four-page joke that used big type to try to hide the fact that no one turned in stories meeting word count. But I didn't have time to dwell too long on *The News*'s shortcomings; Martha opened it to the School News section, where there was a picture of me from sophomore year (the last time I'd shown up for school pictures) and underneath a three-sentence paragraph:

> Regina Shaw, a senior, is officially rich.
> Her mother, Imogene Shaw, won the Arizona
> Five. The amount is estimated to be $2 million,
> according to a source close to Shaw, who had no
> comment at press time.

I read it three times. All the lies read like a foreign language. I scanned for a byline. "Who wrote this crap?"

I didn't realize I had basically blurted out the question until I heard Ms. Moore ask, "Regina, do you have a problem with the readings?"

Lamely, I shook my head. Ms. Moore glanced briefly at the newspaper on my desk, and I shoved it out of sight under my notebook.

I felt another tap on my elbow. I didn't turn around as Martha whispered, "I think Nancy Reilly writes School News. At least she did last semester."

Nancy Reilly. I'd heard that name. My stomach clenched. She was a Bridget groupie.

Reading the paragraph again, I read the lies. And I knew who the source was without even thinking it over. She was addicted to text messaging and making my life hell.

Ten minutes later, I shot out of my seat before the bell had finished trilling. I knew exactly where to find Nancy Reilly. She was in Pete's physics class, which I knew because Pete had gotten stuck with her as a partner this semester. He did all the work and she texted all through class.

As I headed down B Hall, groups of two or more stopped talking whenever I passed by. I wasn't imagining it, either. I would get within five feet of someone and they'd stop talking mid-sentence, mid-word, even mid-consonant. Most gave me a thumbs-up sign.

Me, Regina Shaw. The girl on whose locker someone had

scrawled *Go home and take a Shaw-er* three years ago. The girl who wore sweatpants and fell asleep in class because she worked double shifts at Crapmart. The girl that wasn't asked to sign yearbooks because she worked too much, didn't do any school activities, and wasn't a class brain.

Was it really that simple? Win the lottery and—poof!—become an instant high school celebrity?

I saw Pete by his locker, and my bloodlust for Nancy Reilly changed focus. "Did you read *The News* today?"

Pete gave me a blank look, and I noticed how bloodshot his eyes were. "Saw it Friday. Hank brought it over to give to Mom so she could see if her ad was big enough."

Pete's mom sold homemade jars layered with brown sugar, oatmeal, chocolate chips, and everything else that makes up a cookie; she was a great baker but not so good at figuring out who her demographic was. Hank was the editor-in-chief of *The News*. He was also the guy Pete hung out with when he was off-again with Sarah.

"You've known since Friday?" I felt a headache start behind my right eye. "Pete, we went to mini-golf Friday. And a movie. The entire night was the definition of awkward silences. And you didn't think to tell me about the paper?"

He put a book in his bag and closed the locker. Neither action seemed to have much energy behind it. I even think I heard him sigh. Pete, the nondramatic one. "I was miniature-golfing, Reg. You know I don't think of anything else when I'm going for a hole in one."

I wanted to be mad, but I already felt the tension leaving. Pete had the kind of concentration that had people bending spoons with their minds. I've known this about him since elementary school. Of course, if a *Star Wars* convention came to town and he ran into a Wookie at the Gas 'n Go, he would let me and Sarah know immediately. Pete was weird, not complex.

I banged my forehead against the locker. It felt sort of good, the impact making me forget about the tension between my shoulders. So I did it again. And again.

"C'mon, Reg. I can't handle Sarah being all Sarah and you getting mental on me at the same time. I'm too tired." When I didn't stop, Pete put his hand between my forehead and the locker, and I finally stood up straight. "So what if people know? They were probably going to find out sooner or later. Doesn't the city paper run something when you get the check anyway?"

"We already got our check and no, they didn't run anything."

"No, I mean one of those big Ed McMahon/Publishers Clearing House things from the commercials."

"You watch too much TV, Pete. We didn't get anything like that."

"That's a bummer." His face lit up briefly. "But if you do, I'll take it. I could dress up as Ed McMahon for Halloween, then."

"Halloween's over."

"Oh yeah." Pete didn't say anything for a minute. "There's always next year, though."

The warning bell for second period sounded. "If I get a giant check, it's yours." I held up *The News.* "Anyway, I think this was more than enough attention."

Pete put his arm around my neck. It was more headlock than affectionate. "Why all secretive, Reg?"

I tried to wriggle out from under his arm and thought about Mom and DD's. "Mom just doesn't want everyone to know and start looking for handouts."

He grunted. "Totally understandable." He noogied my head. "By the way, wanna pay for me to go to space camp?"

I licked his arm and he let go, wiping his arm on me. "Let's talk about something more interesting," I said. "Like when you're going to make up with Sarah."

He snorted. "According to her, when hell freezes over and I open a Popsicle stand with Bridget and Lucifer."

"She's still not over the Bridget thing."

He scowled at me. "Of course not. And I've tried explaining to her it wasn't a date."

"Exactly." I knew that Sarah knew that Pete *barely*

knew that Bridget existed. She might be quasi-attractive to someone who didn't know her well enough, but she didn't know the first thing about Ewoks, the Death Star, or the exact moment Princess Leia and Han Solo fell for each other. Sarah? This was her second language. She pretended to hate *Star Wars*, but that was just part of her and Pete's shtick.

"Yeah, well, Sarah thinks there's something going on." He pinched the bridge of his nose with his thumb and forefinger. "I don't know, Reg. I don't think we're getting back together this time."

With the last bell about to ring at any second, I started backing up. Han Solo and Princess Leia got together; so would Pete and Sarah. "Miracles can happen, Pete."

"Yeah? Name one."

I pointed at myself, and for once didn't look around to see if anyone was listening. "Regina Shaw winning the lottery."

Less than twenty-four hours later, everyone knew.

At lunchtime, a drama geek who'd been my lab partner junior year came up to me, even though she'd vowed never to speak to me again when I didn't do my part of the final paper (too much Cashmart overtime) and she ended up doing it all. "It's so cool you won the lottery, Reg!" She was on her way to the trash can with her lunch tray, but she paused long enough to add, "I have another twenty tickets to sell for the senior production of *Our Town* if you need any."

After school, in the parking lot, Tony Roosen came over as Pete and I sat on Pete's hood. "You should really look into a Porsche Carrera. My dad's buddy owns a lot in Phoenix, and I was pretty much raised there. I can help you pick one out, even help you learn stick if you want." This from the guy who egged my house last year. Twice.

And even when I went to the school nurse to get a Band-Aid for the cut I'd gotten from Pete's fender, I wasn't safe. "I'm running a 10K next week for breast cancer. It's tax deductible, too," Nurse Banyon said.

As I made my way back to the student parking lot, even the janitor stopped mopping and told me what he would do with the money: "I'd find myself a deserted island and make sure no one could ever find me and then just count the money over and over again until I died of starvation or thirst."

He was the only one who didn't ask me for something. Not that it mattered. He just had a different way of making me feel in immediate need of a scalding hot shower.

I was staring at every teenage girl's fantasy.

It sat in my driveway, a bright red ribbon tied around it, a bow on top.

A black Land Rover.

Mom skipped out of the house as soon as Pete pulled up to the curb. "Do you like it?"

"Um, do I like shiny pretty cars that are wrapped up in a big bow and given to me? Um, yeah!" I tugged at the ribbon, and it must have been rigged to come apart, because that's just what it did. Every room in the house was under construction, and I had a ten thousand dollar limit on my credit card, but this was the first time I *felt* like we had won the lottery.

"Here's the key." Mom handed it to me, a Land Rover key fob attached to it. In my hand, even the key felt rich.

"This is the LR2, which is the cheaper model, but it just seemed to suit your personality more." My mom was chattering at the speed of a chipmunk. "It has a sunroof, GPS system, satellite radio, two DVD players, even headlights that swivel when you turn the steering wheel." She threw her arms wide, and I didn't know if she was just excited or expecting a hug. I gave her a hug.

And, no, I wasn't trying to avoid a confrontation. I just was feeling an overwhelming need to hug the woman who had bought me

A LAND ROVER!

My thumb was already depressing the unlock button. I opened the driver's-side door, the new-car smell almost making me faint. I'd smelled new-car smell a few times in my life—Pete's dad's Subaru, Sarah's mom's Ford Focus a few years ago, Doc's Oldsmobile when we had to do a paint run. The Shaws had never owned anything with new-car smell before. And Mom spraying new-car scent just wasn't the same.

I slid onto the black leather seat and put the key in the ignition. But I didn't turn it on. I just sat there, smelling and enjoying. In the back of my head, I had a brief thought about how much this car was and the three thousand my mom still owed me for the TV and DVDs.

This was a dream come true, right? I had a new car. A fancy car. Something most teenage girls would sell out their best friend for. But I couldn't silence the tiny voice whining through it all:

Where was my three thousand dollars?

I swallowed hard to keep the question from coming out. I distracted myself by pushing the car's buttons.

"You know who would love a ride in this? Bridget." Mom's face lit up, and she pulled a wad of cash out of the pocket of her jeans. She counted out four or five hundred-dollar bills from it. "Go have some fun. Test-drive it down to Laughlin if you want."

Of everyone I'd thought about sharing my new car with, Bridget came right after digging up Hitler and riding with his corpse. I took the money, shoved it in my pocket, and applied it to Mom's balance of how much she owed me. The tiny bump of money stopped a lot of the anti-Mom thoughts and made me focus on

MY NEW CAR.

"Pete, want to go for a ride?" I called out.

"Can I drive?" He ran a finger over the top of the hood, and then went back over it with the hem of his T-shirt.

"Sure." I grinned. "After three or four hundred thousand miles."

I played with the satellite radio while Pete strapped himself in and Mom talked about all the upgraded features she'd bought. And as she went on, I realized something. My car had a lot more stuff than Bridget's VW.

Driving by Bridget's house wouldn't be too, too far out of my way. And if my horn accidentally beeped as I passed her house, oh well, right?

"Is that duct tape on your phone?" Bridget sat down next to me at a table in front of Sbarro. The smell of pizza called to me, but I'd already given in to two slices. I had my phone open, looking at the time and, yes, there was duct tape holding the battery in. Briefly, I thought how it would be better served on her mouth.

Bridget peeled shopping bags off her wrists and rubbed

at the red marks left behind. "I think there's a cell-phone store in Section C."

My feet hurt, my head hurt, my mouth was dry, and I was dying for a soft pretzel with cinnamon, sugar, and a side of icing. If I'd been with Sarah, I would have just gotten it. With Bridget, whose idea of a snack was a diet soda and sugar-free gum, I didn't act on my craving. Instead, I sucked on the watered-down Dr Pepper in my Mega-Thirst-Quencher.

I should never have gone by Bridget's house. Then Aunt Barb wouldn't have seen me, waved me in, and talked me into going for a test-drive with Bridget. Thank God for Pete. Pete sat in back, keeping Bridget from being too Bridget-y as they argued about how Pete had cheated (Bridget's take) or had rivaled Tiger Woods (Pete's take) at mini-golf.

We ended up thirty miles away in Laughlin, Nevada, a mini-Vegas that had a river running through it. When Bridget saw the outlets, she whined until I pulled into the parking garage. And somehow, I'd ended up playing video games with Pete while Bridget shopped. And shopped.

"I don't need a new phone. I just got mine two months ago." I had dropped it one month ago, but it still worked. If you pressed real hard on the battery pack and used it outside. On a clear day. With no wind.

"You need a new cell." She picked at the sleeve of my long-sleeved shirt. It was one of Dad's Phoenix Suns shirts. "And I think you need to think about wardrobe. The grunge look died in the nineties, and those smelly sweats aren't doing anything for your figure."

I felt my face heat up. "I just washed them," I managed to say. Images of *Go home and take a Shaw-er* flashed in front of me.

"I care, why?" She rolled her eyes. "Sweats are gross in general. Right up there with spandex and polyester." She raised an eyebrow. "Plus, you drive a Land Rover now. That is so not a sweatpants kind of car."

I ran my hands down my thighs, the thin black jersey of my sweats smooth and cool. Laughlin had cinemas, casinos, and lots of shopping. Mom did most of her non-eBay shopping here. The only time I'd been to the outlets, I'd been waiting for Mom to finish gambling. I think I'd eaten about seven slices of pizza and four Cinnabons. I didn't believe in spending a lot of money for uncomfortable clothes. I didn't care how much money I had.

Bags crinkled as Pete, back from the restroom, waded through them and plopped down next to me. "Females, I need sustenance."

"I will only eat sushi." Bridget pulled out her phone and texted. Matter decided.

"I need real food. As in the all-you-can-eat variety. You with me, Reg?" Pete tossed his arm over my shoulders. He'd been doing a lot more touching and feeling lately. It was one of the last stages of the off-again portion of his and Sarah's relationship. This is when he was starting to miss female companionship. Nonthreatening female companionship, which ruled out Bridget.

My phone rang as Bridget launched into a discussion about the ineffectiveness of sneezeguards and why buffets were just a plague waiting to happen. I punched the talk button, grateful to be interrupted from Germs 101. "Hey, Mom."

At first there was silence. "Hello?" I said.

"I thought we had an agreement about keeping the money under wraps."

It was Mom. Angry Mom. The sixty-four ounces of Dr Pepper threatened to come out the way it had gone in. I got up and walked over to a Bridget kind of store, music blaring through the double doors, the lights barely on inside. "You saw *The News*?"

"Oh yes. Your Aunt Barb was quite proud of having us in there." I heard her blow out a long, long breath. "*Waterview Today* wants to interview us, and now every Uncle Tom, Dick, and Harry is going to find us and ask for money."

I barely registered the row of mannequins in front of me, or the overpriced jeans they were wearing. "I didn't tell, though. Bridget told her friend, Nancy Reilly, who—"

"That's not what Bridget said, Regina. She said people overheard you talking about it at the mini-golf place. Rather loudly, too. Is this true?"

"Well, okay, there's a good explanation—"

"I don't care about explanations. You either did it or you didn't, and you just confirmed, in your own words, that you did. End of story." Another deep breath. "*Waterview Today* is sending someone tomorrow to interview us. Do you have something other than sweatpants to wear?"

I looked at the window display of size-zero, faceless mannequins in front of me. "Not really."

"Find something. Use the money I gave you."

I looked around. I think there were some stores that carried clothes for people who ate. And someone must be having a sale so I could hold on to as much of the five hundred as I could. "Okay." But Mom didn't hear me. She'd already hung up.

"So, Regina, any grand dreams about how you want to spend the money?" Ms. Weare smiled, her dentures white Chiclets against her tangerine lipstick.

We were being interviewed in the private dining room at Foster's. Outside, white Christmas lights dangled from the roof, their reflection dancing in the marina's rippling water. I sat up straighter and reached under the table with one hand to adjust the waistband of my new designer jeans, a flash of longing shooting through me for the comfort of drawstring and jersey.

"No big plans yet, Ms. Weare." I'd known Mattie Weare since we moved in three years ago. She lived across from us and freelanced for *Waterview Today*, where she usually wrote for the Calendar section. I guess her living across from us had helped her nail this story. "Maybe some CDs." The Land Rover had a five-disc changer.

Ms. Weare smiled as she scratched down my answer. Out of the corner of my eye, I saw Mom stirring her tea. She hadn't stopped stirring it since we started the interview.

Mom leaned forward and put the teacup down, the bone china rattling on the gold-edged saucer. "Mattie, this will only be running in the local paper, right?" she asked. "I just don't want long-lost cousins in Hoboken, New Jersey, reading the *Arizona Republic* on their computers and hitting us up for a loan."

Ms. Weare smiled and took her glasses off, folded them closed, and let them drop against her chest, where they hung on a beaded chain. "I believe so, Mrs. Shaw. *Waterview Today* is a tiny paper, and pretty much the only news other papers want from us are the details about the water-skiing championships in July."

As Ms. Weare put her glasses back on—it was quite a production, too, since she had to unfold them, clean them, check them in the light for smears and then clean them again—Mom cleared her throat and asked another question. "And, Mattie, is there any way you can also leave out how much we won?"

The older woman slipped her glasses back on and took up her pen and notepad again. "We could give an approximation. Maybe say you won one and a half million?"

Mom laughed. Both Jeff and I looked at her to make sure she was all right; we'd never heard her use that laugh before, like a dolphin caught in a tuna net. "That means we're giving out one and a half million reasons why long-lost relatives want to find my address, pack up their RVs, and camp outside my home until I pretty much pay them to go away." She smiled, as if she was trying to take the edge off her words. She turned to us. "I read about it on the Arizona Lottery site. You know, what to be aware of when you win a large amount of money."

Ms. Weare tapped the end of her pen against the pad.

"What wording are you thinking about, Mrs. Shaw, just so I know if we're on the same page, so to speak."

I had to give Ms. Weare credit. She was a lot sharper than she looked.

"I was thinking that you could say we won *a* lottery."

Ms. Weare's eyes narrowed. "Don't you want me to say you won the Arizona Five?"

Mom fidgeted with the tea saucer, sliding it back and forth on the white tablecloth. "I just don't want any red flags to go up. If we say we won the Arizona Five outright, then people are going to know what the amount is. All they'd have to do is Google 'Arizona Five' and the date we won." She laughed again, and it was shaky. Sort of nervous-sounding. "Remember, Mattie, how we talked about how you'd get the interview and we'd get to keep our privacy? I mean, couldn't you just word it so that it says we won a lottery, but not which one or for how much?"

Ms. Weare folded her hands together. "You're sort of tying my hands here, Mrs. Shaw. I don't know what kind of story it's going to be if I'm not very specific with the details."

Mom grabbed Jeff's hand, which was resting on top of the table. Jeff himself seemed checked out from this conversation. "Jeff, you did pretty well in your journalism classes. Maybe you could help Mattie come up with something?"

Jeff looked as confused as I felt. "Mom, I took one journalism class before I dropped out, and I got a C in it, too." He shifted his weight in his seat. "And I don't think I remember anything other than 'If it bleeds, it leads.' "

"Maybe, Mrs. Shaw," Ms. Weare said, her words crisp and decisive, "we should just put the story on hold for now. This should be a fun story, not your family's worst nightmare." For being the little old lady across the street, Ms. Weare had a backbone. I should take notes.

"Well, I wouldn't exactly use the word nightmare. . . ." Mom hedged.

"Oh?" Ms. Weare readjusted her glasses. "It certainly sounds that way to me." She pushed herself up and picked up the straw tote she used as a purse. "Call me if you feel ready to share your story. Your whole story."

Something passed between them. Not words, not a look, not even a gesture. Tension, maybe?

Mom nodded. "Thanks, Mattie. I'm glad you understand."

The older woman turned and studied us. Me in my new clothes, Jeff in his new sneakers, Mom in her designer dress. "I think I understand perfectly, Mrs. Shaw."

◊ ◊ ◊

"How'd it go?"

I stood on Gabe's front porch, cold and tired and confused by one very weird interview. I wanted to launch myself at his chest, looking especially broad and strong and capable under a white V-neck undershirt.

"Hold me?" I asked, half joking, half serious.

He opened his arms and I hurled myself into him, throwing us off balance. His laughter was deep, rich, and the best thing I'd heard all day.

"Why do you think your mom is so afraid of people finding out?"

It was two hours later, and I was nestled against Gabe's side, content with just breathing him in as we sat on his sofa with the lights off and the fish tank glowing and bubbling in front of us. We'd talked about the trip to Laughlin, about the leak at school, and now we were finishing up talking about the interview. Oh yeah, and we had made out a lot.

"She's just freaked about someone taking advantage of her." I realized I was resting my hand against Gabe's stomach. I'd never done that before. It felt nice. "Ever since she found out Dad cashed out his life insurance, she wants to make sure every single cent she has is accounted for."

I repeated the words that I'd heard from her over and over again. But even as I did, I didn't believe them one hundred percent. I couldn't. I mean, if she supposedly followed every single cent, how did she run out of money for bills and food and gas?

I realized I was now rubbing Gabe's stomach. I raised my head to look at his face, and he was smiling at me. I stopped and buried my hot cheeks and forehead in his armpit. It sounded gross, but it wasn't. Not with Gabe.

"What's with the shyness, Reg?"

I shook my head. No way was I telling him just how new all this was to me.

"C'mon, Blue Eyes. Don't be shy."

I shook my head again, burrowing deeper under his arm.

"Hey, I forgot to ask." He paused until I looked up again. His eyes were warm as he squeezed my hand. "Have you eaten? I know you guys had tea at Foster's, but did you actually have anything to eat? I have some leftover enchiladas Sylvie made before she went to the movies."

Gabe the caretaker. He was only two years older than me, but he acted older. Sometimes even I-need-an-afternoon-nap-and-my-Metamucil old. He'd checked the air in the tires instead of checking out the fancy sound system or GPS system when I introduced him to the Land Rover. He'd massaged my feet when he saw how red my toes got in my new heels tonight. He kept asking me if I was ready to talk to Sarah yet—and that just say the word, he'd drive me to her house and wait in the car.

So, yeah, he might have been twenty years old in terms of body and face, but the mind was like some old person. Like, a thirty-year-old.

"I'm actually not hungry," I said, leaning my head back against his shoulder. "I had some lemon cookies at the interview."

He chuckled, and the vibration felt nice against my back. "You definitely like your sweets, don't you?"

I forced out my own laugh, but inside I was curling into a ball and dying. Did Gabe think I ate too much? That I was fat? I could stand to lose ten pounds, but I wasn't *fat* fat. Just curvy. Normal.

We didn't talk as we sat there, staring at the aquarium, my hand curled between both of his. I don't know what he was thinking about, but I know what I was: *Why does this hot, nice guy like me?*

"Regina, phone."

I didn't answer. Partly because my vocal cords weren't working yet, partly because I didn't know if I was still dreaming or not. And I definitely didn't want to wake up from my dream with me, Gabe, and a box of donuts.

191

"Regina!" Something hit my butt. I pushed straight up, and I felt the string of drool connecting my mouth to my pillow. Based on his position on my bed, Mr. Puffin had been used as a missile. A brief spike of anger surfaced. Mr. Puffin deserved better than that.

"Leave me alone, maggot breath!" I pulled the covers over my head, for a minute forgetting I was eighteen, Jeff was just visiting, we were rich, and Dad was dead.

"Your friend's on the phone."

That woke me up. I scrambled for the cordless Mom had gotten online a couple of days ago. It was from the Museum of Modern Art in New York and looked like a cross between a penguin and a mound of clay. She said it had been a "steal" at three hundred dollars. Which made me think it had really been six hundred.

"Gabe?"

"Did you hear about Sarah?" It was Pete.

"Hold on." I switched ears, sat up, and pulled Mr. Puffin to me. I was wide awake now. "What about Sarah?"

His voice cracked as he said, "She's in the hospital."

Waterview Memorial Hospital was clean, quiet, and painted a horrible shade of Pepto-Bismol pink. I'd only been here once before, when Dad had kidney stones. He'd told us

192

passing them was worse than giving birth. Mom bet the nurses he'd cry when they passed. Mom ended up winning fifty bucks.

"Which room is she in?" I was trying to keep up with Pete, but between his long legs and full-on speed walk, I kept falling behind and had to jog to catch up.

"Two-fifty-two."

Everything about the elevator was slow: the wait for it, the doors opening, the doors closing, the ride up. I thought Pete was going to pry the doors open at one point like Bruce Willis in a *Die Hard* movie.

"Do we even know if she wants to see us?" I asked cautiously, well aware of Pete's unstable mood.

"I don't care." We saw Mrs. Bretton before we saw the room number. She was standing outside, staring into space.

"Hey, Mrs. B." Pete ran to her and threw his arms around her in a bear hug. She looked shocked over Pete's show of emotion. I know I was. "How's our girl?"

"She's doing better." Mrs. Bretton took a step back, possibly to get out of his reach, but also to look at him without straining her neck. "The doctors have her here because of the concussion, but she can go home maybe tomorrow, after they've kept her overnight. Then it's just about keeping water away from her cast."

"Concussion?"

"Cast?" We talked over each other as we tried to digest the extent of Sarah's injuries. "What happened?" I asked.

Mrs. Bretton folded her hands together. "It's silly, really. You know how we've been preparing for the Bake-Off?" We both nodded. "Well, the kitchen was a disaster zone. Oil spills, sugar spills, and no time to properly clean them up as we whipped up our recipes." Her hands moved to her cheeks as she relived the moment. "It was around 4:00 A.M. and we were tired out of our minds. Sarah was bringing me the pie plate, to see how our Blueberry Butterscotch Crumble would look in it, and poof"—she shook her head in disbelief—"she slipped and cracked her head and twisted her arm, fracturing a bone." She put her fingers to her lips, her perfectly manicured nails shaking. "All in one horrible fell swoop."

"Poor Sarah." I put my hand up to my own head, trying to imagine having a hard floor slam into it. "Can we see her?"

Mrs. Bretton took hold of my hand, her skin soft and smelling like lilac. Her voice was low and calm as she said, "She's on some pretty harsh medications. I know that you three have had a falling out, and I just don't want her to have to deal with stress on top of everything else."

I wanted to rush past her and into Sarah's room. But I didn't want to upset Mrs. Bretton more than she already was. "Maybe in a few days?"

She nodded. "A few days sounds fine." She looked around. "Pete?" And then, when she found him, she let out a harsher-sounding "Pete!"

While we'd been talking, Pete had walked around us and into room 252. He had Sarah's hand in both of his while she slept on, unaware that she was finally getting one hundred percent of his undivided attention.

CHAPTER TEN

Genie? Hey, Barb here. I have a great proposition for you.
It has to do with candles, aromatherapy, and a killer Web site.
Take me to lunch and we'll talk, okay?

I LEFT PETE AT THE HOSPITAL, where Sarah was still out of it and Mrs. Bretton sat editing recipes. I told Pete he had to call me when she could answer "Who's the president?" and "What is the name of Reggie's stuffed puffin?" correctly.

I hadn't wanted to leave, but it was already past ten, and I had to add one more source, proofread what I'd written, and print out my paper for Ms. Moore if I wanted graduation to happen. I definitely didn't want summer school to happen anymore. Not when there were better things

(GABE GABE GABE)

to do.

I'd had to go home first so I could change out of the pajama-bottom sweatpants I'd rushed to the hospital in.

Not that there was anything wrong with sweats. But I had a pair of clean jeans at home, the same jeans I'd worn for the interview and that cost more than half my clothes put together. I'd gotten them because Bridget said they made my butt look smaller. And seeing how she didn't say nice things when Mom or Aunt Barb weren't listening, I believed her.

I pulled into the driveway behind Aunt Barb's Mercedes. My aunt was becoming a regular fixture around the house lately as she helped landscape the front yard and oversee the tile guys and helped Mom figure out her wedding colors. I had never seen her as much as I had since we'd won the lottery. It didn't take a genius to figure out why, though. We'd seen her spending Uncle Mark's money for years; it's what she knew how to do.

I speed-walked up the dirt path. The lawn was ripped out, and big buckets of shrubs and flowers and palm trees seemed to take up the entire yard. The Pretty Lady sign was pulled out of the ground and half covered with a bag of manure. Next week, on the day after Thanksgiving, we were getting a flagstone walkway put in. My vent wasn't installed yet, but the front yard never looked at would be complete. Money or no money, some things never changed.

The first thing I noticed when I went inside was that it smelled like pumpkin candles. The second thing was

Bridget in front of a silver rolling rack stuffed with floor-length dresses.

"If you want your pictures to really pop, Aunt Genie, I say go with the fuchsia." Bridget pulled out a vivid pink dress—I guess that was fuchsia—and slung the hanger over her head. She smoothed the dress over her waist, and tulle swished as she walked.

"Excellent taste, young lady." A tiny woman emerged from behind the rack, her hair pulled back into a severe bun and the most perfect-looking eyebrows I've ever seen drawn onto her face. "Mrs. Shaw, have you seen the Vera Wang I pulled for you? The bell bottom of that dress matches the bell bottom of the dress your daughter has chosen."

"Niece," Mom and I said almost simultaneously. Mom added, "My daughter just came in."

"I really like this one, Aunt Genie." Bridget seemed to be petting the dress, especially where it glided over her flat stomach.

"It does look like it would be a perfect fit for your figure," the woman purred. She looked at me, and she seemed to pause too long at my hips. She pursed her lips. "It is not kind to pear shapes, however."

I pulled my oversized T-shirt over my hips before I realized what I was doing.

"Regina likes it, don't you Regina?" Bridget kept petting

the gown, knowing I wouldn't say anything that contradicted her. She was right. Partly because of a three-year-old secret, partly because I wasn't really thinking about bridesmaid dresses at this moment. I glanced at my watch and started toward my room.

"Reggie, I'm glad you're here." Mom took me by the hand and pulled me away from my bedroom and into hers. It looked as if a bridal gown store had set up shop in there. "I need help deciding which one to choose. Your Aunt Barb says the strapless Monique Lhuillier, Bridget is crazy for the Dior with the satin jacket"—she turned and pointed at a dress hanging from her closet door—"but I feel like I should go with the beige Oscar de la Renta. It's not exactly my first dog and pony show, you know?"

"Can we wait until I get back from school?" Tulle, satin, and sequins were everywhere, making this whole Mom-is-marrying-Bob thing real. Mom wasn't supposed to marry Bob. Date, yes. Replace Dad? Never, ever, ever, ever.

EVER.

Bridget flitted by, tulle swishing around her. "Why isn't Bridget at school?" I asked.

"She saw the clothes and she was a goner."

I stopped to think. "Why aren't *you* at work?"

"That's what I wanted to talk to you about." She held my hands in hers, tugging me close. "Bob and I finally settled on a date: Christmas Day. I have a lot to do before then, so I gave my notice at the real estate office."

I mentally did the math. Less than six weeks until the wedding. I didn't do the math about Mom quitting her job, though. She hadn't brought home a paycheck for a while.

Outside, I heard a truck with a loud engine drive by, the kind of truck that'd been stopping at our house once, twice, three times a day to dump off workers to put in new kitchen cabinets, marble in the bathroom, sprinklers in the front yard. "Is he moving in here?" I finally worked the nerve up to say.

"No, no, no, no, no," Mom said with each shake of her head. "We'll be moving into Bob's place down by the lake."

We. It made sense, but it still came as a shock to hear it. I always thought of Mom and Bob as a unit. Not Mom and Bob and me.

"What's going to happen to the house?" I asked.

She shrugged, placing a way-too-young spaghetti-strap dress under her chin. "Keep it."

"As in rent it?"

"No. As in keep it in the family." A small, sad smile appeared. "To remember Dad by, you know? It was his dream house. And I just can't sell it, you know?"

We weren't even going to rent the place? I knew we had

money, but it wasn't like we were filthy rich. A thousand dollars every month from some renter would help out.

It would help my mother pay back my three thousand dollars. Scratch that. Twenty-five hundred dollars.

From the other room, the tiny woman trilled, "Did the dress fit, Mrs. Shaw?"

"I haven't tried it on yet, Margot." Mom rolled her eyes, and thoughts about the house, a renter, and ever seeing my money again were put on hold. "She's a personal shopper from the Vegas Saks, but she's a major pain in my butt. I thought shopping for a dress was supposed to be fun, not some chore." She went over to a dress with a big butt bow and trailed her fingers down the corseted back. "But Aunt Barb convinced me Margot's the best when it comes to wedding dresses and the mature woman." Mom made a face as she said the words. "And it was only twenty-five hundred to get her down here for the day, so at least there's that."

Twenty-five hundred dollars? And that wasn't even including the cost of one of these froufrou princess dresses that were way too young for my forty-something mom. Twenty-five hundred for the services of that troll? Twenty-five hundred that should have been going to *me*? I ignored my heartbeat growing louder in my ears and snuck another look at my watch and thought about that one last source I needed for the paper. I pointed at the beige dress hanging from her closet door and managed to force out, "That one. That's the one you should get."

I started walking out, and saw a few new boxes by the bedroom door. The top one was open, and inside were twelve candles in glass jars. "Wedding favors?"

"Actually, no." Mom came up behind me. "Aunt Barb wants to start her own online business." She pulled out a candle and handed it to me. A label that looked pretty professional and reminded me of the colors in Aunt Barb's house read: *Barb Appleby's Aromatique Candles.* "She wants me to be an investor."

"An investor?" I put the candle back. "Aunt Barb hasn't ever had a job, and now she's asking people to invest in a business which I'm sure she has no idea how to run?"

Mom started putting up earrings next to the beige gown. "She just wants something to call her own. Bridget's out of the house next year, and she'll be left twiddling her thumbs."

Aunt Barb had never really been overly involved in Bridget's life, so I didn't quite understand that reasoning. "How much does she want you to invest?"

Mom shrugged as she tried on a pair of chandelier earrings. "Uncle Mark doesn't think the business will fly, so he's not giving her any money."

"How much, Mom?" Aunt Barb had money. A woman like her always made sure she had cash around.

"Ten thousand."

I bit my lip so hard I tasted blood. What had happened to Mom's no-handout policy? Aunt Barb wasn't some pig farmer from Florida, but she wasn't exactly close to Mom. Except, it looked like, during times of death or money.

Ten minutes later, I had on my expensive jeans and was driving my expensive car to school, leaving behind a house filled with expensive renovation projects and a mother trying on her expensive wedding dress with her expensive personal shopper.

We could finally afford just about anything.

So why was I still thinking about how Mom had given Margot and Aunt Barb thousands of dollars, but she hadn't once thought to pay me back?

"But it's right here. Look, typed and everything."

"You know my policy, Reggie. I'm sorry." Ms. Moore folded her hands on top of her grade book and kept her eyes on mine, ignoring the paper in my hands. A paper with a plastic cover I had even spent $1.49 on.

"But there were extenuating circumstances." I didn't go into details. I didn't want to talk about Sarah in the hospital. She didn't like people to know her personal business; people didn't even know she baked, much less was entering the Bake-Off with her mom. And I definitely wasn't going into

Wedding-Gown-a-Palooza with Ms. Moore. "Trust me, I wouldn't have spent days on this paper just to flake on it at the last minute."

She looked down at her hands, where she twisted an ugly gold ring that looked too tight for her finger. Round and round and round. "I can't back down on this policy, Reggie. Barring death or severed limbs, a late paper is a late paper, and I don't accept them." She seemed to mull over her next words before she finally said, "And you don't exactly have a stellar track record in this department, Reggie."

I flipped through the report as I tried to think of something to come back with. I mean, she was right. But this time was different. I looked at the perfect margins, the perfect spacing, the powerful thesis statement, the reference page it had taken me two hours to format on the new laptop I had gotten just for Ms. Moore's papers.

My mind was coming up with nothing. It was too busy replaying images of Sarah's broken arm, Pete holding her good hand, and Margot admiring Bridget and her perfect stick figure. "So what does this mean?" I finally managed to say.

"It means you will receive a zero on this paper." She gave me a smile that only used half of her face and neither of her eyes. The other half stayed smile-free, like she wasn't going to listen to any more excuses.

"And that's it?" I twisted the report in my hands, the plastic cover creasing. "I'm a couple of hours late and I get a zero?" I tried to search for a solution to get me out of this, and I kept running into Sarah, Margot, and Bridget. Again and again and again.

"I'm sorry, Reggie, but late is late." She didn't look sorry. She looked as if she was already thinking about her next class, her hands stacking a pile of handouts while a sandwich in a Ziploc bag waited nearby.

I had nothing else to say. I wasn't going to tell her about Sarah. I shouldn't have to tell her about Sarah. I had written a really good paper that, for once, I was proud to have my name on. I should get an A based on that, not because I had to be pardoned from visiting my friend in the hospital.

I dropped the paper in the trash can and walked away.

I was almost to the door when Ms. Moore called out, "Maybe we can work something out with extra credit. Reggie?"

I ignored her and merged into after-lunch traffic. I let myself drift through the crowd, allowing myself to be pushed this way and that. I couldn't see ahead of me, but I really didn't care a whole heck of a lot. I had tried, really tried, and this was my reward? An F and summer school?

"Regina!"

I knew that voice. I kept walking and ignored it. Around me, I heard "Hey, Reg" and "Yo, Millions!" I'd never had a nickname, but ever since Pete's buddy had come up with the name, it had been spreading around school. I had hated it at first, but now . . . Now at least people knew my name.

I guess I had slowed down, because Bridget was walking next to me, matching my stride. I guess she'd gotten tired of being fawned over by Margot. Yeah, right. "Did you hear about the class poll?"

Now I knew why she was here. She never missed things like class polls or homecoming-court announcements or student government elections. Bridget was the epitome of what a high school student should be. What a screwed-up world we lived in.

"What about it?" I knew that whatever was making her smile so much wasn't going to be good.

"You're on it," she said. Her smile wasn't exactly evil, but it didn't come from a good place, either. "Wanna guess what people voted you for?"

"Nope." I started walking faster, leaving her behind to stew in whatever it was she had hoped to needle me with. Anything she said was going to just be the rotten cherry on top of my day.

"Most Likely to Never Leave Waterview," she called out from behind me. "Good thing your mom won the lottery, right?"

I ditched the rest of my classes. And right now, I was seriously thinking about ditching senior year.

I wasn't going to pass English. And if I wasn't going to college anyway, why did I need senior English? Why did I need trigonometry? Why did I need school in general?

I tightened my grip on the Land Rover's steering wheel. I could go anywhere—Hawaii, Tokyo, Athens—so what was I still doing in Waterview? I had the radio blasting and the sunroof open, the crisp autumn air breezing through my hair. But nothing was helping. It wasn't even noon, and the day was still one of the worst I'd ever had. The day Dad died was still the worst, followed by the day after Dad died and the day after that and . . .

I forced myself to concentrate on all the reasons dropping out of high school was a great idea. One, I had money now. Two, I had transportation. Three, I didn't have a best friend anymore anyway. Four, I wasn't a brain in any of my classes. My grades were too far gone to even try to raise them now.

But I didn't want to leave. Not Waterview, anyway. Not right now. There was Mom's wedding. There was Jeff.

And there was Gabe. Which meant that I had to stay in Waterview, at least for now.

But I didn't have to stay at Waterview High. I could drop out.

The thought had me wanting to eat my weight in Little Debbies.

Instead of heading home to face Wedding Central, I found myself parked in front of Cashmart. I hadn't been here since I quit. But I had nothing to be embarrassed about. I hadn't stolen anything or stopped showing up or spray-painted *Pig* on Fellers's door like the stockroom guy did last month. Plus, when you live in a blink-and-you'd-miss-it town like Waterview, you don't have a lot of shopping options.

The double doors swished close behind me. The store still looked the same. It even had the same smell: food court popcorn and floor cleaner.

I headed toward Say Cheese!, forgetting whether Gabe had to work today or not. But, I found myself studying the Little Debbie display up front. They were no longer on sale, but Reggie Shaw no longer needed a sale.

I looked around and only saw a mom with two kids poring over a bin of discounted books. It was a weekday morning, which was one of the slowest times of day for Cashmart. Two associates were manning registers at Checkout, but I wasn't going to them. I couldn't take five boxes of Little Debbies through one of those lines.

But I could through self-checkout.

I grabbed a basket and dumped five boxes inside and walked toward the bank of self-scanners. As I was ringing up the second box, I heard:

"Do I need to call a truant officer?"

Gabe stood behind me by the rack of tabloids and gum, giving me that one-dimple grin. My heart sped up to about three hundred beats per minute.

"Hey, stranger." I couldn't hide the boxes, and so I didn't. I just kept scanning them, trying to act like I was scanning notebooks or bags of broccoli. But they weren't notebooks or broccoli. They were junk food, and with each new box I scanned, my heart went up another hundred beats per minute.

"Stocking up for winter?" he asked, his eyes briefly going down.

"You never know when you'll need a Little Debbie fix," I said, trying to make myself sound cute and lighthearted when I was feeling anything but. "Plus, you can't beat five for five dollars."

He looked behind us, where the display was in plain sight of self-checkout. "I don't think they're on sale anymore."

"Oh?" I hesitated, pretending I was mulling over

something I didn't already know. "Well, it's not as if I don't have the money, right? And they're already scanned."

Gabe teased, "Well, if they're already scanned..." He kissed my temple. He kissed my temple? He wasn't repulsed? "Did school let out early today?"

I shook my head and fed a ten-dollar bill into the register. "I'm ditching."

"Is it Senior Ditch Day?"

"Nope." The machine sucked in my bill. "But I think it's Dropout Day." The machine spit out my change, coins clanking in a plastic dish.

Gabe grabbed my bag, and I felt a little sick watching him holding five boxes of food that I planned to eat in under fifteen minutes. He started walking toward Photo, and I walked alongside him even though every one of my nerve endings wanted me to head back to the Land Rover to find a Dumpster to park behind and shove oatmeal pies into my mouth two at a time.

"I don't think I've ever heard about Dropout Day," he said. "Two years and high school's already changed that much?"

"That's because I invented it. I'm not going back to school, so I'm celebrating." With five boxes of Little Debbies.

Gabe stopped walking. "You dropped out?"

"It's not official or anything. I don't know if there's paperwork or if you just stop going or—"

"Seriously. You're dropping out of school?" His head was cocked to one side, and I felt as if he was studying my face, waiting for me to go, "Gotcha!"

"That's the plan." I tried to take the bag out of his hands, but he held on.

"You can't drop out, Reg."

"I'm planning on getting my GED," I said as the thought occurred to me. Graduation might not hold any appeal for me, but neither did having "high school dropout" attached to my name. Then the good people of Waterview High would really think they picked the right girl for Most Likely to Never Leave Waterview and Live in a Trailer.

Gabe stood in front of me, my stash in his hands, and said nothing. He had a look on his face, though, that made me feel as if I had a bad haircut he was trying to make heads or tails of. "What happened?" he finally asked.

"Why do you think something happened?"

"Because you've never once said anything about dropping out of school."

"I've ditched before," I said defensively.

"Yeah, sure, for work. When you had double shifts or overtime." Gabe had a few irritating qualities, including having a good memory for what I'd told him about my life during the pre-lottery days. The censored version. "But you don't have to worry about those kind of things anymore."

No. No, I didn't. All I had to worry about was how I was going to spend my school-free days. "I gotta get going." I wanted a Little Debbie in my mouth. Now. Followed by ten to twenty more. I tried to take the bag from him again.

And again, he held onto it.

"First, tell me what happened."

Based on the stubborn set of his mouth, I knew that me and my Little Debbies were being held hostage. "Where do you want me to start? With Mom and her stupid wedding, maybe Sarah and her stupid stubbornness?" I rubbed the spot between my eyes where I felt little axes pick, pick, picking at my brain. *Me stealing four hundred dollars and kowtowing to Bridget for three long, agonizing years?* "You have to work, Gabe, and this story is way, way too long."

The next thing I knew, he'd grabbed my hand and started pulling me to the automatic doors. He paused just long enough to tell a cashier to page Fellers and tell him Gabe Donaldson had to go home suddenly.

"Where are we going?" I asked. Great. Now I was going to get Gabe fired. Fellers never, ever just let someone go home. There had to be blood and leaking brain matter first.

"Somewhere." He squeezed my hand. "Trust me, it's going to make you feel better."

It was twilight, and the desert was a collage of purples and pinks and browns. And Sarah's house fit right in with its pink stucco walls and tall lavender urns holding cacti and do-it-yourself water fountains that Mrs. Bretton had put together when she wasn't baking, cleaning, or arranging her clothes by color.

"Maybe we should wait." I itched my chin against the side of the seat belt, not feeling the need to leave Gabe's truck whatsoever. I'd told him about Sarah and the wedding dresses and Aunt Barb's stupid candle Web site. I didn't tell him about getting voted Most Likely to Never Leave Waterview or about Bridget blackmailing me. Some things were just too pitiful to say out loud.

"C'mon, Reg. This is the first step of getting you back on track. Making amends."

I shook my head. "I don't want to."

"Regina."

I swung around to face him. "Don't call me that."

"There we go. I like seeing you pissed off." He put his hand up to my cheek. "There's nothing to be scared of. She's your best friend. Pete told me she just got out of the hospital and is a little loopy from the drugs. Get in there and talk to her and use the loopiness to your advantage."

He was right. I had to talk to her. But I couldn't move. It felt like years, not just weeks, since *The Wrath of Khan* and *The Wrath of Sarah*.

I put my hand on the door handle, where it stayed and did nothing. I couldn't do it. I couldn't face the girl who had called me a loser.

"Can we start smaller?" I pleaded.

"What do you have in mind?"

I thought I heard amusement in his voice, but I didn't look up to see. "Telling Margot I hate that fuchsia dress?" I said halfheartedly.

His laugh filled in the truck's cabin, and against my better judgment, I turned to watch his face. His smile was too beautiful, his eyes were too kind, and this whole afternoon had felt too good to be true.

What did he see in me? Yeah, he liked my eyes. Big whoop. I was still me. Me with the ten pounds of extra weight; me, who thought sweatpants were fashionable; me, who was seriously considering dropping out of high school.

Me, who was voted Most Likely to Never Leave Waterview and Live in a Trailer and Raise Toothless Kids.

Me, *Go home and take a Shaw-er.*

Me, the loser.

Sarah's words came back to me, and they were as clear and hateful as the day she'd spit them out. *My problem is that you're the only loser here, Regina. You've known it, this town's known it, but I've been too blind to see it.*

"I can't do it, Gabe." As I said the words, I felt my face crumple and the tears stream down my face. I tried to cover my face with my hands, but he wouldn't let me. He pulled me into his chest and we sat there in the darkness of the truck as I cried, him holding me and kissing my eyes as my new world fell apart.

CHAPTER ELEVEN

Mrs. Shaw? Dolores Baker from Waterview High.
Your daughter missed afternoon classes. Please call
if you'd like to discuss this matter further.

THE WORST DAY SINCE DAD DIED wasn't over yet.

Gabe drove us down the quiet streets of Waterview, the clock saying it was almost 1:00 A.M. We'd decided he'd drive me home, since he didn't feel right taking me back to the near-empty Cashmart parking lot to pick up the Land Rover. "You might start crying and run over a jackrabbit this time of night," he had told me when my tears dried up and I was left with hiccups and a crying-induced headache. "And then you'd cry even harder because you'd killed Thumper."

"Ha-ha." We were now on my street and I was feeling better. Not great, but at least not hopeless, either. Gabe's hand on my knee and Gabe in general made me happy. Gabe, who wanted me to patch up my relationship with my best friend. Gabe, who didn't want me to drive while visually impaired. Gabe, who was sometimes way more mature for his age than I thought humanly possible. And me, Reggie, lapped it up. Too many years with an immature mom, I reasoned.

The house came into view, and the first thing I noticed was how every single light in the house was on, as well as the porch light and the spotlight over the garage. Aunt Barb's car was still there, and so was Bob's pickup truck.

Gabe's truck hadn't rolled to a stop before the front door slammed open and Mom and Bob ran out.

"Regina Eustace Shaw, get in here this minute," Mom shouted.

The looks on their faces made me want to do the opposite: lock myself in the truck and tell Gabe to head toward Mexico.

Bob got to the truck first and yanked open the door. He had my wrist in a firm grip before I even knew what was happening. "Out. Now."

I was too shocked to try to pull my wrist from his hand. Bob, Mr. Comb-over, Mr. Barely Acknowledges Imogene Shaw's Kids, was actually grabbing my wrist? All I knew was I would have tumbled out of my seat if the seat belt hadn't still been latched and Gabe hadn't had his arm around my shoulders.

"Let go! You're hurting her." Gabe tried to pry Bob's

fingers from my wrist, but it was hard with him trying to keep me upright at the same time. I felt as if I weren't even there, as if I were hovering over my body watching this surreal event unfolding in super-slow motion.

"Bob. Bob! Stop it." Mom was there, pulling at the arm Bob was using to clamp down on my wrist. He seemed to let go as soon as she touched him.

I took back possession of my wrist, cradling the part where Bob had bruised it. Gabe turned on the overhead light and gently examined it with his fingers. I leaned my forehead against his temple, trying to remember how to breathe normally again.

"Are you okay?" he asked softly.

I didn't know. I was still floating over my body.

"Reggie?" he prodded.

"In shock," I managed to get out.

Outside, I heard my mother talking to Bob in a low, harsh voice. I couldn't make out the words, but she sounded mad. Good.

Gabe kissed my forehead and anger chafed his words as he whispered, "Want me to kick his ass?"

I laughed. It came out a little hysterical-sounding, though. When I saw him looking at me with concern, I swallowed the new bubble of laughter and forced myself to take a few deep breaths. "Raincheck?"

He winked at me before pulling me across the middle and over to the driver's seat, away from Bob and Mom's powwow on the passenger side. He helped me down, and his hands were still on my waist when Jeff came outside, Bridget following him.

"What's going on with Mom?" I asked when Jeff was close enough to hear my quietly spoken question.

"The school called to say you ditched, and when Mom called Cashmart to talk to you, she found out you'd quit. Then, when you still weren't home by curfew, she got really worried, called Bob, and they've been making themselves nuts ever since." He scowled at me. "They tried calling you. Didn't you hear your phone?"

I shook my head, thinking about the duct tape holding it together. "I think it's broken."

He looked past me at Gabe. "You look familiar."

Gabe kept his arm around my waist, where it tightened for a second before relaxing again. "I have that kind of face." With his free hand, he shook Jeff's hand. "I'm Gabe. You must be Reggie's brother."

"I've heard about you, Gabe." Bridget had made her way over to us. She eyed his arm around me. "You're roommates with Deadhead, right?"

They small-talked about Deadhead and I tuned out. Mom and Bob stood on the other side of the truck, and

Mom seemed to be doing all the talking. "Your friend called again," Jeff said in my ear.

I tried to figure out what he was talking about, and why I felt as if I was experiencing déjà vu. Then I remembered the phone call this morning and Mr. Puffin being launched at me.

"Pete?" I thought about where he'd been all day. "Is everything okay?"

"That's why he was calling. He said that Sarah wants to talk to you."

"Sh—she does?" I said. Gabe gave me a quick squeeze and I looked at his profile. He had a polite look on his face as he listened to Bridget drone on and on about why Deadhead's girlfriend was all wrong for him. But the way his head was tilting toward our conversation made me think he was tuning Bridget out.

A heaviness that I hadn't even realized I felt seemed to lift somewhat.

Sarah wanted to talk. Maybe today wasn't a total loss after all.

The next morning started the same way it always did after people found out about the lottery.

"Yo, Millions!"

"I assume he's talking to you?" Gabe asked. He had picked me up before school, and now we sat in his cab, waiting for the first warning bell to ring. In front of me, some junior on the football team waved at me.

I hadn't wanted to come today, and I still felt the same way. There were only two reasons I was here. One, I hadn't told Mom my idea about dropping out. Two, because Gabe wouldn't let me crash at his place during the day. Not that I had expected him to. Especially after "the talk" last night.

"Curfew is eleven o'clock on a school night, young lady," Mom had started out. "Not eleven-oh-five, not midnight, and definitely not one." We'd relocated to the living room, Mom and Bob on the couch, Gabe and me standing together. Not touching, but most definitely together. Jeff was at the dining room table, a wrought iron and marble concoction Mom had gotten delivered sometime yesterday. Bridget had taken her mom's car and gone home after realizing talk about Deadhead was over with for the night.

"It wasn't intentional, Mom," I said. "I didn't even realize what time it was." And I'd never had a social life that needed curfews before tonight.

"That's the whole point. You should know exactly what time it is. If you don't"— she sucked in a breath through her teeth, like she was trying to rein her emotions in—"it means you're doing something you shouldn't be doing."

"It wasn't like that, Mrs. Shaw," Gabe started explaining. "She's had a pretty rough day and just needed someone to talk to."

"And you were that somebody?" Mom said, her arms crossed, her eyebrow arched high on her forehead.

"Yes, ma'am."

I internally groaned. My mom did not like being called "ma'am." Said it made her feel like a grandma with twenty cats.

"Just what exactly made Regina have this rough day?" She spared a glance at me. "Because as I see it, you had no school and you had no work. It seems that you had a great day playing hooky with your boyfriend."

For a moment, I checked out of the conversation. *Boyfriend.* Was Gabe my boyfriend?

"She wasn't playing hooky with her boyfriend, Mrs. Shaw." As he said the words, my worst fears were confirmed. I ducked my head and tried to will away the prickling sensation in my eyes. "She was trying to get through a pretty rotten day with the support of her boyfriend."

I might have given myself whiplash when I jerked my head back to look at him. He gave me a wink and, even in the middle of this horrible day, I felt myself giving him a tiny smile in return. Not because I was being polite; my emotional state was too raw for that. No, I smiled just out of pure happiness.

"Regina."

I turned my attention back to Mom. She sat on the edge of the couch, her hand on Bob's knee, his hand on top of hers.

"This boy here seems to think you had a perfectly good reason for putting us through this nightmare of a day. Well, we're all ears. The floor is yours."

I opened my mouth, but the words just couldn't come. I was physically, mentally, and emotionally exhausted. "Can we talk about it later?"

"No, we can't talk about it later!" She seemed to take a moment to collect herself as Bob started rubbing her back. Bob, by the way, hadn't looked me in the face since we'd gotten inside.

I felt pressure on my own back and realized it was Gabe's hand. And as I felt the warmth of his skin through the layer of my shirt, I somehow found an energy reserve and started to talk. I told them about Sarah and the hospital, Ms. Moore and the paper, how the paper affected graduation, that I had simply forgotten to tell Mom about Cashmart. I left out the part about being voted Most Likely to Never Leave Waterview.

Because your class thinking it is one thing, a tiny voice squeaked. *Them thinking it means something entirely different.*

We ended the night at around three, with Mom hugging me, telling me Sarah was going to be okay and that we'd figure out English and graduation. Something about how I was entitled to a grade. Bob leaned back on the couch and took it all in, and Gabe sat with Jeff at the table making a house of cards with cardboard paint samples.

I didn't exactly get off the hook, though. My curfew was now nine on a school night since I no longer worked at Cashmart, and Gabe had to face a ten-minute Q&A about how old he was (just turned twenty), what his future goals were (college in a year or two), and if he was aware that I still had seven months of high school left ("Yes, ma'am. Very.").

As I sat at the table, listening to whatever Mom said to me without trying to defend myself or explain my reasons, I noticed *Waterview Today* folded on the table, opened to page six and the headline:

MOTHER WINS THE LOTTERY

Mattie Weare had run the story after all. I skimmed the article when Mom left to take a pee break. It said that we won the Arizona Five, but it didn't say how much. It did use our last name though. Now I understood that I had been the trigger for Mom's nuclear eruption.

Gabe had left soon after Mom's pop quiz but showed up again when I was blowing my hair dry a few hours later. His hair was all over the place and he was wearing glasses instead of his contacts. I was surprised to see him, and told him as much.

"I came to give you a ride to school."

"Jeff said he could drive me." The words came out soft and unconvincing. Gabe was a way better chauffeur than my brother.

Gabe ignored me. "You'll be seeing me after school, too, so I can give you a ride to your car."

"Don't you have work?"

The dimple made an appearance. "I'm taking a mental-health day to get caught up on sleep."

Gabe was going to get fired. I swallowed around a dry marble-sized lump in my throat. Fellers had fired people for missing an hour of work, much less two days' worth. Gabe had deciphered the look on my face. "It's okay, Reg. I have enough vacation days, and I'm not exactly hurting for money, am I?"

The first bell rang and I realized I was still sitting in Gabe's truck. His thumb was making tiny, concentric circles on the back of my hand, and I didn't want to be anywhere else but here, with him.

"You want to go inside?"

I looked at the high school through the window. People were hurrying inside, laughing and hitting each other's arms and tossing around Hacky Sacks. I saw Tommy Baines, the boy I'd beaten in the fourth-grade spelling bee. I saw Jenna Manser, who saw my bra when I accidentally took off my shirt with my sweatshirt in seventh-grade social studies. They were people I'd grown up with since kindergarten. I barely knew them and they barely knew me.

And according to them, they didn't think I'd ever make it out of Waterview.

"No. I never want to go inside." I blew out a pent-up breath. "But I'm going in anyway."

He lifted my hand and brushed his lips against the back. "That's my girl."

"Hey, Millions." Pete gave me a goofy grin as he answered Sarah's front door in a pair of sweatpants and an old T-shirt and bright white sneakers. He hated working out after school, but he did it to build up his endurance for the Waterview Invitational.

Behind me, I could hear my car ticking as it cooled down, as if it were counting down the seconds until I was face-to-face with Sarah again. Seconds that seemed to get shorter and shorter.

"Don't call me Millions." The name was getting on my

nerves. I looked past him, but the house was dark behind him. For one of the first times since Sarah and her mom had decided they were going to do the Bake-Off together, the house didn't smell like pie. "Is Sarah up?"

"Yep." He moved aside, but I stayed where I was. "Reg, c'mon. It's cold and I have the house at a perfect eighty degrees for our convalescent."

I finally stepped inside. It was a small comfort knowing the house hadn't changed while I was away. I could see perfect lines in the carpet from where Mrs. Bretton had just vacuumed. A grandfather clock ticked in the corner, polished to a high gleam. Twenty or so magazines about gardening, home decoration, and baking were fanned in perfect symmetry on the glossy coffee table.

Pete's upbeat attitude wasn't lost on me. "I take it things are going well with you and Sarah."

"You can say we're in talks." He started leading the way down the familiar cornflower-blue carpet. I followed behind him, using a vacuum line as my guide and randomly thinking about how it wasn't as straight as I remembered Mrs. Bretton liking them.

Unlike the rest of the house, Sarah's room was bright and cheery with natural light. She sat on the right side of the bed, on top of her mother's handmade quilt, a remote in her hand and a bowl of popcorn at her side. The left side of the bed was rumpled. I guess talks had been going very, very well if Sarah wasn't making Pete sit on the floor as she'd been known to do when they were off-again.

"Hey." I gave Sarah a small wave. I felt stupid waving, and I shoved my hand into my pocket.

Sarah put down the remote. She didn't smile, but her eyes seemed to grow a little brighter. "Hey."

There was silence as I stood and she sat and the TV mumbled around us.

Pete looked from Sarah to me to Sarah and finally said, "Okay, then. I'm going to leave you two to talk female." He leaned onto the bed and brushed a kiss across Sarah's forehead, and I noticed she closed her eyes as he did, as if she were soaking in the moment. "I'm on a mission to see if your mom stashed any Hot Tamales in the 'bad' section of the pantry."

He left and we didn't say anything. I walked over to a huge basket of flowers with a C-3PO balloon floating above it and lightly punched it. "Pete?"

"The balloon. The flowers are from his mom." Her words crackled as she said them.

"Do you need something to drink?"

She nodded and pointed behind me. "An apple juice would be great."

I turned, and instead of the four-foot dollhouse with

working lights and fully furnished Victorian rooms, there was a mini-fridge.

I'd been gone for two weeks, and already things were changing. "This is new."

"Pete got it for me." She played with the remote, a small smile flitting over her face. "He was afraid I wasn't getting enough fluids."

I opened an apple juice and handed her the bottle. "Who knew Pete was such a caretaker, huh?" As I said the word, Gabe popped into my head. I'd never thought of Pete as a Gabe, but I guess he was. That maybe he always had been but the idea of losing Sarah had made it come out more. If he kept this up, I could see Sarah and Pete's "talks" making their relationship on-again. Maybe even for good.

"I know. I didn't think he even knew that other people got thirsty or cold or needed a foot rub," she said with a faint laugh.

"Mr. I-Don't-Touch-Toes rubbed your feet?"

She nodded. "And he didn't even pretend to gag once."

The way we talked was off. Stop and go, fast and slow. Then again, it was weird to still be standing, to not be on top of Sarah's bed eating a stolen piece of pie that Mrs. Bretton didn't want in the bedrooms, and gossiping about Pete and flipping through TV channels.

I sat on the edge of the bed, staring at my feet, trying

to get back to where we used to be, pre-Bridget. "Pete held your hand at the hospital for, like, two hours straight."

"Mom told me." She turned the remote over and started taking the battery cover off. Then putting it on. Off and on, off and on. Déjà vu. Two weeks ago, she'd been twisting the 7-Up off and on, off and on. "She didn't think it was that cool, though."

No surprise there. Mrs. Bretton had her own unique, type A way of looking at the world. In the time I'd known Sarah and her family, I realized that Mrs. Bretton felt the most comfortable with baked goods, home decoration, and cleaning. She always seemed to like it when Pete and Sarah were in an off-again phase. I personally think it was because she liked Sarah having more time to help bake, decorate, and clean.

"Who knew he had it in him to sit still for so long without some sort of game controller in his hand?" I half joked.

The smile showed up again. The void in my chest was starting to close up, and the room and Sarah began to stop feeling like strangers. This was why I'd come here. Why I was in a room with a girl who had called me a loser and sounded as if she meant it.

Outside, a car door closed. Sarah stopped messing with the battery door and flipped off the TV. "I'm feeling a little tired, Reg."

"Oh. Okay." I got up, suddenly not knowing what to do with my hands or how to use my feet. "So, I'll see you around?"

Sarah smoothed a strand of blond hair behind her ear, her eyes on the TV and its now empty screen. "Sounds good."

What had happened? Ten seconds ago, we were good. But now it was as if Sarah wasn't even in the room anymore.

Before my brain had the chance to tell my feet to get moving, Mr. Bretton walked in. His button-down oxfords and sharply creased khakis made him seem like he was a perfect fit with this house, but his love of ATVs and paint-gun wars made me wonder sometimes how he and his wife had ever started dating, much less get married. "Hey, Reg. Long time no see, kiddo." He swatted the side of my arm with a rolled-up wad of magazines. He moved past me and kissed the top of Sarah's head before dropping the magazines in her lap. His other hand gave her a ribbon-wrapped gold box. I knew that box and its decadent chocolates very intimately. "Thought you and your arm could use some reading material, maybe some sugar, too."

Sarah slid the magazines off her lap and put the remote on top of them. She didn't move to take the box, and Mr. Bretton finally had to put it on a thick stack of magazines on her nightstand. "You don't have to keep bringing me stuff," she said. "I still haven't read the other ones you brought me in the hospital."

"Can't a daddy take care of his little girl?" He ran a hand down the side of her head, cupping her chin. "You feeling better today?"

"Yeah. I am." They stayed like that—him holding her chin and her avoiding his eyes—for a while. Long enough for me to start feeling weird for witnessing it and remember that I was supposed to be leaving.

"I was about to order pizza, Reg," Mr. Bretton said as I got past the bedroom door. "Stay and have a few slices."

"I'm good." I paused and turned back around. "Thanks, though."

"Mom's eating pizza?" Sarah said sarcastically.

"Mom called to say she wasn't going to get home for a while. Something about going down to Phoenix to get some organic peaches for tomorrow," he explained, and his hand smoothed her hair back from her face.

She looked past him at me. I realized I hadn't moved any farther to the front door.

I heard Mr. Bretton saying, "Reg, I know that you and pizza have a close, personal relationship. I'm sure Sarah would want you to stay—right, hon?"

Sarah nodded. It was a hesitant nod, barely noticeable.

I tried reading her expression, but it was an odd mix of politeness and . . . And what? Tension? Discomfort? "You must be pretty tired," I finally said.

"Actually, I'm feeling pretty good." She seemed to be saying something with her eyes. But I couldn't figure out what. Two weeks on the outs, and I couldn't read Sarah as well as I used to. "Dad always orders too much anyway. You might as well stay, you know?"

I took in the scene: the stack of magazines on her bed, the second stack on her nightstand, the gold box of chocolates on top of that, her dad feet away still petting her, pizza coming into a house that rarely got to see fast food, and Mrs. Bretton out even though I never remembered her missing dinner before. Ever. Not even the time she broke her pinky.

The thing that was hanging me up were the magazines and the Godiva. Her dad never gave her presents; that was Mrs. Bretton's department. She would shop and pay for the gifts and then pen his name beside hers.

I didn't feel like a guest anymore. I felt like a buffer between Sarah and her dad. Either way, I wasn't going anywhere.

"Pizza sounds great."

CHAPTER TWELVE

Reg. It's Mom. Use the money I gave you when you're at Cashmart today. I'm having problems with the credit card company and it'll take a couple of days to clear up. Love you.

I'D NEVER BEEN to the principal's office before. But here I was, in an uncomfortable plastic chair, a dusty fake plant on one side, my mother on the other.

"I understand your concerns, Mrs. Shaw," the principal was saying. I'd only seen Mrs. Williams from a distance. Up close, she was younger than I'd thought. "But Ms. Moore told Regina in no uncertain terms that she needed to turn in her paper on time in order to receive an A."

"Yes, I understand that." Mom had a yellow legal pad on her lap, questions filling the page. She might not be great with money, but Mom was a great list maker. "But Regina shouldn't have to miss graduation because of one late paper."

"I understand completely," Mrs. Williams said. I

noticed she started a lot of her sentences with "I understand." I'm glad she could understand Ms. Moore, because I couldn't. "But this wasn't the first paper Regina turned in late. Ms. Moore, would you care to expand?"

I didn't turn around. I knew that Ms. Moore was leaning on a table behind me, but I hadn't looked up at her since we came in.

"Regina knew exactly what was needed of her in order to receive credit for that paper," she said. "She did not meet those requirements, and so her paper received a zero."

Ms. Moore sounded robotlike as she recited pretty much what she'd already told me. I still couldn't believe she was the same person who used to be my art teacher, who found something nice to say about any picture, who never gave anyone less than an A back then.

"A zero," Mom said, "for turning it in two hours late." She turned back to Mrs. Williams. "I thought school was supposed to encourage children, not slam a door in their face when they've made an effort and extenuating circumstances"—she'd told them a friend had been in the hospital, but she hadn't mentioned Sarah's name—"keep them from turning it in at exactly eight A.M."

Mrs. Williams tapped the end of her pen on her desk. "Ms. Moore, Regina received a zero on this assignment?"

Ms. Moore nodded. "She did."

Mrs. Williams continued the tapping. "Mrs. Shaw, Regina, would you excuse us for a moment?"

As we waited outside, Mom and I debated summer school. She was for it, I was against it. I'd stay the summer for Gabe but not for Senior English, the sequel. Our whispers were getting louder and louder as the disagreement grew. Ten minutes later, Ms. Moore walked out of the office, her face red, and Mrs. Williams asked us to come back in. Turned out, Waterview High School had a policy about deducting one letter grade for each day an assignment was late. Ms. Moore had to amend her zero points policy and accept my assignment. Waterview High also had a policy that allowed for one makeup assignment per semester. Ms. Moore would give me my makeup assignment and all would be well again.

With my grade, maybe. But never with Ms. Moore.

I had still stolen four hundred dollars. There wasn't a day that went by when I saw Ms. Moore or heard Ms. Moore or talked to Ms. Moore and didn't think about it.

"I can't believe it. This looks amazing, Reggie." Doc stood in front of the mural at Paws and Claws, shaking her head back and forth. "Absolutely, positively spectacular."

I wasn't supposed to come in today, but Sarah had been sleeping when I went by her house, Gabe was working and would meet up with me for dinner, and a lot of jackhammering was going on at my house lately. So that left at least one haven: the mural at Paws and Claws.

Doc sat in a chair next to me, both of us scrutinizing the mural. Actually, I think I was the one doing the scrutinizing. Doc just looked amazed.

There had been some days when dogs looked like cats and guinea pigs looked like blobs of spilled paint, but in the end, the mural turned out a lot nicer than I expected. You could look at it and even figure out what was what without me having to explain anything.

"I need a picture of this," Doc said suddenly.

"You need a picture of the picture?"

She pushed herself up. "You never know if an earthquake's going to happen."

"An earthquake." I didn't even attempt to keep the doubt and Doc-You're-Nuts vibe out of my tone.

"We are fairly close to California," she said defensively as she went to reception and pulled a small silver camera out of a top drawer. She gestured for me to get up. "Go stand next to it, Reg. I need the artist with her creation." She said "artist" like "ar-teest," as if I was a big deal or something.

I was sticking out my tongue and crossing my eyes when the door opened and Bob walked in. Mom's Bob. Almost-Twisted-My-Arm-Off Bob.

Doc turned around and greeted him, then waited for him to talk about a sick dog or cat. She got a lot of people who came in just to check out prices before bringing in their pet. I didn't get that. Your dog broke his leg or has some sort of growth between his eyes and you're going to see what the price is for helping him? Those people needed to be reincarnated as a neglected pet in their next lifetime. That or a dung beetle.

"Your mom said you might be here." Bob jingled the change in his pockets and looked at the mural behind me. "You did that, Regina?"

I didn't say anything. There wasn't anything to say to him. The guy had almost twisted my hand off my arm and had said nothing afterward. No sorry, no "How's it feeling?"

Doc looked at me, then him, then back to me again. "You need me to stick around, Reg?"

I didn't know. Bob was harmless. At least, he used to be until he got all 'roid rage on me.

"You can stay if you want," Bob said to Doc as he took his coat off. "Plus, maybe it's good that Regina has a witness hearing me tell her what a jerk I've been."

I rubbed at a spot of paint sticking to the side of my hand. The wind today had ruffled the top of Bob's hair, showing his bald spot underneath. If someone had asked me a year ago if this guy had a violent bone in his body, I would have called them an idiot. Bob, with the sad comb-over and soft belly and worn brown shoes? I would have said he could have lost a fight with the Easter Bunny.

"I'm good, Doc. I don't need a babysitter."

Doc nodded and walked to the receptionist's desk. She picked up a file and started flipping through it, but her eyes were still on us. So much for not having a babysitter.

"So." Bob cleared his throat and lowered himself into one of the chairs. "I feel like complete crud."

I started picking up paint bottles and tightening their lids. I'd already tightened them, but I needed something to do with my hands. Plus, I wasn't about to make this a walk in the park for him.

He cleared his throat again and sat back, holding his jacket between his legs. "You know that I have a daughter. Jaclene." He didn't wait for me to respond. "And you've met Jack, her seven-year-old. And you know that she was a teenage mom." He leaned forward. "What you don't know is that right before she got pregnant, she used to miss curfew a lot. And it didn't take a rocket scientist to figure out that she was missing a lot of curfew because she was getting herself pregnant.

"I know we don't talk a lot, Reggie, but I notice things," he said, his eyes still on the mural. "I've noticed that you're smart, a common-sense kind of smart that I've never seen before in another kid. I've noticed that you keep a good eye on your mom when she wants to buy whatever new, shiny, pretty thing catches her eye." He stopped, hesitating over his words. "I've also noticed that you're selling yourself short thinking college isn't for you." He used his jacket to point at the mural. "I mean, look at that. You've got a lot of potential, kid."

I felt the frown on my face, but I couldn't help myself. Bob had never told me any of this. I thought he saw Mom as the perfect woman, and that I was just baggage.

"I've also noticed," he went on, "that you've never ever missed curfew before. That you've never had a boyfriend before, either. So when I saw you get out of that guy's truck and you hadn't been at school or at work and it was two hours past curfew . . ." He rubbed his eyes, and when he opened them, I saw they were watery. "Well, you could maybe see why I snapped. I saw you going down the same path as Jaclene, and I got scared for you." Bob leaned toward me, the space between us closing. But I didn't lean back. For once, I was interested in what he had to say. "I saw you knocked up with a kid, working late shift at Cashmart and Gabe just disappearing into the sunset like Jaclene's boyfriend after Jack was born."

Bob's head dropped, and his shoulders started to shake. I didn't know what to say. Or to do. Bob had always been this constant presence. First as my dad's boss, then as my mom's friend, then as her boyfriend. He was just there. He wasn't someone who was 3-D to me: someone who had bad days or cried or used the restroom.

He looked up and wiped the back of his hand under his nose. "Sorry about that," he said through a watery smile. "Didn't intend to get all weepy on you." He sniffed, and I gave him a tissue box from a table. He nodded his thanks. "Anyway, the reason I came was to let you know that I'm real sorry, Regina. Something sort of primal and horrible came over me, and I never, ever will touch you like that again." He gave me a weak smile. "I told your mom she could call the police if I so much as raised my voice to you." He reached into the inside pocket of his jacket and pulled out a black cell phone. He held it out to me. "I heard about your other one, and your mom and I got you this one."

I took the phone. Is this what someone looked like when they pretended to apologize and fully intended to abuse you again? I couldn't tell. But I knew two things: that his daughter thought he hung the moon and his grandson worshipped him just as much.

A guy with a pattern of violence wouldn't have that sort of love coming his way. A guy like that would be trying to buy their love back. I looked at the phone. And with a much cooler phone than this one.

And then the thought came out of nowhere: *A guy would try to buy their love with magazines and Godiva chocolates and pizza.*

Oh my God.

I was in shock, and Bob was staring at the mural when the bell above the clinic's door tinkled. I looked up and saw Gabe smile at Doc and then turn toward me. The smile disappeared when he saw Bob.

"What's he doing here?" he asked, as if Bob didn't exist. He sat down next to me and put his arm over my legs as he leaned forward, keeping his body between Bob and me.

"Apologizing," I said.

"Are you buying it?" he asked.

I threaded my fingers through Gabe's. I saw Bob try to keep from looking at our hands. "I am buying it." To Bob, I said, "You know when you said I had pretty good common sense?"

His mouth folded up into a half smile. "I think I alluded to you having excellent common sense."

I felt myself giving him a smile in return. "Exactly. So can we just leave it at you trusting me to use common sense in all aspects of my life?"

Bob hesitated, then finally said, "Only on one condition."

"Okay," I said.

"Will you forgive me, Regina?"

"Only on one condition." I waited until he nodded. "Only if you start calling me Reg."

A few days later, it was Thanksgiving eve. At least, that's what my Dad used to call it. He'd fix us a salad and a fiber-rich smoothie for dinner, telling us we needed roughage to make as much room as possible for second helpings, third helpings, and turkey-sandwich dinners the next day.

At breakfast, Mom gave me the list of food she still needed from the store. "And pick up about two hundred dollars' worth of flowers. Bob's place needs some decorations."

Bob had offered to host this year. Our house looked like a war zone, with half-laid tiles, torn-up carpet, and walls splashed with paint samples while Mom decided what to have them painted. The kitchen was almost done: antique white cabinets, stainless steel appliances, granite countertops. All that was needed was tile on the concrete floor.

"Did you say Gabe was coming for Thanksgiving?"

"No, he's going to be in Phoenix." He was spending the day with his family. He'd asked me to come, help him make fun of Sylvie joining a party sorority, but I didn't want to be away from my own family. This was our first Thanksgiving together in years. "But Sarah and Pete are still on." Our yearly tradition started at my house for the noon meal, moved on to Pete's for his family's three o'clock buffet, and then capped off at Sarah's six o'clock sit-down with bone china and crystal and real silver utensils.

Sarah's arm was getting better, and she said that she and her mom were pretty close to finding the perfect apple pie recipe. Our relationship was still far from perfect, but we were talking. It wasn't the old rhythm yet, but it felt like it was slowly getting there. She'd even spoken Yoda to me the other day when we were watching movies in her room. As soon as she had, she'd seemed embarrassed. I quickly told her, "Pass you the popcorn, I will."

Mom was ticking off fingers as she counted. "Is Gabe coming tonight at least?"

"Yep." Tonight was Bob and Mom's engagement party. Bob thought they were too old to be wasting money on such a thing, but Mom had talked him into it by saying she'd pay for everything.

"Excellent." Mom looked at the yellow legal pad she kept her checklists on. "By the way, the workers are coming Monday to install the vent in your room before it gets any colder."

A vent. Three years, and I was getting a vent. I thought about what my life would have been like if I had gotten that vent three years ago—it would have meant my dad was still alive, that I hadn't stolen four hundred dollars from the Art Club, that Bridget didn't own me and my necklace.

But then again, I never would have worked at Cashmart. Or met Gabe.

"And make sure to pick up enough rolls to feed thirteen comfortably. At least one per person, plus extra for people like Jeff who inhale them."

"Thirteen?"

She glanced down at her list. "Well, there's me, Bob, Jaclene and Jack, you, Jeff, Jeff's date Tanya, Pete, Sarah, Uncle Mark, Aunt Barb, Bridget and"—she squinted— "Deadhead? What kind of a name is that?"

Bridget and Deadhead? I guess Bridget had gotten her way yet again. And she might be getting her way once more if I gave into her most recent demand: a trip to Paris. She reasoned my credit card could fit a plane ticket and a two-week hotel stay no problem.

But I hadn't gone through with it yet, even though Bridget had been asking me about it every day, sometimes twice a day, the new Coach bag swinging from her arm. I'd given into all her demands, every last one. So what was stopping me now?

Maybe it was that common sense Bob liked so much about me.

◊ ◊ ◊

Cashmart was bumper-to-bumper with last-minute shoppers pushing carts, carrying baskets, and herding tired children. If one more person bumped me, I was going to seriously contemplate road rage.

"They have pumpkin pies on sale," Gabe said, slowing down as we passed a paper turkey sitting on top of a mountain of pumpkins in the middle of a table heaped with pies.

"We have enough pumpkin pies," I said, leading us down the canned vegetable aisle. "Sarah always brings at least three, and they're way better than any of this store-bought stuff."

I picked up two cans of creamed corn and led us to the bread aisle. Rolls. I needed at least three packages, four if Jeff guzzled down a fiber-rich smoothie today.

We passed a Little Debbie display as we headed toward the dinner rolls. "You good for Little Debbies, Reg?"

"What?" I kneeled and shoved myself halfway into the bottom shelf to get some of the last rolls. I climbed out and dropped them in the cart.

"Little Debbies. Did you need another box?"

I thought about the five boxes that were still in my closet. "I'm not really a Little Debbie kind of person. I was thinking of my mom and Jeff when you saw me buying them." The words rushed into one another as I told the lie.

"Huh." We were caught behind a pileup of carts as we

waited for people to go left or right at the end of the aisle. "Pete says you love them and your family hates them."

I kept my eyes on the list, but the words were blurred and my cheeks were burning. "Pete shouldn't be opening his big, fat mouth."

Gabe's hand slipped under my hair, cool against my raging-hot neck. He kissed my temple. "I know that you eat when you're stressed out. You don't have to hide that from me."

I pulled away and worked on redistributing the contents of the cart—milk on the bottom, bread on top. Anything to keep him from seeing my face. While my head was down, I looked at my watch. "Not a lot of time left before the party." I headed toward another aisle. "I'm going to go get the stuffing and broth. You take the cart, and I'll meet you in line, okay?"

Gabe knew. He knew that I ate crap, and lots of it. He probably visualized me in my closet, stuffing my face and dropping food on my shirt. And he wouldn't be far off from the truth.

I looked up at the aisle numbers, briefly wishing one of the fluorescent lights would fall down, hit my head, and knock me out, sending me to the hospital and waking up with no memory of this mortifying conversation. But then a light would have to fall on Gabe to erase his memory. But not hard enough to hurt him. Just to jostle his brain and erase a few minutes here and there, wherever the keyword *Little Debbie* came up.

The broth and stuffing in my arms, I walked to Checkout, almost dragging my feet as I went. Partly because I didn't want to face Gabe, partly because Doc's prediction might come true and an earthquake would come and rattle the roof.

And I wanted to make sure I was in just the right, light-crashing spot.

The engagement party was on the patio, white linens on the tables, crystal flutes in almost everyone's hand. A professional picture of Mom and Bob sat up front, and a slide show of their vacations and us kids flashed on the ground from a projector overhead. It was cold out, but gas heaters surrounded the place, emitting enough heat to keep us and the string quartet tuning their instruments toasty warm.

"Fancy." Pete stood at my side, a china plate in his hand piled high with shrimp cocktail, mini-quiches, and baked Brie. His arm was around Sarah, who had pasted rhinestones, sequins, and lace onto her cast. The pattern mimicked the pattern in her dress, and I was duly impressed. It looked like Mrs. Bretton was raising a mini-me.

"Very nice," Sarah agreed, looking around. "Is Gabe here yet?"

"Just look for the guy in flannel," Pete said around a mouthful of shrimp. Sarah had told me that Pete had been jealous about Gabe, thinking that Sarah thought he was cuter than Pete. She told me she'd called Pete an idiot and then made out with him. Their relationship was still odd, but it seemed to be based more on respect and humor than intolerance and sarcasm this time around. Whatever the reason, I had a feeling that this on-again stage was permanent.

"He's coming with Deadhead, who isn't exactly punctual," I said, moving to stand closer to a gas heater. I was wearing a maroon sleeveless dress and no sweater and was freezing. But the dress looked better without a sweater, and I wanted to look nice for Gabe, so nice that he'd forget about the whole bingeing-on-Little-Debbies thing when he saw my not-skinny-but-not-obese arms.

Sarah put her good arm around my waist, sharing her warmth. "A guy named Deadhead definitely doesn't care too much about time."

Around us, people with sunburns and ironed T-shirts promoting various sports teams talked and drank and laughed too loud. I recognized a lot of them as people who worked for Bob. For a second, I had déjà vu, thinking about Dad's sunburns and faded Phoenix Suns T-shirt and donkey laugh. It hurt thinking about him, but I also liked thinking about his donkey laugh, and was kind of glad I'd been reminded of that laugh.

It'd been over three years since Dad died. The pain had gotten more manageable, something I never thought would have happened. I no longer felt like a knife was twisting in my gut when I thought about Dad and his traditions or his laugh or what he would have said. Instead, I experienced an ache where the knife used to be, and a warmth, too, grateful for the memories I got to have. Grateful for the love he'd left behind. Even grateful for having known his donkey laugh.

I didn't realize I wasn't listening to Sarah or Pete anymore until I heard them talking about the Bake-Off and using the next two weeks to conduct twenty-four-hour taste tests with Fuji apples, Granny Smith apples, Gala apples . . . Around the twentieth apple, Pete disappeared in the direction of the food. *It's now or never.* I took a deep breath to steady my nerves. Sarah and I had finally found our rhythm, and now I was going to ruin it. But I had to take the chance.

Sarah's life depended on it.

"Sarah?"

"Hmm?" We were sitting at a table, watching the front door for Gabe or my mom.

"I need to ask you something, and—and if I'm totally wrong, I don't want you to be upset, okay?"

She turned to me, her eyebrows almost to her hairline.

"Regina Eustace Shaw, I am deeply in awe of you risking a confrontation. Ask away."

Here it went. "Did you really hurt yourself slipping in the kitchen?"

Part of Sarah's face seemed to shut down. She started playing with the silverware in front of her. "Yes," she said carefully, "I did fall in the kitchen."

I'd known Sarah long enough to know she's supersmart and can talk her way around anything. "I didn't ask if you fell. I asked if you hurt yourself when you slipped."

The string quartet Mom had hired for the evening started into something that sounded familiar, but I had no idea what it was called. It was beautiful, but it was a surreal soundtrack to our conversation.

"What does it matter?" she asked, tapping a knife against a spoon.

"It matters because I want to know you're okay. That no one's hurting you."

She shrugged. "I'll be okay. It's nothing. Just a broken arm. It'll heal."

I wanted to shake her by the shoulders. "Don't forget the concussion. That's serious stuff. People can die from head injuries."

"I really did get the concussion from hitting the floor," she said, still not looking at me, a scowl furrowing her brow.

I gnawed the inside of my lip. Things weren't quite adding up. "Did you really slip?"

Tap, tap, tap. She didn't look up, and something started to build in my chest, and breathing became harder. *I hate confrontations. I hate confrontations.*

"Hey, Gabe's here." Pete stood behind us, pointing at the door we had stopped watching. "And Deadhead looks as if he lives up to his name."

Neither Sarah nor I said anything, or made any movement to indicate we'd heard him. I saw Jeff, in my peripheral vision, come in with his date, Tanya Mathers. They'd gone to high school together, and she now worked at some sort of employment agency.

"Who died, guys?" Pete squatted next to Sarah. "You okay? Are you feeling tired? I can take you home if you want."

She shook her head and pushed the silverware away from her. "I just need to use the ladies'."

Pete took her chair after she left. I looked toward the front, where Bridget was hanging off Deadhead and Gabe was politely listening to her. He was looking at me, though, and smiled at me when I turned his way. I gave him a small smile back, trying not to think about Gabe knowing about me and my binges. Instead, I thought about Gabe and his hand on my neck, Gabe and his checking my tires, Gabe and his almost-always-there smile.

"What'd you say to Sarah?" Pete asked around a mouthful of food.

I shook my head, not wanting to talk to anyone but Sarah about my suspicions. Me asking her those questions hadn't been as bad as I thought, but I still felt a little sick inside.

But I wasn't going to drop it. I couldn't.

CHAPTER THIRTEEN

Imogene? This is Mattie Weare.
The Arizona Lottery Commission called me today and told me
I had to run a correction.
Could you please give me a call back
at your earliest convenience? Thank you.

IT STARTED THE SATURDAY AFTER THANKSGIVING. I'll always remember that day, mainly because it was raining for the first time since last Thanksgiving.

Gabe was at my house, eating a slice of one of Sarah and her mom's pies. Jeff was cooking pancakes, and Mom and Bob weren't up yet. This was Bob's first overnight. I think Mom had noticed things thawing between us and was testing her boundaries.

"So it's Thanksgiving, and your family does enchiladas?"

"Dad was craving them, and since my grandmother's from Spain, it made sense to make them."

Jeff poured the last of the pancake batter in a pan and put the bowl in the sink. He flipped on the faucet, and nothing came out. "Um, Reg, do you know what happened to the water?"

"No idea." I turned back to Gabe, dimly aware of Jeff's question. "But Thanksgiving. Turkey, cranberries, stuffing, that's good stuff. Enchiladas are weird and kind of gross."

Gabe used the back of his fork to smooth the whipped cream on top of the pie, making sure each millimeter was covered. "Personally, I find jellied cranberry sauce that's in the shape of a can far more disgusting."

The phone rang, and as I went to answer it, I shot back with "But you can have enchiladas any day of the week. Turkey and stuffing and pumpkin pie? Once a year, maybe twice if you do it at Christmas, too." I picked up the phone, my mind still on food. "Hello?"

"Christmas, we do lasagna," Gabe said.

"Reggie? Are you sitting down?" the person on the other end said at the same time.

"Gross," I mouthed to Gabe. In the receiver, I said, "Hello? Sarah?"

"Have you seen the paper?" she asked.

"No. You know I don't read it unless you point out some huge grammar mistake to me."

"Go get it. I'll wait."

Waterview Today was delivered to everyone's driveway, free of charge, on Tuesdays and Saturdays.

"Just tell me what's in it." I picked up one of the blueberries Jeff had been folding into the pancakes and tossed it at Gabe. He picked up his fork, a load of pie in it, acting like he was going to flick it at me. "Did you make honor roll again? Because I don't need to read the paper to know that."

"It's too soon for honor roll. And I think you really need to read the story. It's . . . it's not something I can read to you over the phone."

"Okay," I said, drawing out the word. I put down the phone, told the guys I'd be right back, and went outside. The paper was on the driveway—or the mud that used to be our driveway. I ran through the rain, wather soaking through my clothes, and picked up the paper in its plastic bag. That's when I saw it.

Us. My family on the front page. And we were under a headline that read:

MOTHER LIES ABOUT WINNING LOTTERY

Mom sat in Dad's robe, her head on Bob's chest, a crumpled tissue in her hand. They leaned into each other as they sat on the old sofa.

Jeff stood in the middle of the room, his knuckles white as he read from the paper: " 'It has come to the editor's attention that a story we printed last week was inaccurate. A member of the Arizona Lottery Commission informed the paper that Mrs. Shaw did not win the Arizona Five. She did win a portion of the lottery, however; she matched four out of the five numbers. But instead of the $1.6 million she told this reporter and asked to keep out of the paper, she only won $80,000.' "

No one said anything as the words sank in. As the lies sank in.

"Is it true?" Jeff finally asked. He twisted the paper in his hands, and Gabe drew me closer against his side from where we sat on the love seat. I hadn't asked him to stay, but I didn't ask him to leave, either.

Mom sniffed, her eyes red and her hands shaking. "Which part?"

"All of it."

She sniffed again. "It was more like $82,000, but yes, it's true."

I leaned forward, all thoughts about confrontations dead. For once, I didn't analyze the words or how she'd feel when she heard them. "Before or after taxes?"

Mom put the Kleenex under her nose, and new tears started to fall. "Before."

I felt Gabe put his hand at the part where my neck and back met, and I leaned into him. He knew right where the knots were starting to form.

"Why?" Jeff said just one word, but it did the work of a thousand.

Mom shook her head, her hand in front of her mouth. Bob squeezed her other hand. "When she got home and told Reggie about winning, Reggie assumed she had won the big lottery and"— he paused, patting Mom's hand —"and your mom just didn't have it in herself to correct her."

Mom didn't have it in her to correct me? Or was it just easier to let me take the blame for the biggest lie she ever told? This wasn't some pair of five-hundred-dollar shoes that she said she paid two hundred for. This was her telling us she had money for three cars and house remodeling and three credit cards with ten-thousand-dollar limits.

The money hadn't made our lives better. It had made Mom make our lives worse.

For years, I hadn't said anything. And Jeff—big brother Jeff—hadn't said anything. Together, we had let this happen to us. We had let Mom lie to us over and over again, never calling her on it.

Today, it was going to stop. Today, everything I never said was going to be said. Starting now.

"That's rich, Mom. You're the one who lied, you're the

one who's been spending thousands of dollars without any sort of willpower, and you blame me? For once, can't you take the blame? For once, can't you just own up to a mistake and be an adult?"

I shrugged off Gabe's hand and got up. Every one of my nerve endings was frayed and sending me into sensory overload. "How bad is it, Mom?"

Mom stared at me, tears falling down her face like a mini Niagara Falls. Dad's Funeral Bracelet was on her arm, and she was spinning it around.

As the silence stretched on, Bob finally asked, "I'm afraid we don't understand your question, Reggie."

I laughed, and it sounded a little manic. I felt Gabe touch my arm, and I waved my hand to try to let him know I wasn't ready for the loony farm. Yet. "She knows what I mean. She's a chronic spender. That bracelet on her arm? She bought it the week Dad died to remember him by. Even though we didn't have money for Dad's headstone or his casket or . . ." I didn't say anything about the air conditioner. This was about her transgressions, not mine. "She can't save a penny to save her life, and she's been paying thousands of dollars for tile and appliances and cabinets and cars . . ." I trailed off. "Oh God, the cars. They're not even ours, are they?"

She didn't say anything, but the look on her face answered me.

"The costs for the wedding, the twenty-five hundred dollars for the stylist—"

"Twenty-five hundred dollars?" Bob shifted so he could look at her. "You told me three hundred."

No one said anything. And as the silence stretched longer this time, I took the paper and started scanning the article, no longer numb. I had to read the words. I had to make sure that this was as real and horrible as I thought it was. It wasn't until I got to the last paragraph that I realized this horror movie was a double feature.

I barely realized Jeff was talking as I read to the end. "Did you forget to pay the water bill?" he asked.

Mom shook her head. "No, " I didn't forget. The words came out pretty normally. But the next words barely managed to come out between the tears: "I didn't have the money."

Air particles stopped moving, breathing took a hiatus, traffic on I-95 was put on mute. This, this right here, was what I had had nightmares about. Not having money, having something like power or water shut off, becoming a laughingstock.

And my mother just sat on the couch, crying. Like we should be comforting her.

I couldn't stand looking at her. She'd out and out lied to me and told me that the first thing she had done was pay off the bills.

LIAR!

I couldn't stand being in the same room as her.

Or as him.

"I need to go," I finally said. I got up and started toward my room, where my car keys and Little Debbies were.

Just outside my room, arms encircled me, and a face pressed into my neck. "I'm so sorry, Reg."

I shrugged him off. "Don't touch me."

I snapped on the desk light that was still my bedroom's only light. Mom had put up the chandelier, but it wasn't wired yet. Surprise surprise.

My keys were the only thing making noise as I gathered a sweatshirt and picked up my wallet. Not that I needed it or the useless credit card inside. But I had my debit card. It was the key to the money I still had in checking. It wasn't one point six million, but it was better. It was *real*.

"What's going on, Reg?"

I played with the clasp on my wallet, taking an odd pleasure in the snapping sound as I looked past Gabe at the new buttercream color on the hallway walls. "Don't act as if you give a crap about me."

He didn't move. "What are you talking about?" he said slowly, as if he were talking to someone on the edge of a roof, about to step off and plunge to her death.

I snapped off the light and realized my breath was

coming out fast and hard. Gabe still stood in the doorway, outlined by the light filtering through the hallway from the family room.

For once, I was glad my room was cold, that I'd never wasted money on a heater and I never got the vent Mom promised. My body was going through nuclear meltdown, and the coolness might have been the only thing that kept my brain from melting down, too.

I walked back into the family room where no one seemed to have moved, and grabbed the paper. I read the last paragraph out loud through my clenched teeth: "'Mrs. Shaw might not have won millions, but that doesn't mean all is lost for this family. Her daughter, Regina, is rumored to be dating Cashmart heir Gabriel Donaldson. His father, mega-millionaire Ashton Donaldson, told *Waterview Today* that Gabriel is working at the town's Cashmart for a year before returning to college next fall. "No, I haven't met Regina or her mother. But if this girl were truly important to my son, I would have been introduced to her by now."'"

There, in black and white, were the doubts I'd always had. Doubts that were now in our tiny newspaper, on every single person's driveway, getting peed on, getting sprinkled on.

Getting read.

"Reg?"

I was heading back to my bedroom. I couldn't be in the same room with him. Or with her.

My mother had lied. Gabe had lied, and I had no idea why. But that wasn't even the worst part. The worst part was he hadn't told his dad about me. No. No, the worst part was that small voice playing on a loop in my head: *You're too fat. You're too dumb. You're too poor. You have no future, loser.*

I went to the back of my closet and grabbed all five boxes of Little Debbies.

"Reggie?" Gabe. The doorknob rattled, but I'd locked it when I came in. It was still the old garage door, and it was metal, thick, and not going anywhere.

"Reggie, please. Open the door." Again the rattle. I opened the cellophane on the first pie and shoved the entire thing into my mouth. Even if I was tempted to talk to him, I couldn't.

After a while, there was no more rattling. I sat on the bed, pulling Mr. Puffin out from under me, one of Gabe's flannel shirts buttoned up to his neck like a plaid Amish dress. I was on my fifth oatmeal pie when the blind rage started to fade and I saw that Mom had moved all my snow globes onto my dresser so she could paint the room. The miniature casinos in their prisons of water, snow, and glitter looked so peaceful and unassuming. As if they hadn't come from a woman who'd spent her paycheck on the slots instead of the mortgage, on a new pair of Jimmy Choos when I'd been told we didn't have enough money for braces.

Who'd spent every single penny of the lottery on stupid things instead of paying the water bill. Or Dad's student loan. Or me.

I shoved Mr. Puffin against my eyes and concentrated on not crying. Not crying. Not crying.

Crying.

Everything started to change less than forty-eight hours later. Waterview was a small town with small businesses and fast word of mouth.

Before the sun was even up, Mom's Mercedes was the first to go, followed by the plants in the front yard, some of which had been planted. Then, it was the stove and the refrigerator Mom had bought on credit at Larry's Electronics.

For breakfast, Mom took migraine medicine that konked her out and she locked herself in her room. Bob dealt with letting people in and taking stuff out. After an hour, I couldn't take The Great Repossession anymore. The people taking our things was one thing. But the words whirling around in my head while people took our things were worse than anything happening in real time:

Most Likely to Never Leave Waterview.

Mrs. Shaw did not win the Arizona Five.

But if this girl were truly important to my son, I would have been introduced to her by now.

I grabbed my car keys and peeled out of the driveway. I had no idea when my car would get repossessed. I wasn't going to stick around to find out.

"I'm so sorry, Regina." Tanya Mathers sat behind an open file folder, her pen writing something down in the margins of the application. Temp Jobs Inc. wasn't like I had envisioned. It was one big room with a bathroom in the corner, a vending machine in another corner, and a flickering light overhead. Yellowing posters were stapled to the walls, their corners gone.

"What're ya going to do, right?" I grabbed the front of the desk as I barely managed to sit in the chair. "So, anything out there that has a start date of tomorrow? Or tonight. I'm not picky. I just need work."

She looked over a packet of jobs she'd been flipping through as we talked. "The problem is, most of these jobs are full-time. And with you in school—"

"I can manage," I interrupted. "I used to work nearly full-time at Cashmart and go to school. So I know I can do it." I had done it by barely doing homework before. But that wasn't going to be a problem. Homework would never be a problem again. That's why I was here at 8:10 A.M. on a school day.

"The other issue is that the jobs you're qualified for are mainly secretarial, with eight-to-five schedules."

I nodded. "I understand. But I'm okay with that."

She shook her head. "But these employers want someone with a high school education. You quit, and you're known as the girl with the eleventh-grade education."

"That's why I'd take my GED. And I'll tell them that when they interview me."

Tanya studied me, and I'm sure she was wondering if I was serious or not. When I had showed up, reminding her I was Jeff's sister, I had my dead-serious face on. I had lost Gabe and the lottery and my Cashmart job. I was done with losing.

I adopted a firm, businesslike tone, trying to hide the jagged edge of desperation I felt. "This is what I want to do, Tanya. You said you read the paper this weekend. You know exactly what happened." I swallowed, and a lot of the energy I'd come here with seemed to sap out of me. "My family needs money."

What I kept to myself was that I needed money. I needed to know I could build my nest egg and get out of Waterview.

What I didn't say was I couldn't go back to school. I couldn't go with everyone knowing and whispering and writing things on my locker. Again.

Tanya finally nodded and wrote down names and phone numbers on a piece of paper. "Give me until tomorrow afternoon to contact these employers and fill them in on your situation and your plans for the GED." She got up and I followed, and when we got to the door, she patted my shoulder. "We'll get you work, okay?"

"Thank you." I headed outside.

The day was bright and crisp. Arizona falls were like that. Days that felt as if anything were possible.

I looked up at the cloudless sky and gave it two middle fingers.

CHAPTER FOURTEEN

*Mrs. Shaw? Triple-A Towing here. I've got an order here
for a Land Rover. We can do this the hard way or the easy way.
I'm hoping for the easy way.*

IT HAD BEEN THREE DAYS and still no shower. Plenty of
sponge baths, though, with a rag and a bucket of hose water.
Money or no money, it had been almost three years since I
had gone more than twenty-four hours without a shower,
deodorant, a light spray of perfume, and a crisp, clean set
of clothes.

And I hated it. I hated it more than our stuff getting
repossessed, more than not having won the lottery.

Hated. It.

We'd been using the neighbor's hose to get water to
do dishes, to give ourselves sponge baths, and to flush the
toilet. Turns out, the water company can turn off your water
during the weekend but can't be reached until a weekday.

Then they tell you it'll take twenty-four hours to turn it back on.

I got to school early Tuesday morning. Six o'clock early. So early, I was standing outside when the door was unlocked a half hour later.

The computer aide was sitting down to his computer, a cup of steaming coffee on a table that was nowhere close to his keyboard. I had never talked to him; signing in to use the computers doesn't really require much student-aide interaction.

"Hey." I didn't have a backpack with me. I didn't need notebooks or pencils. My books were in my locker. I didn't plan to go to my locker, either, since the school would clean it out anyway.

The aide looked up, his hand moving his mouse. "Yes?"

"I was wondering where I could pick up info about the GED."

He took his hand off the mouse as he rocked back in his chair. "How old are you?"

"Eighteen."

He twisted his mouth. "Well, at least you're old enough. We don't have GED materials here, but the community college does. That's where you test, too."

"Great." I headed toward the door.

"You're Regina Shaw, correct?"

I turned back around. Of course he knew. He lived in

Waterview. He got the paper. Finally, people knew my name, but for all the wrong reasons. "Yes, I am."

"We haven't really talked, but I have a cat. Morris. He's had a bit of a flea problem lately."

This conversation was turning odd. I just nodded, waiting it out, already thinking which roads I'd take to get to WCC.

"I take Morris to the doc over at Paws and Claws." He sipped his coffee, the steam fogging his glasses. "I have to say, I love the mural."

The conversation had officially changed from odd to surreal. "Uh, thanks." I tried to remember if I'd signed the mural. No, no I hadn't. I felt that signing my name was kind of full of myself. "How do you know I painted it?"

"There's an eight-by-ten picture next to it of you and the painting, with a little plaque underneath with your name and date and the mural title."

The mural had a name?

"It's terrific." He wrote something on a piece of printer paper and handed it to me. "If you do portraits, give me a call. My wife would love it if we could hang a painting of Morris over the fireplace."

I was in the parking lot when I saw the Land Rover getting hooked up to a tow truck. I'd been parking it two streets over at home; I didn't here, because I didn't think Triple-A Towing would come at seven in the morning to my high school parking lot.

I just stood there, watching Elvis take away my last ties to freedom. I felt nothing as I watched him work. At least I now knew what Elvis did for a living.

"Regina."

"Bridget," I replied, not turning around. I scanned the parking lot, looking for either Pete's car or Sarah's. Nothing yet. "You know it's only seven, right?"

She pointed behind me, to the career lab. "I promised Mom I'd work on college apps today." She hitched her bag up, the bag I'd bought her, a fake look of concern on her face. I could tell it was fake because when it came to me, she was never concerned. That sounded cold, but it was as if Bridget's genetic code had missed out on the empathy gene. "So I heard about Aunt Genie. That sucks."

I just nodded. Bridget had never cared about the downs of my family before except for gossip material. I wasn't about to give her anything. I kept scanning cars. I was looking at makes and models, not people's faces. I had to get out of here while I still had my pride, as shredded as it was.

I had faith Sarah would get here any minute. She usu-ally came early to type up her papers; lately, her mom had been taking over her computer as she Googled recipes at an almost obsessive-compulsive rate.

I could feel Bridget still standing next to me and that's when I saw it—my necklace. The numbness faded as Bridget rolled the pearl back and forth between her fingers. "I noticed you and Gabe were pretty tight at Aunt Genie's party."

I ignored her. I ignored everything but my pearl twisting between her fingers.

"So, yeah," she said, filling the silence that I wasn't, "I was wondering if you could ask him what the password is to Deadhead's voice mail."

Here I was, my truck being towed, our family on the front page of the city paper, our one point six million fading away . . . and here she was, worried about some guy's voice mail?

"He tells me his ex isn't calling, but she is. I need proof first, though, before I start making his life a living hell." She said more, but I couldn't hear her anymore.

"I'm not going to ask Gabe to figure out Deadhead's password," I said. I think I even interrupted her. I didn't care. I just wanted her to shut up.

She rolled her eyes. "Gabe has to do nothing. Deadhead told me it was based on some inside joke of theirs. Something about Gabe's odometer in that piece of crap he drives."

In front of me, the tow truck turned out of the parking lot, my pretty car behind it, and I was left with Bridget. I looked around. Still no Sarah or Pete. Other cars were here, though. And already I knew things were different. People were looking at me, some who gave me sad little smiles, others who gave me condescending winks, but most who didn't even look at me, their shoes and the dirt parking lot way more interesting.

"When are you seeing Gabe next? Because I'd like to get the password today."

I shook my head and headed over to a bench Pete usually parked by. I sat down. Now I was the one staring at the ground, trying not to fall apart.

And if I said the words aloud—I was no longer with Gabe—then I was really, truly going to fall apart. "I'm not doing it, Bridget."

She didn't say anything at first as the sound of car stereos filled the air around us. "Yes you are," Bridget finally said, confident, but with the itsiest-bitsiest trace of doubt in there. I'd never said no to any of her whims in the last three years. I'd implied it, but I had never out and out said it.

But today was a new day.

"We're even, Bridget." I said the words, even though I knew there was no such thing as "even" to Bridget. There would always be something she wanted and there would always be this secret over my head.

As long as there was this secret, there would always be Bridget.

The thought had me pushing myself up and heading back toward the school. I heard Bridget's feet crunching behind me. "This is going to be the nail in your coffin, Regina," she hissed behind me. "You think life sucks now? Just wait. The girl whose mom didn't win the lottery is about to be the white trash who stole money from the sad little Art Club so that she could get rid of her BO."

I stopped and faced her. I was nothing to Bridget. To her and to people like her. I got it loud and clear the day I was voted Most Likely to Never Leave Waterview.

My attention went back to the necklace. My necklace. The tiny diamond above the pearl winked at me, taunting me just like Bridget.

"It's over," I said. This power struggle, my senior year, this conversation. O-v-e-r.

I took a step toward her, and then another, until I literally walked into her, pushing her back until a trash can kept her from going any farther. I didn't say a word. There was none to say.

"What are you doing?" Bridget's words were breathy, the confidence she always seemed to radiate no longer there.

"What I should have done a long time ago."

I curled my hand around the necklace and snapped it off her neck.

"Ms. Moore?"

Ms. Moore sat at her desk, her bun neat on top of her head. A couple of kids were in their seats trying to finish homework. They looked up briefly, and I knew they knew. But then they went back to their homework, Reggie Shaw just a blip in the middle of yet another endless high school day.

I now had only ten minutes before the first bell rang. Confronting Bridget had taken a lot longer than I'd imagined.

"Reggie." Ms. Moore put down the paper she was reading. "How's the extra credit going?"

I had until the week before Christmas to create a video vignette about *Animal Farm*. I'd storyboarded it, but after today, everything was going in the trash.

"Do you have a minute, Ms. Moore?" I asked. I reached in my pocket and found Dad's necklace. I could do this. It wasn't as if I'd get detention, right? *There's still jail,* a tiny voice said.

Ms. Moore nodded at me, the teacher mask she wore slipping a little. I could tell she knew about the lottery. Of course she knew. Everyone knew. The question was, who had died and *didn't* know.

Behind me, I could hear pencils scratching against paper and pages being flipped through in textbooks. "Actually, do you mind if we go outside?"

"Lead the way," she said.

Once we were in the hallway, where morning gossip and shoes squeaking against tile provided excellent cover for our conversation, I felt my bravado slipping. The longer we stood outside, the more conversations seemed to stutter to a halt and then start up again, this time with the words *Regina* and *lied* and *no money* reaching my ears.

I told myself I didn't care. I was dead to these people. It wasn't as if I was about to get any deader. I tightened my grip on the Coach purse in my hands. The purse I'd taken from Bridget and dumped in the parking lot. I was selling it on eBay as soon as I got home.

There was no good way to start, so I just did. "In ninth grade, remember how I was in your art class and I was in charge of getting the club's money to you?" There was no good way to start, and there was no good way to segue, either. "We took in $1,900 and not $1,500." I paused and took a quick breath, an image of a six-by-six jail cell flashing in front of my eyes. "I stole the difference."

Ms. Moore said nothing, and I wanted to run and keep running until it was three years ago and I could erase everything.

But out of everything she could have said to me, I wasn't prepared for what she said next: "I know."

"You know?" The number of people around me seemed to be growing, their conversations growing louder, my ears burning red.

"I might teach art and English, but I can still figure out my way around a calculator."

My head was spinning. "Why didn't you ever say anything?"

"By the time I figured out that the discrepancy wasn't just a few business owners who'd forgotten to pay us, a couple of months had gone by." She leaned against a row of lockers and shrugged. "Plus, I knew about your dad, and I had a feeling your family was facing some money problems. Everyone always does after a death. So I just made up the difference with my own money."

Around us, people were talking and laughing and occasionally I would hear "Millions" coughed out. But all of that faded away as Ms. Moore's words sank in.

"I don't know when I can pay you back," I finally managed. "We had money and all, but I don't know if you heard about—"

"—about the lottery?" She cocked her head and gave me a half smile. "Saturdays, my husband and I have two rituals: read through *Waterview Today* for grammar mistakes and go to the movies." She reached out and touched my arm. "I'm sorry, Reg."

My throat was closing up. We stood there, Ms. Moore against the lockers, me on the brink of tears, amid a crowd of students that was getting thicker and louder.

"So," she said. "Let's head to class."

I shook my head. She was being so nice. I didn't know how to tell her I was dropping out. So I didn't. "Can't. I have to run some errands today."

Her teacher mask slid back on, and she gave me that look teachers have when they know you're full of bull. "Reggie, life still goes on. I know that it feels as if it stopped, but I promise you, it's still limping along. Missing classes and getting further behind isn't going to help any."

But I wasn't going to get behind. I was just going to cash in, kind of like Mom at her slots after a bad day that had her down a couple thousand. But instead of a couple thousand, I was down over one and a half million. Plus the twenty-five hundred Mom was never, ever going to pay me back.

I almost told Ms. Moore. But I ended up not telling her, because Pete was loping up the hallway.

"I've gotta get going, Ms. Moore. Thank you." And because I had nothing else I could say, I hugged her. Right there in the middle of Waterview High, five minutes before the first bell. I ignored the coughs of "lesbian" and hoped the hug was saying everything I couldn't.

I walked up the Brettons' sidewalk, Pete's car parked behind me, his car keys with a Stormtrooper key chain in my pocket. Pete had told me Sarah was staying home today to work on recipes, something about her mom freaking that they hadn't found the perfect pie yet.

As tiny birds flitted in and out of their bushes and Mrs. Bretton's fountains gurgled softly, I breathed in the day. The windows lining the front porch were open and taking advantage of the Arizona weather.

And that's why I heard it. The crack of flesh hitting flesh.

I tried the door, fear and adrenaline propelling me forward. Locked. I then looked in the window and saw Sarah, her hands shielding her face.

And I saw Mrs. Bretton standing in front of her, her hand raised. "You are totally worthless. Worthless!"

I couldn't breathe and I couldn't talk. But I could pound against the window, even though I didn't even remember raising my arms. They both turned to look at me, and that's when I saw Mrs. Bretton's face for just a second, for the space of a hummingbird's heartbeat. Staring back at me was a stranger. And I would have talked myself into believing I hadn't seen the cold, furious rage distorting her face if I hadn't also seen Sarah's face. Red and wet and scared.

"Let me in, Sarah," I called out.

She shook her head and turned to the wall, covering her face. That's when I became afraid. Sarah never turned away from anything or anyone.

I remembered Pete's keys and flipped through them until I got to the one with the pink rubber ring Sarah had put on it. I shoved it into the knob and walked in. Mrs. Bretton was back in the kitchen, scraping a bowl of batter into a pan, her eyes lit up by something raw and fake.

"Don't you have school today, Regina?" She asked the question as if it was any other day, one when she hadn't just slammed her hand against her daughter's cheek and spat out hateful, unforgettable words.

I ignored her and walked over to Sarah, who was still facing the wall, her hair covering her face and her hand on her cheek.

"Hey."

"Hey," she whispered.

"Do you need me to call someone?"

At first, I didn't think she heard me. Then, I saw the tiny, almost imperceptible nod.

"Your dad?"

More hesitancy, then another brief, barely-there nod. She whispered his number. I just needed the last four. Waterview might have been so small that it had the same prefix for everyone, but it had the same problems that the rest of the world did: liars, dropouts, and child abuse.

I reached for my cell phone, but I'd left it in the car. I walked into the kitchen and took the cordless off the wall.

"What are you doing, Regina?" Mrs. Bretton wiped her hands on a towel and came over to where I stood with the phone. She was tall, like Sarah. She towered over me, which played into the intimidation I was feeling. But I kept dialing.

"I'm taking care of Sarah." I no longer cared about avoiding confrontations. First Bridget, then Ms. Moore, and now Mrs. Bretton. I was getting better with each one, too. "Go take care of your pie, Mrs. Bretton. It may be the last one you make for a while."

CHAPTER FIFTEEN

Hey, Reg. It's S. Just wondering how it's going.
He's a good guy. Be nice to him.

YOU SHOULD'VE SEEN HER. She was like someone in one of your video games." Sarah sat on Pete's car, her feet on his fender, her butt firmly planted on his hood. Pete had his arm around her like she was about to disappear at any moment. He didn't seem to care about the way the hood was crunching under her, either. "Except her boobs were real and she didn't blow Mom's head off."

"I totally wanted to, though." It was lunchtime in the Waterview High parking lot, but it felt as if a lifetime had passed since the Land Rover got towed and I'd gone to the Brettons' and saw Mrs. Bretton going mental on Sarah and called for help. Sarah's dad arrived five minutes later, and he had dragged Mrs. Bretton out to the back patio.

I'd taken Sarah into her bedroom and given her a damp washrag for her face. "She was the one who broke your arm, wasn't she?"

Sarah pressed the washcloth against her face. "She didn't mean to, though." She lowered the towel. "Remember that pie stand she went all the way to Phoenix for? Well, I broke it. And she was really stressed that day and grabbed my arm and . . ."

She put the washcloth over her face again as she turned away. "Anyway, I ended up falling and bumping my head."

"You more than bumped it, Sarah. You got a concussion. You were hospitalized." I pointed to her arm. "She broke you."

The words hung between us, and I knew Sarah understood exactly what I meant, since I wasn't just talking about her arm and head.

Mr. and Mrs. Bretton were still outside talking and yelling when Pete called to ask how the baking was going. We had decided to get out of there and tell him in person.

"Do you think your dad knows about what your mom was doing?" Pete was now asking. He made a fist with his free hand and was tapping his hood with it. I don't think he had any idea he knew what he was doing as the metal dented and didn't pop back out again.

She shook her head. "He knew about her yelling at me. She's always yelled at me. She yells at him too, you know? But I didn't tell him that she grabbed my arm and shoved me in the kitchen." She gave a wry smile. "I told him what I told you. The story she came up with about slipping. I didn't know what else to do. After a while, it was just easier for me to stick with the lie, and to convince myself that's what really happened."

"I think he did know, S," I said quietly. "He gave you an awful lot of gifts. Like he was feeling guilty or something."

Sarah put her hands between her knees, squeezing them together. "He knew but he didn't, you know? He'd ask me if Mom was under a lot of stress, and I'd just say no more than usual. I never told him about her slapping me or calling me names or dumping a pie on me if I screwed up." Pete and I both inhaled sharply over that one. "But at the same time, I was pissed at him for not guessing. How sick is that?"

"It's not sick." It was hard seeing Sarah—strong, feisty, opinionated Sarah—like this. "You were in a bad situation, and you just didn't know what to think."

We sat there, a few minutes left before lunch ended. I knew Pete wasn't going to ask, so I did. "Why didn't you tell us, at least?"

Sarah picked at Pete's pant leg. "Because I didn't know how to say, 'Hey, guys, I'm a Lifetime movie of the week.'"

Pete's fist sank deeper into his hood. "How long? Has this been going on, I mean."

"Two months, give or take," she said. "Ever since we got serious about the Bake-Off." She looked up at the sky, even though the sun was blinding. "Then every little thing started setting her off. First it was not scrubbing the pie pans hard enough, then it was beating the meringue too slowly, and then when the pie stand broke"— she paused, shaking her head at the memory—"she went ballistic."

Pete and I didn't say anything. I mean, what was there to say? *Sorry your mom beat you up?*

"So, change of subject?" Sarah said. Pete put his arm around her shoulders and drew her close to him. "Reg, why were you at my house at eight-thirty on a Monday morning?"

I played with the flannel shirt tied at my waist. One of Gabe's. I could have grabbed a sweat jacket, but I hadn't even thought twice about the flannel. And I was done lying to myself. I was done lying, period. The truth of it was, I missed Gabe. Gabe and his smile, his hands, his words, and his support. *His lies,* that tiny voice reminded me.

"I'm dropping out. I've been thinking about it for a while, and it's now a go."

"Whoa. Stop." Sarah slid down the hood, out from under Pete's arm. "You are not quitting school. Your family's going to be fine, Reg. You guys can get by until June without you quitting school."

I remembered the way I'd had to use a bottle of water crammed in the bottom of my backpack to brush my teeth. My family was not fine.

"I've already made up my mind," I said.

"What'd your mom say? And Bob? And Gabe?"

Mom and Bob were in their own little world, dealing with the repos and the national news organizations that wanted to talk to the woman who'd lied about winning the lottery. The only person who might have cared, he was . . . "It's over with Gabe," I said, forcing myself to smile as if it was no biggie. "And I'm eighteen anyway. No one can stop me."

Sarah reached behind her to Pete. "Give me your cell phone," she told him. When it was in her hand, she started dialing. "Hello? Hey. Can you page Gabe Donaldson for me? Thanks."

I saw what she was doing, I heard what she was doing, yet I still couldn't believe she was doing it. This was a new level of ballsiness, even for Sarah.

"What are you doing?"

"Helping you think better," she said, leaning away from my outstretched hand. "Gabe? Yeah? Hey, it's Sarah, Reggie's friend." She slapped at my hand when I frantically reached for the phone. "She needs to talk to you, but she doesn't know it yet," she said as I shook my head and kept mouthing *No, I don't* at her. "But she never listens to me and we both know her mom's in la-la land. Can you come get her from school? Yeah? Awesome."

She hung up, and I think my brain had officially shut down. Otherwise, I would have thought about what she had just done and walked into traffic.

To me, she said, "Remember how you came to my house today?"

Numbly, I nodded.

"Well, it's my turn, okay?"

"Your turn to do what?" I asked robotically. She had just called Gabe. The one person in the world that I didn't want to see me like this, to see the full extent of how big a loser I actually was. And it sounded as if he was coming. The same guy who hadn't told his dad about me.

"To save you from yourself."

I heard her, but the words didn't make sense. "Why do you care? I'm just a loser." I threw the word back at her. A word that never left, that seemed to resurface in my brain every five minutes or less.

"And that's what kills me!" Sarah screamed at the sky. "I call you a loser when I'm mad, and that's the one thing you hear. The one thing! After years of me telling you that you could be so much more, that you can do anything, and this is the one thing that sinks in?"

She waved the cell phone in front of my face. "And I called Gabe because you are crying out for help. We know that you would've taken Pete's car to WCC and signed up for the GED if that's really what you wanted to do."

"Yeah, she's right, Reg," Pete agreed. "You wouldn't have gone to Sarah's if you were serious. I mean, what, you've known Sarah since first grade? When has she ever let you do something stupid? She's a pit bull about that kind of stuff and you knew that. You *wanted* to be talked out of dropping out."

Sarah gave him a look like he was Han Solo and she was Princess Leia. So much for Mr. Non-Communicative.

"Whatever, I gotta get going." I stood up, scanning the parking lot. No Gabe. A little part of me was relieved, but there was also a little part of me that was disappointed.

"Yeah?" Sarah raised an eyebrow. "You walking?"

I'd forgotten about the no-car situation.

"Pete, I need to borrow—"

"No," he said.

"No?"

"Sarah would kill me."

"I would." Sarah nodded.

Behind me, I heard an engine vibrating. An engine that you usually hear in old trucks.

"Anyway," Sarah said, turning me around, "your chariot awaits."

It had been at least three years since I'd been to the beach. I lived four miles from it, but it might as well have been four hundred. Working double shifts and overtime at Cashmart kept a girl from working on a tan. But here I was, finally at the beach on the day that my freedom was about to disappear again.

I sat on top of a picnic bench, the breeze off the lake cold. I wrapped my arms around myself, and even though I couldn't see Gabe, I could feel him somewhere behind me. I watched the lake lap the sand, not wanting to talk. Afraid to have Gabe finally confirm all the horrible thoughts I'd been having since I ate five boxes of Little Debbies as he pounded on my bedroom door.

I realized on the drive over that I wasn't mad at him anymore. After the day I'd just had, him not telling me he was heir to one of the biggest fortunes in the world just didn't rank up there with my mother lying to me, Waterview finding out about it, Mrs. Bretton slapping Sarah across the face, and me quitting school so that I could get the water turned back on.

A concept that I'm sure Gabe didn't have the faintest idea about.

"You're missing work," I said, stating the obvious, but my brain could only handle the obvious.

"And you're missing school." His words came out flat, monotonal. Like he had somewhere better to be. I swallowed hard and focused on the lake and the couple of boats that were out today, driven by people who had the day off or were just playing hooky. People who didn't have a care in the world.

The table vibrated under me, and I saw a mom-type running toward us, picking up a soccer ball that must've hit the corner. "Sorry about that. He's not too good with his aim yet." She turned and went back to a little kid who looked three or four.

Somewhere to my left, Gabe said, "Remember that kid with the red hair and the two huge rabbit teeth?"

I felt myself smiling. Despite everything. "Yeah. He just wasn't going to smile for his Mom's Christmas pic, no matter what."

"Yeah." Gabe climbed onto the table, sitting down about a foot away. "And then you realized he was a soccer fan."

"Who doesn't love soccer?" I said, thinking about that day. "But I got him to smile."

"Yes. Yes, you did." Gabe rubbed the palms of his hands together, his eyes on the lake in front of us. "I can't believe you actually slid across the floor on your stomach."

"Hey, he was a soccer goalie, I used to be a soccer goalie, and there was a pretend ball that needed to get stopped. And it worked, thank you very much."

"It did."

The breeze was getting cooler, and I crossed my arms over my chest, rubbing them. I felt Gabe turn to look at me, but I kept my eyes on the water.

"You fully committed to get him to smile," he said, matter-of-factly.

"Of course I did. What's the point of half-assing it if you can go all the way?"

Gabe didn't say anything for a full minute, but he was nodding at something that seemed to be running through his head. "So why are you quitting high school when you're, what, seven-eighths of the way through it?"

I rolled my eyes. Gabe had officially taken up Sarah's baton.

"I have no choice, Gabriel." I purposely used the name that had been in the newspaper article. "In case you forgot, my family has no money, and the money I had been saving? Mom borrowed it for a flat-screen TV, and she never paid me back, and I have a feeling she never will. That's my mother. I knew better and yet I gave her that stupid money."

More silence, more keeping my eyes on the water, willing the stinging to stop.

"You can't come back to Cashmart, Reg," he said, so quietly that it took a moment to figure out that he was the one who had said it, not just the tiny voice in my head.

"I wasn't planning on going back to Cashmart," I said angrily. "I need to work full-time, and I have a feeling Mr. I-Own-Cashmart isn't going to let me come back." I wouldn't have come back even if Cashmart was paying twenty bucks an hour. I couldn't be around Gabe like that, seeing him and knowing that we were done. There'd be no more late-night talks, no more jokes, no more quick kisses in the Say Cheese! storeroom.

Don't cry, don't cry, don't cry.

"You know why I'm not letting Fellers hire you back, right?" He didn't wait for my answer. "You were too comfortable when I got there. You never would have left, and I thought the Photo Goddess deserved better than that."

"It seems good enough for you," I snapped back.

"Because I have to work there for a year before I start back up at school." I felt him look at me, but I didn't turn to meet his eyes. "Dad wants me to understand the business from the bottom up so I'll know how to take over when it's time."

The wind was picking up, and I focused on not thinking about the flannel wrapped around my waist. I was halfway hoping he didn't notice that I was wearing it. That I had needed to have something of his tied around my waist today.

I tried to distract him. "Must be nice to have had a good life waiting for you after school."

"It is, and it isn't. I don't like the idea that I really have no other future but Cashmart. I was really pissed off when I was in tenth grade and wanted to be a doctor."

That had me looking at him. "You wanted to be a doctor?"

He nodded. He pulled up his sleeve. "You're not the only one who has a hard time talking about painful things, Reg." He pointed to the EVD tattooed on his inner elbow. "My mom—Evelyn Victoria Donaldson—died of cancer when I was in tenth grade. She'd had it for a long time, and Dad was busy with his multimillion-dollar career. So I was the one who made sure she took her pills, got her to chemo, wiped up her vomit. I wanted to be a doctor because I wanted to help other kids from having to go through losing their moms."

I bit the inside of my cheek, and I realized Gabe wasn't a control freak because of an overblown ego. He'd had to grow up fast and hard because he needed to take care of his mom.

"Do you still want to be a doctor?" I asked.

"Nah." He smiled, and his dimple came out. I loved

that dimple. Whenever I thought of Gabe, I thought of his smile, that dimple, our talks, the smell of musk and rain. I felt a sharp pain somewhere in the vicinity of my heart as I thought about no longer having any of those things anymore. "I used to, but I wasn't good enough at chemistry. And when anatomy came junior year of high school, I couldn't dissect the cat. Did you know they use a cat in anatomy? Yeah, no way was I going to do that when Oscar was alive and well at home."

He picked up the sleeve of the flannel I was wearing. I don't even think he knew what he was doing as he ran his finger over the hem. "And then I realized I was pretty good in my economics class, that I could run a small business model better than anyone else, and that the stocks I picked for a stock-portfolio assignment did really, really well. And I realized I had a natural talent for that sort of thing."

He looked at me, the sleeve still in his hand. "And that's why it bugged me so much to see you at Cashmart being so good with photos, really having an eye for it, and planning a life as a department store manager."

"That bugged you?"

"Well, yeah. Fellers had told me how the girl in Photo wanted to take on a managerial position one day, maybe even turn manager of the store, and that I shouldn't be surprised if she was cold to me, since she'd wanted the photo manager position. Then I met you." He shook his head and smiled. "There was no way you were going to be happy as a manager. Your talent lies in how creative you are, like getting that kid to smile or even getting that stupid rat to calm down. So I played the Gabriel Donaldson card," he said, puffing out his chest and deepening his voice as he mocked himself, "and wrote you up."

"But the district manager was there. . . ." I trailed off. A district manager wouldn't have told Gabe Donaldson, Cashmart heir, anything.

"Nope. I just told Fellers to say that. I also told him he had to back me up, saying that he made me write you up."

Part of me thought he was a total control freak. The other part of me realized why he was such a control freak. I should have been mad, but I wasn't. I'd wanted the photo manager job for money, plain and simple. But I'd had no long-term plans. I could very well have stayed at Cashmart—maybe even Waterview—for ten, twenty years, because it was easy and because it was there. "Why do you always think you know what's best for me?"

"Because I'm older than you," he said simply.

"That's really annoying."

I thought I heard a brief laugh. "Duly noted."

This was way too much information to absorb in one sitting. I put my head on my knees, listening to the wind snapping palm trees overhead. I shoved my arms under me, trying to warm up so that I could think.

"Why didn't you tell your dad about me?" I forced out.

I felt something cover my back, and the flannel Gabe had been wearing was now on my back. I tried to shrug it off, but Gabe put his hand on my back to keep it where it was.

"My dad isn't the most present guy you've ever met. He wasn't there for my mom, you know? So we haven't been exactly close for the last five years or so. We talk business and that's about it." He bumped my elbow with his. "And I did invite you to Thanksgiving. You're the one who said no, remember?"

As he said the words, I did remember. *I am not going to ugly cry. I am not going to ugly cry.* "Why are you here, Gabe? You broke up with me."

I felt him lean against me, and his lips touched my ear as he said, "Um, no. You're the one who broke up with me, remember? I wasn't the one who locked the door."

I didn't have the energy to lift my head, so instead I rotated it until my temple rested on my knees. "What was I supposed to do? You li-lied." *Don't ugly cry. Don't ugly cry.*

"I didn't mean to, Reg," he said earnestly, his face inches from mine, so close I could see the green flecks in his hazel eyes. "But how does someone share something like that?

Do I just blurt out, 'Hey, my dad owns Cashmart. So, what movie do you want to see today?' I didn't handle it well, but I didn't keep it from you because of some ulterior motive."

"Well, you're off the hook." The tears started to run. So did my nose. So much for not ugly crying. "You don't have to pretend to be interested in the girl who inhales junk food and whose water got turned off and who stole four hundred dollars freshman year because someone wrote on her locker that she smelled."

There. Everything was finally out. I had nothing left to hide, nothing left to lose as I said, "You don't have to feel obligated to stay with—the girl voted most likely to never leave Waterview."

The foot of space between us disappeared as his arm went around me and his other hand cupped my face. His nose and lips burrowed into my neck, and his words vibrated against my skin. "Shut up. Just shut up. I love everything about you, Reggie. The junk food, the crazy mom, everything. And if you stole four hundred dollars, knowing you, you had a pretty damn good reason." He pulled back, and I saw that he meant every word he was saying. "You are gorgeous, with a heart that's bigger than anyone's I've ever seen and with a talent for art you better not waste." He laughed quietly. "I'm playing my 'I'm older than you' card, by the way. I hope you're cool with that."

CHAPTER SIXTEEN

*Reg? It's Bob. I got your first cell phone bill, and I
noticed you've barely used it. Make sure you have it with you at
all times, okay? Jaclene's old car isn't reliable all the time, and I
don't want you stranded without some way to contact us.
Well, all right, then. See you tonight.*

SO, EUSTACE. Are you happy?"

I was in Gabe's arms, swaying to an old song by some
dead guy. We were in Bob's backyard, Christmas lights
hanging from the stucco wall, a potluck spread out over
three tables, a computer acting as DJ.

"Define happy, Ernest." We'd been playing a particularly
vicious version of Truth or Dare, and now neither of us
would stop using our horrible middle names. But it was
okay. The day had been almost fairytale-like, going to Bob's
for Christmas breakfast, going to Pete's to watch *How the
Grinch Stole Christmas* for the four-hundred-and-fifth time,

going to Gabe's apartment and meeting his dad, who'd come up for the day with Sylvie. His dad giving me a big bear hug when I was leaving, telling me how his son ever managed to hook up with a doll like me, he didn't know. Gabe had rolled his eyes, but I appreciated his dad trying to make up for his quote in the paper.

"Let's start small and work our way up," Gabe said. He squeezed my waist. "Are you happy that your legs work?"

A puff of laughter blew out. "Uh, yeah. I'm happy my legs work."

"Are you happy you're dancing?"

The smile hurt my jaw, it was that wide. "Yes."

"Are you happy you're dancing with me?"

"Oh." I pretended to mull over the question. He twirled us in a tight circle, and I had to grab his arms to steady myself. "Yes! I'm very happy about that. I thought that was part of the dancing question anyway."

People were starting to move inside, most dressed in green velvets and red satins. It was dusk, and the temperature had started to take its usual day-to-night forty-degree dive. I was wearing Gabe's jacket, though, and was warm. Being pressed against him didn't hurt, either.

"Are you happy your mother's married?"

I looked behind me, where Bob sat next to Mom and laughed over something Jeff was saying. His daughter and grandson sat at the same table, and were laughing, too.

"Yes, very much so." And, it was true. For the first time in years, we were starting to feel like a family again. We'd moved into Bob's house a week ago and had already instituted Game Night, which consisted of Bob beating us at Monopoly, Bob beating us at Liar's Dice, Bob beating us at Carcassonne. It wasn't so much Game Night as Bob-Demolishing-Us Night. But it still felt nice, whatever it was. Even Jeff had been coming home more often; he kept saying that one day Bob would lose, and he'd be there when it happened.

For a while, I was worried Bob wanted to call off the wedding. I was worried up until he kissed my mom about thirty minutes ago after the whole man/wife thing. But I think I finally knew why Bob was with Mom. It'd taken me a while, but I think he was a lot like Gabe. He was a caretaker. He took care of Jaclene and Jack, and now he was taking care of Mom.

"Are you happy about the dress you're wearing?" he asked softly.

"Very," I whispered back. I'd found the dress in the back of Waterview Bridal Clearance, seventy-five percent off. One for me, one for Bridget. It was made for a busty girl, cut generously in the front and low in the back. It was perfect on me, sort of lumpy and dumpy on Bridget, who'd been scowling all night. That could have been either from the dress *or* not being the usual center of attention *or* Deadhead ignoring her and chatting up one of the cute girls from Mom's old real estate office.

"I like it, too." He put his hand under the jacket, placing it on my bare back. "Are you happy that you didn't drop out?"

I shrugged but leaned closer so I could hide my smile against his shoulder. Everyone had been one hundred and fifty percent against me dropping out of school: Mom, Bob, Jeff, Gabe, Pete, Sarah.

Even Doc got in on the dropout discussion. I guess the aide from the computer lab had come in for a Morris checkup and told her about me and the GED. That same day, Doc showed up in her scrubs in the middle of us packing up the living room.

"Please tell me you are not doing something as stupid as dropping out."

"I am not doing something as stupid as dropping out," I'd agreed. That had taken the steam out of her, and she sat down on one of the taped-up boxes, her bad leg straight out.

"Well, good." She looked around. "You're not moving out of Waterview, are you? People are going to forget about the story soon enough. I heard Elvis is running for the city council."

I wrapped newspaper around another snow globe. This one was from some medieval-themed casino, where I had hidden in the gift shop and tried on earrings while Mom gambled for four hours straight. I was eleven at the time. I had a feeling I'd be leaving these snow globes packed up in Bob's garage until Mom forgot about them and I could throw them out.

"We're not leaving Waterview. We're just moving to the other side of town, into Mom's fiancé's house." Bob had told Mom she was selling the house. Not asked, but told. Demanded, actually. He was calm as she pleaded with him, asking him to give her time to say good-bye to Dad's memories. He'd kissed the top of her head and told her no, that the house was going and so was her room filled with her eBay junk. They couldn't afford two mortgages and, for Bob's sanity, he couldn't deal with her having two husbands.

He'd told me and Jeff that he was going to split the profits from the house between us. He figured that we'd each get about fifteen thousand, after he paid off Dad's forty-thousand-dollar loan. Fifteen thousand! Jeff wanted to use it for a down payment on a house. I had an idea what I wanted to use my money on, but I was still getting my ducks in a row, and I didn't want to tell anyone about it in case things didn't work out.

Bob had also told Mom that she was going to start going to Gamblers Anonymous. And that's what sealed the deal for me about Bob. He didn't ask if Mom *wanted* to go; he told her she was going. The sick thing? The closest meeting was in Laughlin, in a strip mall across from one of the casinos. Bob planned to drive her to the meetings, stay with her, and drive her home. He told her that it wasn't because he didn't trust her, but he didn't trust her addiction.

After I assured Doc I really, truly wasn't going to drop out, she said, "I want you to do another mural for Paws and Claws. And this time, I'm paying you by the hour."

I thought about how much I owed her. "Doc, I don't think the mural I finished is worth six thousand dollars. I'm not taking your charity."

She dug inside her purse and pulled out a crumpled sheet of printer paper. "Yeah? Do you still think that after you see this?"

I saw it was a price sheet from someone's Web site. Pet Portraits by Catherine. My jaw dropped when I read it. "A thousand bucks per animal?"

"Exactly. And look at her work." She handed me a stack of printouts stapled together. As I flipped through them, I couldn't help but think that they looked like something you'd see in a paint-by-numbers book. "Your stuff's better than that."

I continued to look at the paintings. "So, a thousand bucks per animal, huh?" I pretended to do the math in my head. "So, what, I did eight animals, but we'll say the gerbil only counts as half an animal. So that means you owe me fifteen hundred dollars?"

"According to this woman's prices, yeah."

I found myself smiling so much that I had to move my jaw from side to side to stretch my cheeks.

"I can't afford those prices, of course," Doc said, "but I thought maybe you'd want to charge me twenty bucks an hour for this next mural?"

Twenty bucks an hour? After two years making barely seven an hour at Cashmart? My thoughts raced. I could do it after school, and with Doc closed weekends, I'd be free for whatever. For whomever. I'd be able to save money again. And not for bills—Bob had taken care of those now that Mom's bank account was closed and her credit cards were cut up.

"Deal," I'd said.

"Hey." Gabe brought me back to the present, and I realized the song was now a Christmas song. "This is a yes-or-no game. No shrugs allowed." He paused. "And in case you forgot, I'll ask again: Are you happy that you didn't drop out?"

He watched me with a hint of worry in his eyes. I couldn't believe he still thought I might quit school. Especially ince he'd heard me talk to Sylvie this morning about the Art School in Phoenix. And last I heard, you needed a high school diploma to get in. Talent, too. And for once, I think I had some. Maybe even enough talent to get a scholarship, or at least to get enough jobs to put myself through school, debt-free.

I tickled his stomach, and he drew me closer as he tried to protect himself and kiss my neck.

"Yes, I'm very, very happy that I didn't drop out."

After a few minutes with his lips brushing my neck, he pulled back. "Reg?"

"Hmm?" Gabe's lips were nice. My neck missed them.

"Merry Christmas." He handed me a small white box tied with a deep red velvet ribbon.

"What's this?"

"Why don't you open it?"

I didn't reach for it. "You already gave me something, Gabriel." I stroked the diamond-and-pearl pendant at the base of my throat.

"Fixing a clasp is not a present." He pushed the small box toward me. "I promise, it isn't anything big."

I took the gift. I shook it. It was a lot smaller than the gift I'd given him earlier: a case of Reese's Peanut Butter Cups. King-sized, dark chocolate, white chocolate, miniatures. The works.

305

"It's to get you started thinking about stuff beyond Cashmart and Waterview and the stuff with your mom."

I opened the box, his arms still around me as we swayed to the music.

Inside was a plastic snow globe, the kind you put your own picture into. It was filled with water, snow, glitter, and a picture of Simon the Rat.

"I thought it'd be nice to commemorate the day we met," Gabe said. "And I know how you like snow globes."

I hated snow globes. They had represented the years of gambling my mother had done until we were almost broke. But I didn't tell him I hated snow globes. I didn't want to ruin the moment. But I would one day. I was no longer a big fan of avoidance. Instead, I whispered in his ear, "Well, I definitely liked the day we met." I looked up until I could meet his eyes. "You could maybe say I loved it."

I was touching up my makeup in Bob's bedroom mirror when Mom came in, the white suit we'd gotten her on clearance gliding over her figure. We still had a weird something going on between us, the last few weeks filled with tense silences and doors being closed too loudly. I searched my brain for something to say. "Are you enjoying yourself, Mom?"

She went into the closet and came out with a gold-threaded shawl. "I guess."

I turned to her, my happy mood fading away. "What do you mean, you guess?"

She sat on the bed and shrugged. "A computer's playing our music, our food was brought by our guests, and our honeymoon is going to be here while you, Jeff, Jaclene, and Jack go up to Lake Tahoe to see Bob's parents. Where's the great in that?"

"I think people are having a great time."

"But I wanted something nicer." Her eyes glistened, but I didn't even feel the slightest bit bad for her. "The dress, the string orchestra, the fancy food, and the custom-made fondant cake." She wiped her nose with the back of her hand. "Our engagement party was nicer than this. And it sucks that Barb isn't here."

I never knew what would set me off with my mother. But now I no longer had to suck it down. "You're sad Aunt Barb isn't here? She's not here because you can't loan her the money for her start-up. What kind of sister holds a grudge for something like that?" I drew in a breath. I was far from finished. "And are you really talking about the engagement party that you used the last of our money on? That engagement party?" I gestured outside. "Personally, I love having a potluck and a computer as our DJ. Because you know what? I love knowing that our water's going to stay on and a roof is going to stay over our heads.

"You've gotta stop living in some fantasy world where you have unlimited amounts of money. I mean, it got so bad that you lied to us. You lied to the town."

"I didn't lie—"

"Stop it!" I shouted. "Just stop it! You messed up, Mom. You messed up and you need to know that. And you need to know that you started messing up when you took Grandpa Shaw's money."

"What?" She looked startled. "I don't know what you're talking about."

"I'm talking about getting money when I was born, and you using it for whatever instead of putting it in my account. How much money did you steal from me, Mom? Beyond the money you kept borrowing and borrowing and borrowing from me? I mean, I know you're never going to repay it. That's just not who you are. But, c'mon, at least own up to the lies."

"I didn't steal your money, Regina." And the look she gave me? Pure anger. She was angry with *me*?

I left the room. I hated confrontations. I hated them. But I was done avoiding them. I came back, a Converse shoebox in my hands from my bedroom I hadn't unpacked yet. "You haven't stolen any money?" I opened the lid and dumped the contents into her lap. Hundreds of receipts came out. *Hundreds*. "Every single receipt in there is money you've borrowed from me. For Starbucks, for your cell, for electricity, for mortgage. For the air conditioner you should have paid for." I let the box drop to the ground, the receipts surrounding us like that dumb snow in those snow globes Mom loved so much. "And you know what? I've been too afraid to tally up everything. I think I'd puke knowing exactly how much I've given you over the years and will never, ever see again."

Tears filled her eyes. But I was on a roll. And I knew the tears would dry and she still wouldn't understand what I had been trying to say. But the important thing? I was saying it. Finally.

"I love you, Mom. But I need you to stop lying to yourself. I need you to start being a better person who is responsible with money so that Jeff and I can have a chance at . . . at . . ." I didn't know what to say. At feeling normal? At having a family?

I didn't want to dumb down my words to make her feel better. She'd had three years of that, and it hadn't helped. "You screwed up, Mom. Big time."

TWO WEEKS LATER

Hello? Sarah? Wakey wakey. It's Reg.
I'm bringing coffee.
See you soon.

THE LINE STRETCHED FROM THE ROW OF DOUBLE DOORS, down the concrete stairs, and almost to the end of the student parking lot. People wore sweatshirts, flannels, and long pants. Some even still wore flip-flops.

It was mid-January, and Waterview was officially experiencing winter. Today it was sixty degrees, and I was glad I had layered two flannels together. I wore them over the pair of designer jeans I'd bought in Laughlin, the last pair of jeans I would be buying for the next ten years.

"I don't know, Pete."

"C'mon, Reg. Humor me. What do you think?"

Pete, Sarah, and I sat on the ground, with me on top of one of their SAT books because the concrete was freezing my butt.

"Cup is to saucer," I finally said.

"See?" he said to Sarah. "Told you she's a genius with these multiple-choice tests."

"I think I was the one who pointed it out to you back in seventh grade," Sarah said.

This was usually about the time they started going back and forth with insults. Instead, Pete gave her a quick peck. "Yeah, I think you're right."

Behind me, someone called out, "Won any Monopoly money lately, Shaw?"

Someone else chimed in, "Didn't you hear? Millions's new nickname is Pennies."

A few people laughed. A lot, though, were studying last-minute questions and didn't pay attention.

I didn't react. I never did. And it wasn't because I wanted to avoid a confrontation. I was all about confrontations if the situation warranted them. But in less than six months, high school would be over. I would probably never see most of these people again.

"We're going to the Bake-Off later, right?" Pete asked. "You're going to meet up with us, Reg?"

I nodded. "Of course. Wouldn't miss it." Sarah had decided to enter the Bake-Off by herself. Her mom was in an anger-management thing in Montana, and she'd been there for four weeks now. Mrs. Bretton needed to complete at least eight weeks before she was allowed to come back home and be anywhere near her daughter. That was according to Mr. Bretton. According to Sarah, she'd gotten a postcard from her mom that read: "I love you." The rest of the space was devoted to a picture she had drawn showing Sarah how she should display her pie at the Bake-Off.

The doors at the top of the stairs opened. We got up, and the line started to slowly move forward. I could feel the tension, just like at the last SAT. Me, I was relatively stress-free. And lately, I didn't feel like eating five boxes of Little Debbies. I hadn't for about a month, since we'd moved into Bob's and Mom had been going to Gamblers Anonymous, and I'd started another mural for Doc.

"You got everything you need?"

"Five number-twos, water, an apple, and a granola bar." I pulled Gabe's mini-snow globe out of my pocket. I'd decided that this snow globe was a keeper. It represented future dreams, not lost dreams. Plus, Simon the Rat seemed to be winking at me. "And this for luck."

We were now at the bottom of the steps. "Luck ha[s] nothing to do with it," Pete said. "Smart you are."

I smiled at him and walked up the rest of the stairs by myself.

The SAT, art school, and the future awaited.